# Happy MESSY SCARY Love

## LEAH KONEN

Amulet Books • New York

Library of Congress Cataloging-in-Publication Data
Names: Konen, Leah, author.
Title: Happy messy scary love / by Leah Konen.
Description: New York, NY: Amulet Books, 2019. | Summary: Olivia plans to spend her summer in the Catskills, binge-watching horror movies and chatting with her online friend Elm, but things get complicated when she sends Elm her best friend's picture and she runs into the last person she thought she would ever see in real life.
Identifiers: LCCN 2018047037 | ISBN 9781419734892 (hardback)
Subjects: | CYAC: Online identities—Fiction. | Horror films—Fiction. | Catskill Mountains Region (N.Y.)—Fiction.
Classification: LCC PZ7.K83514 Hap 2019 | DDC [Fic]—dc23

Text copyright © 2019 Alloy Entertainment, LLC

alloy**entertainment**

Jacket illustrations copyright © 2019 Mary Kate McDevitt
Book design by Siobhán Gallagher

Printed and bound in U.S.A.
10 9 8 7 6 5 4 3 2 1

Amulet Books are available at special discounts when purchased in quantity for premiums and promotions as well as fundraising or educational use. Special editions can also be created to specification. For details, contact specialsales @abramsbooks.com or the address below.

Amulet Books® is a registered trademark of Harry N. Abrams, Inc.

**ABRAMS** The Art of Books
195 Broadway, New York, NY 10007
abramsbooks.com

This book is dedicated to anyone who's ever nerded out in secret—
here's to not being afraid to be who we are

> JIMMY
> You know, they say you miss a hundred
> percent of the shots you don't take.
>
> ONYX
> Would you mind sparing me the basketball
> metaphors until *after* we've made it out of
> here alive?
>
> —*The Bad Decision Handbook* by O. Knight

# I Know What You're Doing This Summer

"What are you doing this summer, Olivia?"

They're the words I dread, scarier than any of the movies I watch at night, any of the Stephen King novels I read, or even that true crime documentary I watched in April.

We're sitting in the gym at Xaverian High School in Brooklyn—me and Katie, and the other girls from French class, waiting for the final assembly, one little event that stands between us and the glories—or pitfalls—of summer vacation. Our French teacher, Ms. Padma, let us out of class early, and now the five of us are surrounded by a plethora of chairs waiting to be filled. The air in the gym is stale, wood floors dusty, metal chairs screechy, as if the school is ready for us to get out of here more than anyone.

I scratch underneath my collar as Tessa stares, waiting for an answer. My uniform is itchy and the thought of my sad little secret makes it itchier. "I already told you," I say, plastering on a smile in lieu of a real answer, and then quickly—oh so quickly—looking away.

If I were in a horror movie, if we were trapped in this school with some crazed killer or monster on the loose, this is where I'd suggest to the crew it would be a good idea to split up. Of course, that's a total trope and never a good idea, but then I wouldn't have to answer

Tessa's question—or look at any of their eager eyes. The ins and outs of everyday high school are way worse than anything waiting for you in a horror flick, that I know for sure.

Tessa cocks her head to the side, her glossy hair cascading across her shoulders. "No, you didn't."

I know what each of them is doing, since they've all been talking about it, ad nauseam, for the last few weeks:

My best friend, Katie, is going to the acting program at the New School that she's been dreaming of for years.

Tessa and her family are doing a house swap, trading their tiny Brooklyn apartment for a "pied-à-terre," whatever the hell that means, one block from the Eiffel Tower.

Fatima is interning at an NGO in Africa.

Eloise is leading meditation workshops at a "mindfulness sleepaway camp" in Vermont.

And me, well . . .

"I'm keeping busy," I say, tugging at a particularly unruly curl and scratching at my chin. Since I found out I didn't get into NYU, I've mainly kept the questions at bay by saying how things were "still up in the air," but it's evidently too late for that now.

"Busy?" Tessa asks with a laugh, and I realize it's exactly what my uncle says, the one in Iowa whose schedule revolves around telemarketing work and feeding his four cats. *Keeping busy.* What you say when you have nothing to keep you busy at all.

"Wait, weren't you going to that NYU screenwriting program?" Eloise asks. Her voice is even-keeled, calming. Of course she's going to be a meditation instructor. It's a perfect fit.

"Jealous," Fatima says. "I was in the Village last weekend, and the dudes there are just . . ." She brings her fingers to her lips. "Mwah!"

They laugh, but internally I cringe. I won't be anywhere near Greenwich Village this summer, that's for sure.

Back in January, when the future had seemed all bright and glowy; when I had twenty-seven words written and at the top of my Google Doc, titled *The Bad Decision Handbook*; when the pulsing of the cursor was encouraging, not chastising—I'd told everyone who would listen: *I'm applying to NYU's screenwriting program this summer! I want to write horror movies! I swear, they're more freeing and feminist and just . . . awesome . . . than any other genre. Forget Wes Craven, George A. Romero, and all the dudes who've dominated the genre. There's a new crew of ladies in town, and I'm going to be one of them!*

I'd had big plans, plans so large and daunting that it somehow became impossible to get past word number twenty-seven. It's not that I didn't want to write. It's more that I didn't want to write anything *bad*. So I spent a lot of time doing research—er, watching horror movies.

And then suddenly, without even realizing it, it was March, and the deadline was quickly approaching. The fifteen-page sample I needed to submit was no more than a couple of "*FADE IN*"s and "*INTERIOR CABIN – DAY*"s and one line of voice-over—"*I didn't believe in monsters until I visited Shadow Lake*"—which even I knew was just about the worst way to open anything on earth. Hello, heavy-handedness! On top of that, it felt like my one bad line of dialogue had become an actual monster, reminding me that no way, no how, was I cut out for this.

Even worse, I couldn't help but think about freshman year, my heart thumping wildly as I stood on that stage, stumbling over my lines for my audition for the school's production of *Dracula*, and of the cast list posted outside the drama room.

It didn't matter that I had a screenplay idea that had been bouncing around in my head for months—I didn't have a single thing to show for it. When March 15 came along, I did submit my application—my parents had written the check and everything—but I can hardly even remember what I wrote. Run-on sentences, things jotted down way too fast, racing against the clock of a deadline. I pushed it off so much, I didn't even give myself a shot.

The girls are still waiting for an answer, and Katie, blond hair stick-straight and skin clear as anything, shoots me an understanding look with her gray-blue eyes. She's the only one who knows the truth about what I'm doing this summer. And it is, drumroll, please . . . a big fat pile of nothing in the big fat middle of nowhere!

I'll be up in the Catskill Mountains with my mom and dad, at this little cottage in the middle of the woods, where my parents and I spent six weeks last summer, right after they bought the place. Even though the internet is hardly fast enough to handle my very full queue on Netflix, Amazon Prime, and HBO Now, I'm secretly kind of relieved. It's nothing compared to what my friends are doing, but at least I'll be away from the pressure of Brooklyn. Maybe I'll even actually make progress on the screenplay that wouldn't be.

Besides, the internet isn't too slow to get on Reddit. I snap at the elastic band on my wrist, pushing down the anticipation of a new Reddit message I'm awaiting from a certain someone, and I look at Eloise. "They've got a really strict admissions process . . ." I let the words hang in the air.

Then, just in case: "I didn't get in. I'm going upstate with my parents."

A shuffle as the gym doors open and students pile in, and yet there is an excruciating quiet as my confession hits these girls, my friends.

Katie, as per usual, saves me. She laughs, mouth wide-open, voice bubbly and light. "Who needs a stupid program to write? Last I checked you've got a computer like the rest of us—and a place to get away from it all. I'm pretty sure Greta Gerwig didn't write *Lady Bird* in an *NYU* program. No joke, she only turned to acting when a bunch of stupid playwriting programs wouldn't take her. And look how she turned out!"

The girls laugh, a chorus of "yeah"s and "you're totally right"s. Then the seats fill up, and our principal takes the stage, and I'm off the chopping block for the moment. Except I have to admit to myself that if I couldn't even manage fifteen cohesive pages for the application, I probably won't get very far on my own.

Still, I've got to hand it to Katie. As usual, she's saved the day, evaded the awkwardness, made it all okay . . . for a little bit at least. Katie, the natural star, the one who always knows the right thing to say and do. She's the *best* best friend a girl could ever ask for.

She may not totally support my horror addiction, but she supports me, and that's all that matters. It's no wonder I love her so much.

# One New Message

My after-school routine is always the same.

Katie and I walk to Third Avenue in Bay Ridge, Brooklyn, then turn south, weaving though the thrum of people and activity. Past delis and bodegas receiving deliveries of beer. The Thai place that always smells like basil. The shawarma spot that features meat spinning and dripping in the window, strangely appetizing even under those harsh yellow lights. Bars opening up for happy hour, setting chairs out on the sidewalk and using chalkboard signs to turn their daily specials into witty puns.

At Eightieth Street, Katie and I burst through the doors of our favorite Mediterranean deli. A rush of AC greets us, relief from the oppressive early June swampiness. A glass case displays shelf after shelf of deliciousness: dried apricots, hummus smooth as butter, pastries dappled with poppy-seed sprinkles. Aliyah is at the counter, and she smiles warmly as she grabs her tongs and puts a pair of spinach pies into two wax-paper bags. "Today has to be the last day, right?"

Katie nods and then pouts. "No more spinach pies for us until September."

Aliyah only smiles and adds an extra pie in each of our bags.

We pay separately and head back out. Katie digs into hers right away, taking a huge bite. I nibble at the edge of mine, savoring the salty dough.

We walk briskly, like all New Yorkers do, and when we reach Eighty-Second Street, Katie pauses. "I know you don't want to talk about it, but are you okay?"

Katie has learned by now that any discussion of summer is off-limits. She wants to go all touchy-feely on me, analyze *why* I procrastinated so long, *how* I'm feeling when my friends are doing so much more than me, but I don't.

I wrap her in a big hug. "You're the best," I say. "For saving me earlier. Greta Gerwig and all that. I'll be fine."

Her smile comes right back. "Good, then come over later. We have to celebrate the end of our imprisonment."

I half want to laugh. Xaverian High is hardly imprisonment.

"You have spinach under your lip," I tell her. Katie laughs and flicks it away, rubbing her fingers on the tweed of her skirt. I wrinkle up my nose at her grooming methods, but she only shrugs. Even though it's got to be high eighties, her skin is clear and sweat-free, apart from the faintest sheen on the top of her forehead. "I think my parents want to do dinner somewhere," I say, shifting my weight from foot to foot. "But I'll swing by afterward."

Katie nods, and then hugs me again, fiercely. "See ya," she says, and she turns, but then immediately swivels back. "Oh, and don't forget, it's my turn to pick the movie."

I raise my eyebrows. "How could I ever?"

From Katie's turnoff, it's ten more blocks to my house. I walk them quick as I possibly can, much more quickly than I did with her.

In minutes, I'm here, my home on Ninety-Third Street. I grab the key from my pocket and let myself in through the side entrance, stepping into the hallway. When most people think of Brooklyn, they think of fancy apartments; but we have a house. It's old and dusty, but a house all the same—most everyone lives in houses in our neighborhood in Bay Ridge. I dash through the kitchen and up the stairs as fast as I can—my parents won't be home for a few hours.

In my bedroom, I tap at the button on my window AC unit. It grumbles to life. I squirm out of my awful uniform—white short-sleeved shirt, sweater vest, tweed skirt, items that were *not* designed for a summer in Brooklyn—and pull on shorts and a tank top, propping myself up with pillows on my bed.

Posters stare back at me: *Psycho*, *Get Out*, and *Nosferatu* on one wall. *Let the Right One In* and *It Follows* on another. I hear a rumple of glossy paper as I sink further into the bed: behind me is the best one, an oversized poster of *Carrie*, my all-time favorite movie.

My phone dings with a text. It's from my aunt Chrissy, who also lives in Brooklyn, a short bike ride away in Sunset Park.

*Happy last day, girlie! Summer is here, YOU DID THAT SHIT!*

I laugh. My aunt Chrissy, a freelance creative director and card-carrying cool girl, is just about the furthest thing from a fuddy-duddy old aunt you could possibly imagine.

I text back, saying thanks and shooting over a GIF of a tongue-wagging dog.

She writes back right away. *Ready to be up in the woods?*

*Yes but I wish you were coming, too!* I write. *I'm gonna miss you*

*You, too, my love!*

I tap at the home button on my phone, putting her messages aside for now. Then with tingling fingers, I open the Reddit app.

I'm already logged in under my handle, CarriesRevenge01. I could go straight to the Horror Movie Appreciation subreddit, but I don't.

Instead, my eyes focus on the envelope icon in the bottom right corner. It's bright orange. Happy orange. *I have a new message* orange.

I relish in that prickle of excitement deep in my belly. Then I pause before tapping into my inbox, glancing through all the posts and articles on my homepage—cute dogs, political news, funny memes.

It's silly, I know, how much an internet message excites me. So silly I haven't had the guts to tell Katie about it.

It started back in February. I was a longtime lurker on the threads, always using them to find horror movie recs. But as the deadline for my NYU application quickly approached, I made my first post. I'd been feeling hopeless and wanted the low-down—how bad would it be if I didn't get into the NYU program?

*Did most horror movie directors go to film school?*

The comments on my post were exactly what I needed to hear:

*No! In fact, very few did! Most of them don't have time for that shit. They're too busy making movies.*

*Stanley Kubrick was turned down from every college he applied to—he was an awful student.*

*Many did but it's definitely not a requirement. (But putting yourself out there and making the damn movie is.)*

And then, a comment from a user named ElmStreetNightmare84:

*My aunt is a budding horror director (no joke!) and she went to college but she studied, I kid you not, biology (vom). Now she directs indie horror herself, she's living the dream! Basically, nothing is required but passion when it comes to this kind of stuff. Though I hear a lot of programs are good for one thing . . . getting you to finish your project. Personally, I'd love to go to film school if I could find a way to swing it.*

Elm and I didn't start messaging right away. Plenty of people left comments—that's what you do on a thread like this. But after that first question, I became more active in the group. I started posting regularly about my favorite movies, commenting on threads when people asked for recommendations.

Then, one afternoon, shortly after I turned in my mess of an application, I made a post about found-footage movies, the kind where all the action is supposedly recorded by one of the characters, like on a home movie or with the camera on your laptop. Most movies like this are pretty cheesy, with overly shaky camera work and bad dialogue, but I was on the hunt for some good ones.

The responses to my post were swift and overwhelmingly negative. People went on and on about how it's the worst genre of all time and how *The Blair Witch Project* basically ruined horror.

Then I saw that orange envelope. A direct message, not part of the thread. From ElmStreetNightmare84.

*Ouch, you'd think by the responses that you'd asked for recommendations of movies where cute little dogs die (which is actually a thing, and I HATE it). Anyway, since it's Battle of the Braggarts out there, thought I'd write to you personally.* Creep *and* Creep 2 *are GREAT found footage if you haven't checked them out already! Give 'em a watch. (Or don't, if you don't wanna.) That's the joy of movies: You get to choose what you like!*

*P.S. I saw you were talking about film school in an earlier post? Are you applying to any? I've been thinking about it myself but am on the fence . . .*

*Oh and P.P.S. Sweet handle, love* Carrie*!!!*

I wrote back, thanking him for the recs, admiring his use of the word "braggart," telling him I was in the process of applying to an

NYU summer program for high school students, and shooting him over some recs of my own. When I watched and loved the movies he recommended, I wrote him again, telling him so. He did the same for me. After a few messages, and a few complaints about AP US History, we discovered we were the same age, a happy realization, since the subreddit was mainly dominated by real adults. Our genders came out naturally in an exchange about feminist horror and the lack of women directors.

Back in March, just after I submitted my half-assed NYU application, we only messaged every week or so. But around the end of April, our correspondence became more of a daily habit, something I looked forward to every day during school, while teachers droned on, and Katie updated me on all the drama in her drama club (spoiler alert: there was a lot). Even more, the messages became a distraction from the fact that my summer plans had blown up in my face, that all of my friends' futures were so much more promising than mine.

More than all of that, Elm is something just for me, not my parents, not Aunt Chrissy, not Katie, just me.

I stare at the envelope.

One new message.

I tap.

# Hi, Carrie

Sure enough, it's from ElmStreetNightmare84, sent this morning at eleven a.m.

*Okay, okay, on your recommendation, I did re-watch* Get Out *last night. I mean, I loved it the first time, but you couldn't be more right. Every line! Every. Single. Line. It's no wonder he got the Oscar for writing. Side note: Did you know that only six horror movies have ever even been nominated for Best Picture? It's a shame, I tell ya, a total shame.*

*All right, my rec is this—don't follow me to a cabin in the woods and murder me, but it's NOT EXACTLY HORROR THIS TIME. I know, I know. But it's a thriller (that counts, right?). It's called* Victoria, *and the whole thing takes place in, I kid you not, ONE SHOT. It's nuts.*

*Can't wait to hear what you think. Seriously. You are the Queen of the Quizzically Terrifying IMHO (even if this one isn't quite as terrifying as others).*

*Peace!*

*Elm*

Queen of the Quizzically Terrifying: six out of ten stars, not one of his best nicknames, to be honest—he's either getting soft or has run out of alliteratives—but it's still very, very sweet. In the past he's called me Empress of All Eerie, Monarch of Monsters, and Feudal Lord of the Fear-Inducing, which remains my personal favorite.

Here's all I know about Elm:

He lives in North Carolina.

He's seventeen.

His aunt is an indie horror director.

His favorite food is mac and cheese.

His horror movies of choice are closed-door mysteries, the kind where people are trapped in a house together and have to figure out who did it. Very classic.

That's pretty much it. Though I could practically create an algorithm designed around his specific movie tastes, when it comes to the nitty-gritty real life details, I know so little. His name, for one. If he has a job. Where he wants to go to college. He's mentioned an interest in film school, but never really elaborated.

His knowledge is equally limited about me. He knows I live in Brooklyn, that I'm seventeen, and my aunt is a freelance creative director (we went off on a tangent about cool aunts once). He's heard about my daily, post-class spinach pie; and he's clear on the fact that I don't have a favorite horror genre: ghost stories, zombies, murder mysteries, creature features—I'll do them all, as long as they're good (and sometimes, even if they're not that good; it's an addiction, after all).

My thumbs hover over the keyboard on my phone, trying to think of exactly how to describe the movie he recommended to me yesterday morning, the one I stayed up until two a.m. watching in the basement, the one his aunt had passed along to him.

*I'm so glad you enjoyed* Get Out, Round 2! *Your rec was equally delightful. The story was just so, how do I even describe it? It got under your skin. I need more recs from your aunt, especially since summer vacay has officially started. Are you guys out of school yet? My friend and I had our last spinach pies of the year this afternoon :(*

*Anyway, have you ever watched* Rope? *It's an old Hitchcock with Jimmy Stewart and some other guys whose names I do not recall. It is SO GOOD. I think it's right up your alley, the whole trapped in one room/home thing. I tried to get my friend to watch it last week (it's not gruesome at all, so I thought she'd be fine with it), but she called it boring . . . OY. Honestly it's hard to get her to watch anything that's not straight-up Oscar bait.*

*I will totally be checking out* Victoria *but not tonight. The aforementioned friend wants me to come over and celebrate the "end of our imprisonment," as she has been referring to it for months, so that means I'll most likely be watching something with Meryl Streep, or "National Treasure Meryl Streep," as she calls her. Her Meryl obsession is as bad as my horror obsession, so it can get a little old.*

*Talk soon!*

*Carrie*

I tap Send.

Yes, we are Elm and Carrie to each other—that's it. And I love it; it's half the fun. There's an anonymity there, something I don't get at school or with Katie or my parents. Freedom.

After all, you can only go on about horror movies for so long before people lose interest, call you morbid, and think you're a freak. Not with Elm. Even my parents, who pride themselves on being supportive, will give me a funny look if they walk into my room during a particularly gruesome scene. And of course they *always* walk in at just the worst time.

On top of that, I can't disappoint him, because he doesn't know me. He accepts me, even the parts of me that don't shine quite as brightly in real life. Sheltered by the glow of my phone's screen, I'm not afraid to say whatever comes into my mind. A cheesy joke or nerdy bit of humor. An honest feeling or realization. There are no consequences. No high school theater directors staring slack-jawed as you mess up your lines. We're modern-day pen pals, nothing more. And as much as I know having an online pen pal is still rare and nerdy AF in today's age, it makes me happy, so happy.

I jump as my phone dings, an unfamiliar sound. In the bottom corner, a notification has appeared. *ElmStreetNightmare84 would like to chat.*

I hesitate. We're so safe in our world of messages. Live chatting, that's a whole other thing. Still, I want to know what he has to say. I tap Accept.

*ElmStreetNightmare84: Hi Carrie*

The name, said so casually like a greeting, makes me smile just the tiniest bit. I turn around, glancing at my movie poster behind me.

*CarriesRevenge01: Hi Elm*

Then nothing. Just those stupid little dots. Why, suddenly, does he want to chat? What changed?

Finally:

*ElmStreetNightmare84: I was on here and I got your message! Thought you might be on too—hope it's not too much of an imposition, popping in like this*

*ElmStreetNightmare84: I promise I'm not watching you through the screen like some crazy horror movie stalker ;)*

I laugh at his cheesy humor. He keeps typing.

*ElmStreetNightmare84: My methods would be way less cliché anyway, believe me*

*CarriesRevenge01: How do you know I'm not watching YOU through the screen? I have no problem with clichés :D*

*ElmStreetNightmare84: Sorry, but I expected more of you, Justice of Jump Scares*

I roll my eyes.

*CarriesRevenge01: You're such a nerd*

*ElmStreetNightmare84: Guilty as charged! So school's out, huh?
Me too. What are you up to now?*

I hesitate, feeling that hot sting of failure again.

*CarriesRevenge01: Oh, you know. All movies, all the time.*

*ElmStreetNightmare84: Duh! I forgot about your film program.
NYU, right?*

All at once, I realize he's completely misunderstood me.

I should correct him. I should correct him right now.

*ElmStreetNightmare84: I'm actually interning at this indie film
collective up north, the one my aunt's a part of. Not as cool as NYU,
but still . . .*

*ElmStreetNightmare84: Anyway, speaking of movies, I had a
question for ya*

*CarriesRevenge01: Shoot*

*ElmStreetNightmare84: I was watching this doc about old peo-
ple who go online just to make friends with teens . . .*

I feel instant relief. Discussion of summer plans is over. Back to
banter about movies we've watched. I can do banter. I can do banter
well, if I do say so myself.

*CarriesRevenge01: You caught me! Despite what I told you, I'm
actually sixty-five.*

*ElmStreetNightmare84: Wow, oldie! I'm only sixty-three! Eesh.
It's almost five. Isn't it your dinnertime right now?*

*CarriesRevenge01: Nope, I already ate. Early Bird Special ends
at 4:30*

*ElmStreetNightmare84: lol*

*ElmStreetNightmare84: Really though, we should trade pics,
you know, to confirm that neither of us are sexagenarians*

*ElmStreetNightmare84: (which sounds way sexier than it is)*

My stomach twists, and it's not from the spinach pie. Suddenly, it feels like things are moving too quickly, going from easy and anonymous to anxiety inducing, just like that.

Photos are a different level. Photos have flaws, pimples, and pores. You can't capture your witty banter, your love for 1930s noir, in a photo. Photos are for people like Katie, who know how to perfectly shoot a selfie practically out of the womb.

I steal a glance in the mirror, which only confirms what I'm feeling. There's a bright red pimple on my cheek, one that's probably going to leave a mark, and my hair is going every which way, curls refusing to be tamed. There are circles under my eyes from staying up late to watch the movie last night, begging for some under-eye concealer. I know it shouldn't be that big of a deal, but there's something nice about it being like this, where there aren't faces to names, where it's only our words that matter.

My heart beats quickly as my fingers hover over the keyboard, trying to think of a way to say no without making it sound like I am a sexagenarian. But then—

*ElmStreetNightmare84: Here, I'll go first!*

His photo appears. Elm is on my screen, smiling all wide and goofy.

My heart beats faster. Beyond the playful grin, it's impossible not to realize it:

Elm is actually . . . kind of . . . really hot.

His hair is messy-cool, falling just past the top of his forehead, and his kind brown eyes peek behind glasses, the good kind of glasses, the ones with thick round frames that make him look intellectual but still very attractive. His teeth are straight—he definitely had braces at some point. There's not a single pimple on his face—it's clear apart from a hairline scar just under his left eye—and he's wearing a gray T-shirt with a crossword puzzle on it. At the edges of his arms, you can see hints of muscle.

It's not like he's the most gorgeous guy in the world or anything, but if I saw him around Brooklyn, well, I'd definitely be looking twice.

I won't lie, there are times, over the last month, when I'd imagined what he looked like. Part of me wanted him to be cute, wanted it really badly, in fact. But now that he is, it's a little unnerving. It's easier to be charming if you've got absolutely nothing to lose, when you don't know there's a hot guy on the other side of the screen.

Another message pops up:

*ElmStreetNightmare84: Your turn*

I take a deep breath.

*CarriesRevenge01: Sure, hang on a sec*

I hold up my phone and push the button.

It's all wrong. My nose looks huge, my eyes too wide, zombie-like.

I shake my head and hold my phone higher this time, push the button again.

But it's wrong, too. My pimple stands out, my curls look awful, all messed up and weird.

I try another one. And another. But it's no use.

His pic was so . . . cute. So easy and relaxed. Taken instantly. Snapped and sent, just like that.

Now he knows I'm sitting here toying with my selfies. He knows I lack the confidence to shoot off a simple photo.

I shake my head. All I know is every second makes the whole thing more awkward.

I need to get the hell out of Dodge, like Marion Crane at the beginning of *Psycho*.

*CarriesRevenge01: Sorry gotta go, will send one later!*

Before he can say anything else, I close the Reddit app and toss my phone across the bed, as if I can trap my insecurities, lock them away inside the tiny pixels of my screen.

# Vertigo

I hear the twist of the key in the door right on schedule, just a minute after six o'clock. Within seconds, my mom has poked her head into my room. "Happy last day, Tiger!" She beams. People always say we look alike, from our hair, curly and unmanageable, to our eyes, wide and round, to our oily Irish skin. My mom's skin is fine, now, but if you look closely under the light, you can see her history: years of the same acne that currently plagues me. "I got us a table at Spumoni Gardens."

"Oh wow," I say, instantly glad I didn't finish my spinach pie. L&B Spumoni Gardens is only the best restaurant in all of Brooklyn—and maybe the earth. Best pizza. Best pasta. Best eggplant. Best everything.

She tilts her head. "Don't tell me I don't ever do anything nice for my daughter."

"Thanks, Mom," I say. "Chrissy coming, too?"

"Of course," she says. "Now get into some real clothes. Dad will be home within the hour."

As promised, Dad gets home at seven, but Chrissy doesn't show. At seven fifteen, I shoot her a quick, *Where you at*, but when I don't hear back, my mom insists we go.

"We're really not going to wait for her?" I ask as I climb into the backseat of my parents' Subaru.

My mom's in the driver's seat and my dad's on his phone, likely reading yet another article from the *New York Times*—one he'll want to discuss at length at dinner. "I don't know what to tell you, Olivia. I told her about the reservation. She'll just have to meet us there."

I pull out my phone, type, *Can you meet us?*, but just then, the car door bursts open. "What, were you trying to ditch me? On my favorite niece's last day of school? Rude, you guys. Rude."

Chrissy thunks her messenger bag down, bursting with her laptop, sketchbook, charcoal pencils, and loads of receipts and other paraphernalia, and pulls the door shut behind her. She's wearing a striped dress over ripped-up tights (Chrissy always wears tights, no matter the weather) and thick black boots.

Chrissy looks like my mom and me—everyone says that, too—but at the same time, she's so different. Her hair is longer, looser, and straight enough that she can pull off bangs (I tried to emulate them two summers ago, to epic failure), but it's not just that. She's got this whole aura about her that's just . . . cool.

She squeezes my shoulder. "You know I wouldn't miss it for the world, darling."

"Appreciate your promptness, as always," my mom says.

"Was the R train acting up?" my dad asks, much more kindly.

Chrissy tousles my hair. "No, I was actually in the nabe already. I was finishing up some quick edits on my laptop at this bar—you know the one on Eighty-Fifth, the one Danny used to own? And I was ready to go, but then there was this rush of people—after-work crowd, I guess—and the bartender took a million years to close my tab. I was telling him, I've got to go celebrate my niece, but—"

"Working at a bar," my mom says, her voice trailing off.

"The ceiling's being fixed at my studio," Chrissy says. "I told you that. They found asbestos last week."

My mom sighs, backing out of the driveway. "And I told you that there's a new coworking space opening up right by you—all women."

Chrissy catches my eyes—we both know the truth about my mother—she expects perfection. She prides herself on being the toughest-grading art history professor at Pratt, and her high standards extend to real life, too. She wants Chrissy to be the Perfect Role Model Aunt. For me to be the Perfect Daughter with the right balance of extracurriculars, social activity, and grades.

"This works for me, Cam," Chrissy says finally. "And saves money on coworking fees."

Dad looks up from his article and turns to face us, smiling, as always. "May I please request no sisterly bickering before Spumoni Gardens? I need the mental space to prepare my stomach for the onslaught of deliciousness."

We all laugh then. Dad always knows the right thing to say.

The restaurant smells like tomatoes, basil, and oregano. And cheese, lots and lots of cheese. The hostess leads us to a table in the corner, and we squeeze in, Chrissy and I hugging the table to avoid bumping into the people next to us. It's loud in here, as usual. A cacophony of voices, clattering dishes, wineglasses clinking together. Family and friends celebrating. My dad, Iowa-born-and-bred, takes in his surroundings. You can tell that even after living here for years, the bustle and pulse of everything still awes him.

My mom grew up in Brooklyn, in the very house we live in, actually, though you'd hardly know it. She went to Iowa for undergrad and graduate school, where she met my dad. He was studying journalism; she was studying art. They got married in Iowa and had me there, nascent years I don't remember; but I like to imagine they were spent frolicking through cornfields.

When I was five, my mom got offered a job at Pratt. Journalism was "making its slow and agonizing crawl toward extinction," as my dad says, and so we moved. My mom's parents were retiring—they live in a beach community in Florida now—and their old house became ours. We've been here ever since.

We go to rural Iowa to visit my dad's parents every Christmas. We drive from the airport, on highways surrounded by actual cornfields, and what I notice more than anything else—when my grandma and grandpa aren't asking me what it's like to grow up in "the Big Apple"—is how quiet everything is. It's the same as it is in our house in the Catskill Mountains. Quiet that stretches out, wraps itself all around you.

"What are we going to order?" Chrissy asks, rubbing her hands together. "Or perhaps more accurately, what are we *not* going to order? Because I want just about everything."

I request the pizza, Dad wants to make sure we don't skip over linguine and clams and eggplant parm; Chrissy has to have the scaloppine; and Mom isn't sure if we really need a whole bottle of wine or if we should just do glasses. Eventually, the makings of a proper order form, and Mom delivers it, line by line, to the guy in a Spumoni Gardens T-shirt who looks about two years younger than me—and like he stepped out of central casting: Pizzeria Boy. Outside, I see a tour bus pull up and people pile out, heading to the area of the restaurant where you can get pizza to go—some of them are probably from Iowa. You can't be the best food in Brooklyn without getting your share of tourists, I suppose.

Mom and Chrissy talk about their mom, my nana, who recently applied to be on the board of her condo association in Florida, and all the drama that's ensued, as if our lives were actually turning into a *Seinfeld* episode. Dad, in a shocking turn of events, tells us about the *New York Times* article he'd been reading in the car, a piece on the incubation lab for many a famous Broadway project. I stay quiet as the conversation ping-pongs back and forth.

Unlike a lot of people my age, I don't dislike spending time with my family. I don't think they're lame or boring or anything. To be honest, I like listening to their conversations, hearing Dad go on about how in the world we can save journalism, occasionally wishing he'd never traded it in for marketing director of a start-up, or Chrissy talk about her escapades (which Mom always side-eyes her for) and her ad campaign of the moment. I even like hearing my mom detail the goings-on at Pratt and the bureaucracy of academia. When we're all together like this, it just works.

The hardest part isn't that I don't think they're cool—quite the opposite. The hardest part is that I wonder if I'll ever be as cool and successful as them.

The food comes out and we dig in, family-style. Sicilian pizza, the crust crispy and buttery on the bottom, tomatoes tart and crushed to perfection on top. Forkfuls of linguine and layers of eggplant; bites of chicken marsala and pork scaloppine. I sip my dad's wine to wash it down, because after they've each had a glass, they grow slightly less uptight about the rules. The sauce, the cheese, the pasta—all of it is like a big warm hug after today.

My mom is pouring herself a second glass when she eyes my dad. "Shall I?"

"Go ahead," my dad says. "Tell her your news. Tell her what you found for her."

I don't let them see it, but I feel a prickle of excitement in my gut. I set my fork of linguine down on my plate, eager. My mom has contacts in the art world, contacts she alluded to when I told her I didn't get accepted into my program. I was sure it was too late for her to drum up anything, but maybe I was wrong. Maybe something actually panned out.

"Well, since it didn't work out with NYU—"

"Screw that bougie-ass school," Chrissy says. "They don't know what they're missing."

"Chrissy!" my mom says, horrified.

She only shrugs. "What? It's true."

"Well, anyway, like I was saying, since it didn't come to fruition, I put some feelers out, like I said I would." She takes another sip of wine. "You're in luck. One of my contacts came through."

I feel a sense of overwhelming relief, and I tell myself never to doubt my mother and her methods again. My dear mother and her art world contacts.

"Wow," I say, jumping out of my chair and wrapping her in a hug across the table. "Thank you so much, Mom."

I sit back down and try not to focus on how much she looks taken aback. I make a mental note to thank her more, whoops.

I pick up my fork and take another bite of linguine, swallowing it down quick. Our town in the Catskills, Woodstock, is artsy. And Hudson, just across the river, has lots of galleries. I imagine returning to Xaverian High, telling all the girls about the summer I spent interning at a gallery or museum. It wouldn't be a bad thing to have on a film school application, would it? Art and cinema go hand in hand. Maybe even something with the word "collective" in the title, like Elm's place. I wouldn't be a failure after all. I'd be a cool gallery girl. Perhaps I'd start drinking almond milk. And reading the *New Yorker*. And using the word "ubiquitous." Might even wear a beret, unironically. "Er, do we need to go shopping or anything? I don't have a ton of, you know, professional clothes. Or maybe there's not a dress code? I don't know what the art scene is like up there."

"Easy there, killer," my dad says.

"Huh?"

My mom slowly sets down her wine. She and my dad exchange another glance.

"Go ahead," he says again.

These two are full of surprises, like a horror movie that won't end. What is it that they're not telling me?

"It's not in the art world," my mom says cautiously.

"Oh," I say. "Oh my god, it's not in film, is it? I know the Wood-stock Film Festival is probably beginning to plan already."

"Not exactly," my mom says.

"It's still great, though," Dad says, finishing off his scaloppine. "Really."

My heart sinks. The "really" is like a nail in the coffin. He wouldn't say it like that if it were anything that didn't need a true hard sell . . .

I glance to Chrissy, but she only shrugs. She doesn't know what they're up to, either.

"My old high school friend Marianne lives up there now," my mom says.

Marianne? I've never even heard of a high school friend Marianne. Boy, she must have really had to dig deep.

"Marianne?" Chrissy says. "You guys are still in touch?"

My mom nods dismissively. "Yes, and—"

"Wait, I think I saw something on Facebook. I don't get it. Doesn't she—"

"She owns a zip-lining company," my mom interrupts, her voice unnaturally bright.

My fork clangs against the plate.

I turn to see Chrissy, jaw agape.

"Zip-lining?" I ask. "Like, harnessing your body to a string and catapulting through the air for no reason?"

"I suppose that's the gist of it," my mom says with an awkward laugh. "Anyway, we got you a job there."

"A job? Like manning the zip line? Did you tell her I'm not exactly . . . outdoorsy?"

My mom brushes bread crumbs off the table with one hand, *literally* brushing my concerns aside. "They'll train you properly, I'm sure."

"And that I'm not into heights?" I don't have full-on vertigo or anything, but heights are not my thing. Five minutes at the top of One World Trade Center, and I wanted to be back down. Stat.

Chrissy grabs her glass of wine, takes a gulp. "*That's* what you got her? Geez, I thought at least it would be a restaurant or something. Making the poor girl work at a place she's afraid of? It's a little much, even for you, Cam."

My mom's eyes shoot daggers at Chrissy, but she doesn't respond.

"Chrissy's right," I say. "If it's just about a job, I can work at a restaurant. Or a shop or something."

My mom crosses her arms. "Have you applied to any restaurants or shops, Olivia? Woodstock is small. I'm sure everything is all booked up for the summer. Jobs don't just grow on trees, you know. Plus, this will get you out of your comfort zone."

"Oh, come on, Cam," Chrissy says. "This is supposed to be a celebration. Did you really have to tell her like this?"

"Can you stay out of it?" my mom snaps.

My dad takes a deep breath. "Enough, you two." He turns to me. "Olivia, it's all incredibly secure. Most of the time, you'll be on the base of the mountain anyway, checking people in and sending them up and all that. Don't worry, we looked into it."

I look from my dad to my mom and back again. "So that's it?"

Silence as they stare at me. Yes, that's it, their eyes say. That's definitely it.

I rack my brain, trying to think of an excuse. "I was thinking about working on my screenplay, you know," I blurt out. "Taking some time to actually write."

My mom smiles. "That's perfect, actually. Marianne said she doesn't need anyone until high season, which isn't for a couple of weeks, so you'll have time for all that."

I stare at my mom. I want to shake my head, tell her no way, no how, but how can I? I'm the one who procrastinated the NYU application, the one who didn't try and figure anything else out.

"All right," I say finally. "If that's what you really want."

"It is," my mom says. "Now, let's not let this ruin our dinner. Shall we look at the dessert menu?"

Beneath the table, Chrissy reaches out, grabs my hand in hers, gives it a squeeze.

Sometimes I swear she's the only one out of all of them who gets me.

# What Would Meryl Do

It's nine by the time they drop me off at Katie's, a colonial brick home set back from the road with a little patch of lawn and everything. I dash up the walk, the Subaru idling behind me, and knock three times. In seconds Katie is at the door, waving hello to my parents and ushering me in.

I step into the hallway I've come to know so well. Everything in Katie's world is shiny and new. The tiles are this cool slate color, and the floors are dark chocolate hardwood. The walls are painted a perfect neutral gray that a decorator picked out.

"Hey, Olivia," Alice, Katie's mom, says from the leather sofa, where she's snuggled up with their dachshund, Cooper. "Happy last day!"

Like Katie, Katie's mom is pretty awesome. She's a writer, for one thing, with a stash of her own books sitting in the color-coded bookshelves in their living room. But more than that, she's not uptight at all. She watches loads of TV, including the really dumb reality stuff. She's always taking the two of us to the newest Broadway shows. And she and Katie have all these mother-daughter dates together—Russian Tea Room, mani-pedis, that kind of thing.

"Hi," I say as I follow Katie to the kitchen: a big open room about twice the size of my family's, covered in white tiles that make it look like the walls in the subway, only fancier.

Katie reaches for a bag of popcorn, tossing it into the microwave.

"Please," I say. "I can't eat for days after the meal I just had."

She ignores my objection, pushing the start button. "You'll want some, trust me."

Katie knows me inside and out, better than any of the other girls at Xaverian High. Tessa is always joking that Katie is the assistant manager of my life, running the day to day. When we're out together, she usually ends up choosing where we go, where we stop to eat, and what have you. It sounds weird—and maybe it is—but I kind of like it that way. The pressure is off of me to take the reins.

Besides, when I try to do things on my own—case in point, NYU—I always find a way to screw them up.

Katie grabs two glasses from the cabinet and fills them up with the sparkling water that's always at her house, then pushes one over to me.

"Where's your dad this time?" I ask, taking a sip.

"Tokyo," she says. "Eating sushi every day. Asshole."

I laugh, and she does, too. Her dad travels a lot, but he's not one of those absent fathers married to his work or anything. Sometimes he even takes Katie on his business trips, if she can get time off school and isn't in the middle of school play rehearsals. It's part of why Alice feels different from most moms. When Katie's dad, Peter, is gone, it's kind of like they're sisters or something. Katie's an only child, like me.

Up in her room, we arrange ourselves on the sofa, the steaming bowl of popcorn between us. Katie's bedroom is huge, like a teenager would have on a TV show. It's painted the same pale shade of gray as the rest of the house, but with bright colors everywhere—a multi-colored bedspread her dad picked up from Morocco, a blue velvet sofa in one corner that's set up perfectly for watching movies on her huge TV. The walls are lined with shelves topped with different curiosities from all over the world. A Mardi Gras mask. A wood carving from Indonesia.

Katie reaches behind her and dims the lights, then flicks on the TV and queues up Netflix, hand already digging into the popcorn.

"I have bad news," I say.

She chews her popcorn quickly and swallows it down with sparkling water. "Oh god, what?"

"Nothing horrible," I say. "I just . . ."

"Spit it out, Olivia."

I sigh, grabbing a brightly colored pillow her dad brought back from Thailand and hugging it to my chest. "My parents are making me work at a *zip-line company.*"

Katie's mouth pops open. "What? Like, to fly through the woods?"

I nod. "Helping people catapult through the air."

Katie laughs. "Let me guess, your mom cooked this one up."

"She thinks it will get me out of my comfort zone," I say. "Direct quote."

Katie pauses, hand hovering over the bowl of popcorn.

"What?"

She grabs a few kernels. "I don't know. Maybe it will."

"What do you mean?" I ask.

She sighs. "I mean, maybe you need a little push." She smirks. "Even if it is off the side of a cliff. I mean, fear of change or success or whatever is obviously an issue for you. You completely self-sabotaged the whole NYU thing."

"Ouch," I say.

"What?" she asks. "It's true. I told you not to wait till the last minute. I worked on my application to the New School for ages. If you want to do something, you have to, you know, *do* it."

She's right, I know this, which is why I can't argue. And since she's Assistant Manager of My Life, I do look to her for advice. Still, she doesn't understand. I'm not naturally fabulous at things like she is. The *Dracula* auditions proved that. Had I not procrastinated, I still might not have gotten in.

"Anyway," Katie says. "It's up in the mountains. I bet there will be hot guys working up there. Maybe one of them can help you with your *pulleys* or whatever."

I laugh, reaching absentmindedly for the popcorn. If I were Katie, maybe I could simply distract myself with thoughts of all the cute boys that may be waiting upstate. Not only is she gorgeous, but she's a natural extrovert, and I am decidedly not—it's no wonder she's inherently good at acting. She has that je ne sais quoi, charm and beauty that lights up the room, draws people closer—like moths to flame. "You know how I am around new people," I say. "I get all awkward. Besides, I hardly think I'll attract a guy by having a vertigo-inspired panic attack when I'm trying to do my job."

Katie smirks. "Come now, don't be dramatic. That's my role."

"Fine," I say. "But you have to at least come up on the weekends, give me something to do that's not fear-inducing."

Katie purses her lips. "You know I can't."

"Why?"

She ticks off her fingers. "First off, I'm going to be mega busy with whatever sort of productions they have us doing. Secondly, this summer is all about making connections, Olivia. I can't just come upstate every weekend while everyone else in the program is becoming besties. WWMD."

What Would Meryl Do, a common refrain of Katie's, one used so frequently that Fatima even translated it into French—*Qu'est-ce que Meryl ferait?* Tessa and Eloise have grown completely tired of it, but Fatima and I still (usually) find it endearing.

"Maybe Meryl would connect with her acting roots in the cool, refreshing mountain air," I say.

Katie shakes her head. "I'm sorry, Olivia, but this is *everything* to me. I have to give it my all. Come on, let's start a movie, okay? I'm sure everything, even zip-line running, will feel better once you're up there."

Without waiting for an answer, she flips through her Netflix queue, landing on *Kramer vs. Kramer.*

"Really?" I ask. "We've watched this one already."

Katie pouts. "Not for at least a year! You said it was my pick, anyway. She kills it in this, and I need to brush up on how to play a really negative character for auditions and stuff." Without another word, she presses Play and grabs another handful of popcorn.

We're not two minutes into the opening credits before Katie pauses it, turning to me. "I'm sorry," she says. "Do you really not want to watch this?"

I shake my head. "No, it's not that," I say. "I'm just mad at myself . . . I should have tried harder. I shouldn't have procrastinated."

Katie holds up a finger. "Look, I know I just gave you a little tough love, but what's done is done. There's no point in dwelling on regrets, okay? I know I sound like your mom and all, but I really think this will be good for you. When you're not sending people through the air, you can have some peace and quiet to work on your screenplay. I wasn't bullshitting this afternoon. Lots of people do their most creative work outside the confines of schools and programs."

I nod. "You're probably right. I just have to write the damn thing, stop putting it off."

Katie grins. "Exactly! WWMD doesn't just apply to actors, you know. It's a whole spirit of living. Going for the gold, that kind of thing. You know Meryl was in *She-Devil* and *Death Becomes Her* practically back-to-back. She could have been written off as someone limited to campy comedic horror—no offense."

I laugh. "None taken."

"But what did she do? She kept on fighting, and within a few years, she was killing it in *Bridges of Madison County*. It put her back on the map! It helped make her the national treasure that she continues to be today. Never forget, Olivia. This is only your *Death Becomes Her* moment. This is only one step of your story."

"I'm no Meryl Streep," I say.

Katie raises an eyebrow. "We all have a Meryl inside of us, Olivia. You should really know that by now."

I force a smile, but what Katie's forgetting, or what she's pretending to forget, is that I already *had* my *Death Becomes Her* moment.

It's half of what's made it so easy to self-sabotage in the first place.

# The First Death Becomes Her Moment, Explained

I was the one who told Katie about the *Dracula* auditions freshman year. It was me who convinced Katie to try out, who watched different *Dracula* adaptations almost every night, getting into character. For Katie, it was nothing more than an afterthought.

I was all set. I'd memorized the monologue of Lucy, the female lead, her character weak as anything after Dracula lets her blood: "Oh, I do feel so thin I barely cast a shadow . . ." I'd practiced it: in front of the mirror, in the shower, after pausing *Dracula* on my laptop, whispering it to the posters on the walls in my room. Not to mention, it was horror, something I'd been obsessing over since middle school.

It's not like I expected to get the part of Lucy—I was only a freshman and totally new to acting—but I was hoping for a vampire, at least. I was hoping for something.

Katie and I went to the auditorium together, sat in the itchy fabric seats, waiting our turns. She held her monologue in her hand, on fresh white paper, as if she'd only just printed it at the school library. Looking it over, she mouthed the words to herself.

"Didn't you practice?" I asked.

"A little," she said. "But I'm mostly doing this for you, anyway."

I shook my head, mentally running through my lines again. I didn't need a sheet of paper. It was all there, etched into my brain's gray matter. I'd done a video recording that morning. I'd aced it.

"Katie Dry," Ms. Sinclair, the drama teacher, called. Katie stood up, walking down the aisle and up the stairs to the stage slowly, casually, as if she didn't have a care in the world.

She took one glance at her paper, then folded it quickly, shoving it into her pocket. She cleared her throat, and then she started.

It was strange, as her best friend, to watch her. She didn't sound anything like herself, truly. It was almost like she opened her mouth and another person came out. One who was sad, scared even, but witty and cheeky all the same. But the weirdest part was, she didn't sound like she was acting at all. She was a natural. Her delivery was seamless. Beautiful. When she finished, there was a collective pause, as if we were all waiting to see if she had anything more to give us that day.

She didn't even say thank you, just walked off the stage, back along the aisle, and plunked down next to me. "How did I do?"

I could barely get a syllable out—how in the world could you describe perfection?—before they called my name. "Olivia Knight!"

I jumped up, climbing the steps quickly, and stood in the middle.

But the lights were so bright, Ms. Sinclair's eyes too piercing. Everything looked different from up on the stage. And I couldn't get Katie's performance out of my head. It was blindsiding. She was so natural, so easy and cool, without even trying. Flashing to all my practices, my whole interpretation suddenly seemed overwrought.

"You can go ahead," Ms. Sinclair said.

I cleared my throat. "Oh, I do feel so—"

I froze. Suddenly, I couldn't remember. I do feel so *what*? I wanted to fill in the blanks with other words: "scared," "embarrassed," "ashamed."

I took a deep breath. "Oh, I do feel so . . ."

It wouldn't come. I didn't even have the damn thing printed out, didn't have something to check.

"Take your time," Ms. Sinclair said. "No rush."

I nodded, tears welling my eyes, then spit out the words. "Oh, I do feel so thin I barely cast a shadow . . ." This time it came, though it was garbled. I flubbed lines left and right, skipping around. When I was done, I scurried off the stage as fast as my legs would carry me. It was only back in my seat that the hot salty tears kissed my cheeks.

"It wasn't that bad," Katie said. "Really. You got through it in the end."

We both knew she was wrong.

I hoped that maybe Ms. Sinclair would throw me a bone, give me Vampire Number Six or something, but I didn't even get that.

Katie was cast as Lucy. Of course she was cast as Lucy.

I was given the position of stagehand.

The rest is history. Katie killed it in the production, while I moved the props around, setting a chair just right so she could properly deliver her lines. Afterward, she dove head first into the world of acting, while I realized that if I wanted to channel my movie love into something, it had to be in a different way. I'd always been a big reader—writing felt natural. I began to research screenwriters, to watch even more horror, to think about film school, to jot down script ideas, write my own scary short stories.

Still, there was always that feeling—of failure, of loss, most of all, of having the rug yanked from under me.

I'd thought I'd had *Dracula* in the bag. I'd tried so hard, I'd practiced so much, but when push came to shove, I'd made a fool of myself.

It's hard to get the guts to trust myself again.

# What Would Meryl Do: Part Two

The movie is better than I remembered, and come eleven, Katie and I are hugging each other goodbye while Alice calls me a Lyft.

As I walk up my driveway, I can see that most of the lights in the house are dark, but when I get inside, I notice a light on in the basement, hear the din of TV. Chrissy and my mom can agree on one thing—their love of *I Love Lucy*. It's one they've imparted on me, one that's kept all of us up many a night. I head for the stairs, eager to join them and forget everything that happened at dinner. But as I reach the first step, I hear talking, louder than anything on the TV.

"You should never have questioned me like that," my mom says. If it weren't for her tone, I would hardly be able to tell it was her. She and Chrissy have almost the same voice, but Chrissy doesn't talk like that, all judge-y and uptight.

"I'm sorry," Chrissy says. "I was only saying . . . You're obviously trying to push her, but is this really the right way? Signing her up for something she's legitimately scared of? What if Mom had made you, I don't know, work at a spider exhibit?"

They're talking about me.

"Can you not be completely ridiculous for one second?" my mom says.

"I'm just saying," Chrissy goes on. "Our parents let us find our own way. They didn't force it."

"Well, maybe if they had forced it, you wouldn't be pushing forty-five and still stumbling home from bars at three a.m."

"Jesus, Cam," Chrissy says. "That's totally uncalled for. It's my life, okay?"

"I'm just pointing out that you're still living the life you were twenty years ago. I'm not."

"Yeah, I know you're not, Cam. Neither am I, actually. All I care about is what's best for Olivia. That's all I was saying."

"Yes, and by saying it, you've completely made me the bad guy," my mom says.

"I didn't mean to—"

"Besides, what's best for her is to get out of the damn house. She's been wasting away in front of the TV and internet all year. I don't want her to do the same thing but with mountains in the background. She needs this, and if you were her mom, you'd know that. But you're not, okay?"

"You don't have to be so cruel about it," Chrissy says.

"If you wanted your own kids," my mom says, "you should have had your own. Don't try to parent mine."

Silence. And then a shuffle of steps.

Quickly, I turn around, rush to the front door, pull it open and shut—loudly—as if I've only just walked in.

"Olivia," my mom says. Her lips are pressed tightly together, but in her eyes, there's a sheen of moisture, like she's about to cry if she doesn't hold it together properly. She forces a smile. "How's Katie?"

"What are you doing up?" I ask.

"Chrissy and I were just watching *I Love Lucy*," she says. "She's got to work early, though. She's about to leave."

Chrissy comes up the stairs next, her lips pressed together just like my mother's. But she smiles when she sees me. "How was your movie?"

"Good," I say quickly, feeling my face go hot at all I've just heard. "I'm tired, though. I'm going to bed." I dash up the stairs before either of them can say anything else.

Back in my room, I shut the door tight and get on my laptop.

I can't get my mom's words out of my head.

*She's been wasting away all year.*

That's what she thinks of me. My own mother, who is supposed to, you know, love me unconditionally and all that. She thinks I'm a total loser.

An awful thought strikes me. *Is she right?*

I grab my phone and open Reddit. I should write to Elm, apologize for getting off so suddenly earlier.

I create a new message, unsure quite what to say. Everything I can think of sounds just awful.

*Sorry for not sending you a photo . . .*

*I was preparing to stuff my face with Italian food in a sad attempt to avoid the mess I've gotten myself in.*

*My best friend has decided that this is my* Death Becomes Her *moment, and honestly, she's kind of right, except I've already had one of those and that was embarrassing enough.*

*My mom thinks I'm wasting away, and my self-esteem admittedly ain't the greatest right now!*

A chat pops up, blinking at me.

*ElmStreetNightmare84: Hey stranger, still waiting on that photo ;)*

*ElmStreetNightmare84: Unless you are sixty-five, which is cool and all, just, uhh, lemme know, OK?*

*ElmStreetNightmare84: Also, with no photo to go on, it's like I'm*

*trapped in a room with a two-way mirror . . . you can see me but I*
*can't see you! AND THE POLICE COULD GET ME AT ANY MOMENT*

He's right. No photos would be one thing, but since he's gone ahead and sent his with the promise of mine in return, our whole balance will be off if I don't immediately send one over.

Katie's words pop into my head. What Would Meryl Do? She'd probably just send the damn photo and not give it another thought.

Only Meryl, like Katie, is blond and beautiful. With easy popularity and natural confidence. The type to deliver a *Dracula* monologue flawlessly. If I were Meryl, or Katie, this whole thing would be a hell of a lot easier.

A text appears. From Katie. **Miss you already.** It comes with a photo of her smiling—half silly, half cute. Katie knows how to take a proper selfie. She knows how to not fail at summer before it's even started.

Alice would never say about Katie what my mom said about me.

Heart racing, fingers tingling with nerves, I make a snap decision, because What Would Meryl Do only works if you're someone like Meryl.

I go back to the Reddit app, and before I can stop myself, I load Katie's photo into the chat with Elm and hit Send.

He writes back immediately.

*ElmStreetNightmare84: Well hello there, Carrie, nice to meet your photo! Glad to see you are indeed not sixty-five!*

*CarriesRevenge01: Indeed I am not! Got to go to bed now. Talk tomorrow!*

I close the app, already partially regretting what I've done.

I know it's wrong, I know I shouldn't have, but just for a moment, it was nice to pretend I was as beautiful and pulled together and self-assured as Katie.

It was nice to pretend I wasn't wasting away.

I half want to message him again, tell him it was a lie, but it would sound ridiculous at this point. Embarrassing.

Besides, it's only a silly little online friendship. He'll never find out, and Katie won't, either.

It's not like we're ever going to meet in real life.

# The Bad Decision Handbook

You could definitely set a horror movie here, that's for sure.

I gaze out the window of my room, just after eleven a.m., the third morning of my Catskills summer, and all I can see is trees and the light trickle of the stream that borders our property. The cottage is small—only two bedrooms plus the attic—one you reach by a drive that winds in the shape of a snake. It's got green slats on the outside and all sorts of wood on the inside, uneven planks on the floor, rough-hewn beams on the ceilings. Last summer, I did my best to make this room mine, adding horror movie posters, knickknacks I picked up in town, and two coats of purple paint, which came out darker than I intended and only served to up the creep factor, which I secretly kind of love, despite my mom's attempts to get me to brighten it up with a lighter accent wall.

If the horror movie were *actually* set here, a group of friends would arrive for vacation, or a reunion, or a weekend far away from their parents if they're teens—or their regular lives if they're in their thirties—or what have you. Only, and here's the kicker, there would be a deranged killer, either lurking in the woods (*Friday the 13th*), or maybe even inside, among the people who've gathered here (*The Invitation*). Or maybe there's not a human killer, maybe there's a body snatcher deep in the forest, just waiting to take over one of the cabin's inhabitants (*Honeymoon*), or perhaps there are flesh-possessing demons, gearing up for their rise from the ground (*The Evil Dead*). Sometimes, you'd even get them all, a mixed bag of horror movie tropes, wrapped up into one delicious package (*The Cabin in the Woods*).

Of course, here there are no monsters like that. Here there is only one presence casting shadows over me—the screenplay that's still waiting to be written.

Even though I told myself I'd write every moment I could up here, yesterday and the day before didn't exactly go as planned. I traded writing time for helping my parents get the house in order and accompanying them to antiques stores, finishing off each night with horror movies that skip endlessly, given the slow internet.

But today I'm going to change that. I have to.

Groggy but determined to get in at least one line before noon, I open up my laptop and load my screenplay. The first thing I do is cut the mess of words I practically vomited onto the screen the day I submitted my NYU application, moving them to another document. I'll deal with that cluster later. For now, I'm starting back on the only thing that's even remotely decent—the first page.

*INTERIOR CABIN – DAY.*

The cursor blinks demonically at me, a challenge.

I rest my hands on the keyboard, ready to go, but my fingers tense up.

I glance to the title of my screenplay, at the top of the page in capital letters.

*THE BAD DECISION HANDBOOK*

My stomach feels weighty as a brick and my eyes beg me to return to sleeping. The idea is there, in my head—a satirical horror, playing off all the bad decisions characters typically make in horror movies—but actually writing it, that's a different story. The longest cohesive thing I've ever written is an essay on Emily Brontë. It was eight pages, double spaced, and filled halfway up with Heathcliff quotes. Right now, walking out to the backyard, digging my own grave, and carving up a headstone that says SHE WANTED TO BE A WRITER, ONE DAY seems easier than typing even a single word into this damn document.

I should be able to do this, do what every other writer in history has done and use my time "away from it all" to create something worth-while. The whole Stephen King up in Maine thing.

I stare at the cursor.

Problem is, I'm not Stephen King. The blank page makes me feel frozen, like in one of those dreams where you can't move. Or in a hor-ror movie, where the quaking main character knows that the killer is *just* around the corner but they, for whatever inane reason, stand there, stock-still, refusing to run.

Or a *Dracula* audition, lines erased from my brain.

I slam my laptop shut, push it aside, and get out of bed.

"Morning, sleepyhead," my dad says as I walk into the kitchen, looking up from his iPad. He and my mom are sitting at the round walnut table, drinking coffee and taking in the view of the mountains from the front window, like they always do. "The mountain air has got you sleeping, hasn't it?"

The truth is, I spent half the night trying to watch a movie, but it took me almost three hours to get through it, because our janky internet kept skipping. Once I finished, of course I had to chat to Elm about it. I finally signed off sometime after three a.m.

"The air *is* nice," I say, pouring coffee into my mug and adding a big splash of French vanilla creamer and three sugars. I make myself a bowl of cereal, then sit down between them, filching a piece of turkey bacon off my dad's plate. "That said, the internet is slower than the R train. I was up half the night trying to get my movie to play."

My mom crosses her arms and raises her eyebrows. "Would *you* like to fix it, Miss There's Always Something?"

I ignore her jab. "Sure," I say, forcing a smile. I stir my cereal and take a bite. "Take me to Best Buy, and I'll get us a Wi-Fi signal booster. I'll go today if you'll go with me."

"Internet's fine for me," my dad says, tilting his iPad toward me. "By the way, there's an article in today's *Times* about the economics of independent cinema. You might want to check it out."

"Thanks, Dad," I say. "I'll give it a read." I take another bite of cereal. "It's just, it's different when you're streaming a movie than reading an article. I could barely get anything to load last night."

My mom taps her spoon on the side of her cereal bowl, almost like she's trying to hypnotize me, like the mom in *Get Out*, and come to think of it, she probably is. To somehow convince me to be the active, hike-loving, ultra-productive daughter she never had. Chrissy is always telling me how my mom was always a go-getter, even when she was young, whereas Chrissy was the one who watched too much TV and drank too much light beer. "I don't want to tell you what to do, but maybe you should spend a little less time on the internet?"

If I had a nickel for every time she's told me she doesn't want to tell me what to do and then proceeded to do exactly that, I could pay Jordan Peele to write the damn screenplay for me. I take another bite of cereal. "And fill my time how? The job doesn't start for a little bit, right?"

*Writing your screenplay, you idiot.*

My parents exchange a look. "Well, the thing is," my mom says. "Marianne actually called this morning, saying she might need you sooner. I know I said it wouldn't be for a couple of weeks, and I know you wanted to work on your screenplay, but if you're up for it, she needs you."

I stare at my cereal bowl. On the one hand, the thought of willingly subjecting myself to the zip-line job—and earlier than necessary, at that—seems hellish, but all the same, the last forty-eight hours have been . . . difficult. There's been nothing to do, I can barely even get a movie going, and the silence, the emptiness and stagnation of it all, it's weighing on me. My chats with Elm are bright spots, but though he does check in during the day, the messages are few and far between. He's busy most days with his internship already in full swing, and it's not until the evening that our chats kick into full gear.

Plus, if I have something to do, I don't have to feel quite so bad that I'm not making any progress on my screenplay.

"Okay," I say. "I guess I can start earlier. I mean, if she really needs me."

"Perfect," my mom says, clasping her hands together. "Marianne says you can come in for training this afternoon."

# Fresh Meat

As a reward for my "flexibility," my parents make the twenty-minute drive down to Best Buy to get the signal booster, ensuring I'll be able to actually watch Elm's recs after my zip-lining shifts (oy). Afterward, we go by Target, stocking up on shorts and tees and comfy sorts of things to wear to my new place of employment.

We stop for a bite at this breakfast-all-day place in Woodstock the three of us are obsessed with, and after walking around town a bit—past galleries I won't be interning for, the record store that my dad can't pass without a stop, and the housewares shop where everything looks like it came out of a photo shoot about living in the mountains—it's one thirty, time to go. My training shift starts at two.

Scheduling-wise, I have to admit it's kind of perfect. Elm works from eleven to six most days, and since I never exactly disabused him of the notion that I'm at the NYU program, I've been careful not to be too quick to reply to his chats when I'm supposed to be in class, or workshopping, or doing one of the other amazing things I might have been doing this summer.

We get up the mountain roads easily, even taking the back way. My dad goes on the whole time about how wonderful it is to have all-wheel drive (I swear to god, if he could choose between a Porsche and our Subaru, he'd choose the latter). Eventually, we reach Hunter's Main Street, speckled with ski shops and pizza joints. We turn, climbing up the road until we reach a large building that must be the lodge, with huge windows and an undulating roof that mirrors the curve of the mountains behind it.

My mom points ahead. "Marianne said to go to that building just next to the lodge."

"Who do I ask for? Is Marianne there today?"

"Not sure," my mom says with a shrug. "I'm sure you'll figure it out though."

"Have a great first day!" my dad says as I grab my backpack and step out of the car. "We'll be back at six to pick you up."

I approach the door of the building my mom pointed to, but she has to be wrong—it looks like a ski shop closed down for the winter. Discount jackets and knit beanies. I turn back, scanning the parking lot, but the Subaru is already gone.

I pull out my phone. It's 2:01. Shit.

I walk to the left, toward the lodge, but the buildings are similarly empty.

2:03. Double shit. Here I am, already late for my first shift of a job my mom got me as a favor. I quickly return to the sad abandoned ski shop, dark and foreboding, the tense stillness of a setting right before all hell breaks loose. I pull on the handle. It's locked.

"What are you doing?"

I jump. Turning, I spot a girl about my age, maybe a little older. Her red hair has been looped into French braids that hug her scalp and land on her shoulders; she's got a nose ring and rows of studs crawling up her left earlobe; her hazel eyes are rimmed in dark kohl liner; and freckles cover almost every inch of her face and arms. She looks like a punk-rock Pippi Longstocking. She's wearing a Zipline Experience T-shirt, no less than four carabiners hang off the belt loops of her jean shorts, and a walkie-talkie beeps from her hip.

"Sorry, I—"

She crosses her arms. "Trying to break into the ski shop, load up on nylon gloves?"

"No—"

The girl bursts into cackling laughter, tossing her head back like some kind of cartoon villain. She stops, abruptly. "Sorry, I'm an ass. Are you Olivia?"

"Yeah, how did you . . ."

"Come on," she says, walking past me. I follow, and it's easy to keep up. She walks much slower than I do, than anyone in Brooklyn does. "You're looking for the check-in office, right?"

"I think so."

"It's right around here." She grins. "We've been looking forward to your arrival."

*Looking forward to your arrival?* I half want to tell her that she sounds like the bad guy in a movie. I mean, come on. That's the kind of line I'd find way too cheesy to ever put in a script, given that it's basically dripping with impending peril, the kind of line that would have popped into my head anyway and paralyzed me with writer's block.

"Er, you have?" I ask as we round the corner, approach a door with a sign above. ZIP-LINE CHECK-IN HERE.

"Of course we have," the girl continues. "Apart from one new guy, it's the same exact crew as last summer, and we're desperate for fresh meat."

*Fresh meat.* There she goes again. It would be fun to set a horror movie at a zip-line course, come to think of it. So many options. Some Sasquatch-style monster living up in the mountains, or a maniacal killer sabotaging the safety equipment. Or, everyone trapped in the abandoned ski lodge, doors locked, wondering who the killer could be. That's what Elm would do, if he were going to write it. There'd be some accident on the course, they'd be gathered in the lodge, the power would go out and the doors would lock from the inside, and only then would they realize that the accident hadn't been an accident at all, that the killer lurked among them, wearing the same Zipline Experience T-shirt and carabiners as everyone else . . .

The girl pauses outside the door. "I'm Steinway, by the way," she says.

"Steinway?"

"It's my last name. Like the piano, which I also play." She tosses her head back in laughter again. "Oh boy, you already think I'm way too much."

I shake my head. "No, not at all."

She smiles and opens the door. "Follow me."

Inside, the place is nothing like the ski shop. The room echoes with voices, with groups of kids and adults, people on vacation or at least on vacation for the day.

Steinway walks through rows of T-shirts and gear for sale to a wrap-around check-in desk in the back. She hinges up the corner of the desk and lets herself in. I follow.

There's a guy at the counter, typing into a computer caked with dust.

"You can put your bag and stuff here," she says, opening one of the cabinets.

I toss in my things and she hands me a clipboard. "Oh, and sign this. Just your basic waiver. Now, let me find you a T-shirt." She kneels down, opening and shutting cabinet doors.

Clipboard in hand, I gaze at the line of people, then back at the counter guy. "Does he need help?"

Steinway shakes her head. "They're all going on the two-thirty tour. Tennyson will check them in. There's time, my friend, plenty of time."

"Okay," I say. I scribble my signature on the waiver, not reading it too closely, but sure that if I massively fall to my death out there, it will not be Zipline Experience's fault at all. Then I shove my hands into my pockets, not quite sure what to do. Tennyson is tall and skinny, has to be at least six-foot-five, with hair that looks like it hasn't been washed in a while and a bandana tied around his neck. If I'm not mistaken, he smells the teensiest bit like weed. Not that I ever smoke, but I've come to recognize the scent from walking around Brooklyn.

"Aha!" Steinway says. "Medium okay? It might be a little roomy, but it's all I have."

She hands it to me, and I pull it over my tank top. It is roomy, but now at least I don't stick out like a sore thumb.

"Tennyson, this is Olivia," she says, even though he looks way too busy to bother with me.

Still, he turns around. "Olivia! Our new recruit. Come to spice up the boredom of always having the same old gang. And a lady, no less, to balance out our demographics. We need more ladies up in here, am I right?"

Steinway rolls her eyes. "That's sexist."

"It's sexist to want *more* women? How?"

She shrugs. "I don't have the time to educate you right now. But you sound like an idiot."

Tennyson sticks out his hand anyway. "Tennyson, here, like the lord. Lord Alfred. The poet."

"We get it," Steinway says.

"Anyway, most people call me Ten. Have since I was a kid. Can't mess with perfection, I guess."

Half of me feels like I need to switch up my name just to have something to say when I introduce myself. *Olivia*, but you can call me Liv, Livvie, Via? No, *Olivia*, but you can call me Carrie, like my favorite people do.

Tennyson (Ten?) goes on: "And don't listen to Steinway. She's happy to have more ladies as well—right, Steinway?"

The girl, for the first time, turns red, her freckles almost disappearing, but she quickly recovers. "You're an idiot," she says. "Come on, Olivia. Let's get away from this bureaucratic check-in bullshit and on to the real stuff. The main course is amazing. Hope you're not afraid of heights!"

I swallow, my throat suddenly tight, and follow behind her.

Whatever my mom once thought, she certainly can't accuse me of wasting away now.

# Elm Street Nightmare

We walk down a wide hallway and toward a door that reads EMERGENCY EXIT ONLY.

I can't help it, I imagine the camera shot. The open, empty corridor, a fluorescent light flickering, making an awful sound you can't tune out, like David Lynch is always doing in *Twin Peaks* and the like.

Then a girl or a guy, or maybe both, running down the hallway. You don't know who's behind them, but you know *someone* is.

Hell, maybe that's the way I open the screenplay. Not with them arriving at a cabin, not with my bullshit line about monsters and Shadow Lake, but with them running down a cavernous hallway, the viewer dying to know how in the world they got there. And me, knowing. Me, discovering along the way. All "in medias res," like my English teacher was always going on about.

Who knows, maybe I'll even add a character who plays the piano. Someone friendly and easygoing, but with a little bit of a secret you don't find out until later . . .

I feel a tingle in my fingers, the tingle I always get when I have a good idea. Steinway walks toward the door and pushes. Nothing happens, no sound at all, the sign no more than a weak deterrent for visitors trying to use the wrong door; immediately, we're back into the daylight.

*God*, it's freaking beautiful.

Out here, you can't see any buildings, only mountains. But it's not like the mountains you see from our house, all far away and in the distance, etched into the horizon like a painting. This is different. The mountains are *right here*, demanding to be noticed, to be appreciated. Ski lifts run lazily, carting people up the mountain. In front of us, some sort of rope-course tower looms, kids playing on it, their laughter spilling down like droplets of water.

The sun is high, and the sky is oh so blue, and it feels like—it's crazy, but it feels like when I wander down to the East River on my own to look at all of Manhattan stretched before me. Like it's not the middle of nowhere, it's the middle of *everything*. I remember this feeling last summer, when we first got the house. Only, I'd been so distracted by the NYU drama this year, it's like I totally forgot about it.

"You have to excuse Tennyson," Steinway says. "I swear to god it's like he's never been around a bi girl before."

I shake my head. "*That's* what he meant? Kind of offensive, no?"

Steinway adjusts her braids. "He doesn't mean to be a dick, really, or else I've grown numb to it, but yeah, totally inappropriate. You get used to it, I guess. I swear he thinks one of these days I'm going to tell him he's the tall stoner I've always been dreaming of."

I laugh, and Steinway presses a button on her walkie. "Steinway to Jake. Come in, Jake."

There's a grumble of static and then a beep. "Go ahead, Steinway."

"Hold two thirty for Newbie. Headed skyward for FF. Over."

"Roger that. Over."

Steinway presses another button. "Over and out."

I stare at her as we keep walking, more than a little impressed. She somehow managed to make this whole thing sound like some sort of covert op. "Skyward is that?" I point to the ski lift about fifty yards ahead.

"Deductive reasoning," Steinway says. "Good."

"FF?"

"First flight. Well, first flight here, for training, to be more precise. Anyway, you don't have to use the lingo. It just helps us pass the time. You've worked at a zip-line place before, right?"

I shake my head.

She walks toward the rope tower, but again her gait is slow and easy, like there's no rush, no rush at all, even if Jake, whoever he is, is holding the group for us.

"Or summer camp or anything?"

"Nuh-uh."

She pauses and turns, one hand on her hip. "But you've *been* to summer camp, done the whole zip-line thing, right?"

I scratch at the back of my neck. The sun, so majestic, suddenly feels too bright, like I can't keep any secrets, or maybe it's Steinway, who doesn't seem like she has much of a tolerance for bullshit, like she could see right through it. "Not exactly. I'm not from around here. I live in Brooklyn."

She laughs. "How did you get this job anyway?"

Now it's my turn to blush. "Nepotism."

Steinway bursts into that cackling laughter once again. "Oh my god, I love you already."

I feel that tingle in my fingers again, but this time, it's not because I've had a mini breakthrough on the Screenplay That Will Never Be. It's the same tingle I got when I first met Katie, when we found ourselves in the cafeteria at Xaverian High, two of the only people new to the whole parochial school thing. We were public school girls, all through middle school—PS 170 and PS 185 respectively—we didn't come from the same schools everyone else did. Meeting Katie was like finding an ally, someone who gives you that feeling, like they can see you, really see you, for who you are. It's the feeling I get every time I hang out with Chrissy. And the feeling I get when I talk to Elm.

Sometimes, all you want in the world is to be seen like that. Sometimes, it feels impossibly hard.

"My mom knows Marianne, the owner," I say. "From way back when, I guess. I haven't even met her."

"She's great," Steinway says. "Everyone's great. Even Tennyson, when he's not being an idiot." She points up to the rope tower. "All right, so since you're not an experienced guide or whatever, you'll most likely be running the check-in desk like Tennyson is today, but you'll sometimes be in charge of supervising Ropeland, our name for the tower. It's mainly for kids who aren't tall enough to do the zip line. There will always be one of us up there actually leading them through it—that guy up there is Joe—he helps out here occasionally. Anyway, mainly you just stand at the bottom and blow the whistle if anyone gets rowdy or tries to go up when it's not yet their turn. Occasionally, one of the instructors might need your help with something, but for the most part you just chill. Got it?"

I feel a tickle of relief in my stomach. So I won't be up on some platform in the middle of a forest, sending people flying into the air. I can handle this. I can definitely handle this.

I gaze up at the tower, about as tall as a small apartment building. My stomach aches just looking at it, but I tell myself it's not a big deal. I can totally help out up there if an instructor needs me. *Can't I?*

"It's not often that anyone needs help, anyway, so don't worry too much. Come on."

We walk past the ropes course and toward the ski lift. There's a line, but Steinway walks to the front. A girl is standing there, in the same

T-shirt as us, chipping red paint off her nails and occasionally looking up at the line in front of her.

"Cora, this is the new girl, Olivia. Olivia, Cora. I'm going to take her up, show her the course."

"Roger," Cora says, still chipping away at her nail. Then she lifts her head, calling out to the crowd of people: "Hold the line!"

We walk in front of everyone, and in seconds, a seat swings around, thunking at our thighs, and Steinway is pulling the bar down, the ground no longer beneath us. We're floating up the mountain.

I steal a quick glance down, and my stomach does a somersault. I've been on ski lifts before but I've never liked them. Why aren't there seat belts, for one thing? Why don't the bars go all the way across? So many questions.

"Cora's cool, but she's a little low-key right now because she just broke up with her long-term boyfriend," Steinway says. "She for some reason thought they were going to get married? She's only twenty-one, but alas."

Steinway's feet dangle back and forth as we continue up and up.

"Christ, you look kind of green. You don't get motion sickness, do you?"

I shake my head.

"Afraid of heights?"

"Well . . ."

"No, you're *not* serious. You *have* to be kidding."

"Not *totally* afraid."

Steinway raises her eyebrows. "Why are you here, again?"

For a second, I almost think I can tell her, up here on our bench in the sky, where nothing else really matters. That I failed at finding my own plan for the summer and that my mom was left scraping through her contacts to find something for me to do. Then I lose my nerve. "I told you," I say, deadpan. "Nepotism."

Another laugh, more chuckle than cackle this time. "Well, just try not to think about the distance between us and the ground too much, I guess."

She pauses, and so does the lift. Our bench keeps swinging, and my stomach churns. The lift starts back up, this time with a jolt. "Today's going to be a baptism by fire," Steinway continues.

"What do you mean?"

"Marianne likes all the newbies to do a zip-line course. It's usually considered a perk, because most people like zip-lining. Most people who opt to spend their summer working at a zip-line park, at least." Another raised eyebrow. "So anyway, you'll get used to it? I could make up something to tell Marianne, but it will only be delaying the inevitable. She's going to want you to do it."

I shake my head. "It's okay," I say. "I'll do it."

Comfort zone, I remind myself. This is about getting out of my stupid comfort zone. I'm sure nothing will happen, no *Final Destination* moment that sends me flying, my body crushing into a cavern, bones crunching.

The lift quickly approaches the summit of the mountain. Steinway lifts the bar over our heads.

"Hop off in three, okay? One, two, three!"

The seat practically pushes us off, and my feet once again connect with ground. Up here, it's not so bad. The mountain is big and wide, no different from the ground below. It's not like I'm standing at the edge of a cliff or anything. Plus, Steinway is incredibly cool, and I already feel like I can be myself here. This is good. One go at the zip line, and I won't even have to deal with heights again. I'll just check people in and occasionally supervise the ropes course. I can do this. I *know* I can do this.

We walk, about fifty yards ahead, toward a guy who's standing, his back to us, the same walkie-talkie connected to his hip. A crowd of people has already gathered around him—must be the others on the tour. I can do this. Just don't think too much, like Steinway said.

"Jake's also new-ish," she says as we get closer. "I'm going to take the lift back down, but he can get you all set up for the tour. You'll be going with the two-thirty group."

"Jake!" she calls as we reach him. "This is Olivia! She's going to do the two thirty with you."

From the back I can see that he's tall, shoulders wide, hair curly and unkempt.

He turns, and I stop, frozen to the spot, my heart beating wildly.

The curly hair, the eyes, wide and kind and familiar, taking me in.

Me, who he doesn't recognize, who he wouldn't recognize, couldn't recognize.

I very much recognize him.

"Hi, Olivia," he says. "Welcome." He sticks out his hand.

I stick out mine, too. "Hi," I manage, though my head is spinning, my brain struggling to compute—to comprehend.

Jake, the guy I'm looking at, the guy who's going to lead me on a tour through the trees . . .

Jake is *Elm*.

ONYX
You're asking me to go out, on my own,
jump headfirst into the great unknown with
a psychopathic serial killer on the loose?
Isn't that a bad decision?

JIMMY
Exactly.

—*The Bad Decision Handbook* by O. Knight

# First Flight

"Ready to zip-line?" Elm, I mean, Jake, asks.

"Uhh," I say, suddenly unable to form a proper sentence.

It *can't* be Elm. Elm is interning at an indie film thing. With his cool aunt.

Elm has never mentioned upstate New York, not even once. Elm doesn't exist in this world, mine. Then I remember, in a flash. He said he was going up north.

Still, it can't be. North is huge. Like ten states, at least—maybe Canada. Even upstate New York is massive, filled with so many places that aren't here. And he never talked about zip-lining, only his internship.

I rack my brain, trying to remember exactly what the photo looked like, desperate to pull up Reddit on my phone and check. But I can't—even if that weren't rude AF, my phone's not on me. It's back at the check-in office in my backpack in the cabinet.

"Don't worry about her," Steinway says. "She hasn't zip-lined before. She's just a little nervous."

"Never zip-lined and working at a zip-lining company? I love it," Elm-Jake says.

"Right?" Steinway says. "Bold, this one."

Steinway turns to me. "I'm going to go help Tennyson with the next round of check-ins. You should be finished by four thirty. Come back down and find me when you're done."

"Yeah, she can show you the rest of the *ropes*," Jake says.

A pause and then Steinway laughs, elbowing him lightly in the ribs. "Dude, any more dad jokes and I'm going to start calling you Freddy again."

Jake shakes his head, but laughs along with her, and Steinway turns to me. "Anyway, you good?"

I nod, even though I'm not good, not at all. I'd thought I'd do one or two zip lines, but two hours' worth? The prospect is terrifying.

Not to mention, if Elm-Jake is really both Elm and Jake . . .

No, I tell myself. He can't be. It's not possible. Elm is toiling away at some film collective somewhere. Vermont, maybe. Elm is placing elaborate Starbucks orders for indie directors, carrying cardboard trays of paper cups.

Elm is not the guy standing in front of me, waiting for me to answer Steinway's question.

"Of course! I'm great!" I say, laying it on a little thick.

Steinway narrows her eyes. Maybe too thick.

"Er, I'll come find you when I'm done," I tell her, my face going hot.

"Perf," she says, then turns on her heel and saunters away.

"All right, let's get you a harness," Elm-Jake says. Or is it Jake-Elm? Which is the real him? Damn it. Which is the real me? Am I Olivia-Carrie or Carrie-Olivia?

*Stop it*, I tell myself. *You're making this more complicated than a Christopher Nolan screenplay.* (Side note: *Memento* was a great horror movie.)

I glance around. The crowd of people are waiting for me, of course they are. Steinway said so herself on the walkie. "Yeah," I say. "Let's harness up!"

Jake, who I will refer to as just Jake, at least until I've had a chance to double-check—grabs a harness from the pile that sits at his feet. He kneels down and holds it out. "Go ahead. Step in."

I'm reminded of Katie's dog, Cooper, the way Katie holds out the harness for the little brown thing.

I do, and he shimmies it up my legs, around my thighs, being extra careful not to let his hand brush my skin even the tiniest bit. Once it's up, he begins clipping buckles. One of his hands has the slightest shake to it. He's nervous—why? Then I remind myself. He's new, too.

He looks up, smiling briefly, then fastens the last buckle and begins to pull at the straps, making everything super tight. I look down. My semi-cute jean shorts have taken on the look of a denim diaper, bunched up and squished just so.

Jake gives a final tug to the straps and, hands still now, he hooks on a carabiner, which connects to a silvery rope and another carabiner, twisting them both so the lever isn't exposed.

"There's no way that can come undone, right?" I ask.

"No way," he says, smiling at me again. Then he gives the harness a few tugs that make the shorts situation somehow even more awkward than before. "Safety first. That's what my pop-pop says." He smiles, but then looks away, almost bashful. "Now you just need a helmet."

He begins digging through his pile and comes up with an electric-yellow one. I put it on, but it's way too tight.

I hand it back to him. "Sorry, but my head's kind of big."

He laughs. "No *biggie*."

I pause, staring at him, trying to figure this situation out.

"I know, I know," he says. "Dad jokes. I'll stop."

It's not his cheesy humor. It's only that I wish my head were more normal-sized, like Katie's. Even more, I wish I hadn't sent that photo of her. I wish I could wrap my supersized head around what is really going on right now. Have I stepped into a parallel universe, all *Twin Peaks* Red Room kind of thing, and in this universe the wildest coincidences are entirely possible?

The wildest coincidences are right here in front of me, digging around for an extra-large helmet?

"Here," Jake says. "This one might work."

It does. I clip it tight, and Jake gives me a smile, a smile that looks *exactly* like the one in the photo he sent me. Still, the nerdy glasses are missing, one tick mark in the *Jake is not Elm* category. Besides, the world is full of doppelgängers. Just the other day, I got stopped outside of the downtown Brooklyn Target and a girl swore up and down we'd met at band camp in Vermont. It's too big of a coincidence. It can't be him. He's just an attractive (and a little awkward) new coworker who's seen me in a denim diaper and knows my head is about three sizes too large.

Then I see it, glinting in the bright mountain sunlight.

The scar.

A little ridge, right under his left eye. Just like in the photo.

"All right, two thirty!" he yells. "Welcome to the New York Zipline Experience. Are you *ready* to zip-line?"

A chorus of claps and *woo-hoo*s.

"I can't hear you!" he calls. "Are you *ready to zip-line?*" He sounds like a pro, even though he's new. I wonder briefly if he's worked at a place like this before.

The chorus grows louder, and I make my way to the side.

"First, uhh, a few safety things," Jake says. "Never, I repeat, never, try to unhook or adjust your equipment on your own. Second . . ."

He continues on, delivering a verbal disclaimer, but his words turn soupy in my head.

Jake is Elm. Standing here in front of me. Someway, somehow.

"Okay, two thirty, let's do this," Jake says, eyes flitting around the space, as if making sure everyone's listening. He shifts his weight, ever so slightly, from foot to foot. "Follow me," he says, after just a beat too long, and we walk across the grass and toward a cluster of trees. It's crisp up here, despite being the thick of summer, the mountain air a hell of a lot more pleasant than the air in Brooklyn in June. As we approach, I see a wooden platform, the shiny silver rope that must be our first zip line.

"Bryson is waiting for you guys just on the other side." Jake turns, giving a large wave to the dude who must be Bryson. "Who wants to go first?"

An older woman, who has to be at least sixty-five, steps up.

Just in front of me, a girl my age cheers. "Go, Grandma!"

Jake grabs the lady's carabiner and hooks it onto the rope above, then twists it and gives it a tug. "Ready?" he asks.

"Hell yes!" she shouts.

"Put your hands here," Jake says, showing her where to hold her rope. "And then you're good to go."

She takes a deep breath and then, just like that, jumps off the platform, a high-pitched wail of thrill echoing through the canopy of trees.

"Next!" Jake calls.

I hang out in the back, staring at my carabiners, wondering if they can break, as each of the other people in the group goes ahead of me. I suppose getting crushed into the bottom of a mountainous ravine is one way to fulfill my parents' desire for me to "get out of my comfort zone."

Finally, I'm the only one left.

"Lucky number eleven," Jake says.

"Isn't it lucky number seven?" I ask, feeling like I really do need luck right now—all the luck I can get.

Jake shrugs. "It rhymes, at least. Another bad joke, I suppose." He smiles, instantly calling that photo back to mind. "But, come on. Let's do it."

I step up onto the platform, feel sweat beginning to pour from beneath my helmet.

Jake's eyes catch mine, and for an instant, his own awkwardness fades away. "Wow," he says, voice soft, eyes wide with concern. "You really are worried, aren't you?"

"I know it's stupid," I say. "I know that it's safe and you double-checked everything, it's just—" I gulp. "It's the heights thing. I don't know."

My face goes hot and suddenly, inexplicably, I half want to cry. Here I am, the girl who watches horror movies on the reg, sees women and men fight back against their attackers, outsmart their killers, face down their biggest fears, and yet I can't even get on a zip line, one that a *grandmother* just did, no problem at all.

"Hey," Jake says, putting his hand on my arm, my skin turning warm at his touch. "Hey, you're shaking. It's okay."

"I know."

He holds me steady. "No, I mean. It's okay to be scared. This is going to sound stupid, and I can't believe I'm even telling you this, but I used to be *deathly* afraid of the dark."

I laugh weakly. "When you were five?"

His hand drops from my arm, and he stares at the ground. "When I was fourteen," he says sheepishly. "I almost had a panic attack when the lights went out at a middle school dance."

"You're messing with me," I say.

He looks up then. "I wish."

"I guess you should never be a movie theater usher then."

He laughs. "And I guess you shouldn't work at a zip-line company—oops, too late."

We both laugh then.

"It won't be as bad as you're imagining," he says. "Besides, I only sleep with a night-light like one out of two nights these days."

I burst out laughing.

"Hey, I landed one," he says.

"You did."

He tilts his head to the side. "Are you okay to do this?"

I nod. "I can try."

"All you've got to do is step off that platform. The equipment does the rest."

"Okay," I say.

"Here," he says. "Er, if it's not too weird, take my hand."

I do, and it's warm, and we walk up to the platform together, and it's so strange, because I've been talking with him for months, and I felt like I knew him so well; but in a weird way, it's like none of it compares to us holding hands right now—how much you can learn about someone in just one touch.

"Don't look down," he says. "Only up." He gives my hand a squeeze, and I squeeze back, and for a second, I feel only safety, because he's here with me.

"Ready?" he asks when we've neared the edge. "I'm going to stop forcing you to hold my hand now, but I'll be right behind you."

I don't want to do it. I want to turn around and take the ski lift down, tell anyone who will listen that I'm quitting on the spot. I want to go back to Brooklyn and my old, predictable life.

Only I don't have a choice now. I'm up here, all hooked in, and I promised my parents I would give this a shot.

I have to. For them—and for me.

I take a deep breath.

I unclasp my hand from his, and I look up, not down, at the sky, blue and beautiful.

"You got this," I hear behind me.

*I've got this*, I tell myself. I'm not going to be afraid anymore. I'm not going to be stuck.

Eyes locked straight ahead, I take a step.

Like that, the ground is gone from beneath me, the air is whooshing around me, the line is buzzing above me, metal on metal, and the sky is everywhere, open and welcoming and complete—

I'm flying.

# Freddy

My heart is still beating fast, a feeling of elation, of freedom, running through my blood as Bryson helps unhook me. He's short and stocky, with a shaved head and tattoos snaking up and down his arms.

We stand, untethered, on a wooden platform that connects to another wooden platform via a rickety rope bridge. I pause, looking around me.

I did it. I freaking did it. I went for it, and it didn't blow up in my face.

No flubbing up an application. No stumbling over lines.

I flew.

Now to just tackle the rope bridge ahead of me that looks as if it wants to fall apart at any minute.

"How was it?" Jake asks, stepping onto the platform and unhooking himself.

"Good," I say. "Awesome, actually. Though, to be totally honest, the bridge over there is another story."

"Right?" Jake asks as he ambles up to me. "I've only been here a week, and I already hate that bridge. Heights or no, it gives me the willies. But, far as I know, no one has died."

I feel a chill crawl up my spine.

"Relax," he says as he reads the look on my face. "I was only kidding. I do that, if you've noticed."

I laugh. "Really? I missed that."

He laughs, too. "Seriously, this place doesn't mess around with safety. I promise."

I watch as Bryson helps the group of zip-liners cross, one by one. It's slow-going, and I have a minute alone with Jake as we make our way toward the group. "Thanks," I say. "For helping me back there."

"I was right, right? It wasn't as bad as you imagined?"

I shake my head, reaching out to steady myself on a tree. "Yeah, it was kind of amazing, actually."

He beams. "I knew you would like it."

My eyes land on his scar again—proof, staring right back at me.

Still, I want to hear it from his mouth, I want to find a way to ask him, to hint at our conversations without giving myself away. I need code lingo, like Steinway on her walkie. I look straight ahead. About half of the group has crossed the bridge.

Something subtle. If I can throw myself off a cliff, surely I can ask him a question about his life. "So . . . do you like movies?" I ask.

Immediately, I want to chastise myself, palm to forehead, only I'm afraid if I make any sudden movements, I'll lose my footing and fall to my death, even though the edge of the platform is still several feet away.

Jake only laughs. "I do," he says. "I do indeed."

"Horror?" I ask. It's stupid, so obvious. All my cards, revealed at once. But I want to hear it from him.

Jake's mouth forms a grin. "How did you know?"

My heart thumps in my chest. How did I know?

*I've been chatting with you since March. Hey, old friend!*

*I sent you a pic of my best friend because I was not #facegoals that day you asked.*

*What Would Meryl Do only makes sense if you're as cool, popular, and easygoing as someone like Meryl!*

*Hi, my name is Olivia, and I'm a horror-holic. Thus I know you from the Reddit horror community we both frequent.*

"I just . . ."

"Oh yeah," Jake says. "Steinway threatening me with her dumb nickname."

*Nickname?* "Right," I say, racking my brain for what it was.

It hits me just as he says it.

"See, I made the mistake of telling her, early on, that my favorite movie is *A Nightmare on Elm Street.* So she started calling me Freddy, for Freddy Krueger. Only I made her stop because Freddy is a super weird name."

I swear to god I feel the blood drain from my face.

"Oh shit," he says. "Your dad's not named Freddy, is he? I'm sorry."

"No," I say, forcing a smile. "No, I don't know anyone named Freddy."

"That's a relief," he says, scratching at the bottom of his chin. "Anyway, if she were going to give me a movie-inspired nickname, it should be Elm. That's my handle on Reddit anyway." He grins sheepishly. "Sorry. Nerd alert."

I swallow, my breath shallow, and suddenly I feel like I can't move. It's really him.

I mean, I knew it was him. I recognized his face. I saw his scar.

But still, holy shit, it's *really* him. No freakishly similar doppelgänger with a freakishly similar scar.

Just Jake. Just Elm. Only merged into one, standing in front of me, confused.

"What is it?" he asks. "You look, I don't know, surprised. Tell you the truth, I thought I was giving off pretty solid nerd vibes already."

For a second, I want to confess everything. That it's me, Carrie, and I love horror as much as he does, and I have new recommendations for him, that I can deliver in person now instead of online.

I want to tell him that it's serendipitous, almost, the way we've been thrown together like this. Like Jigsaw in the *Saw* movies, someone pulling the strings—only not in such a gruesome and nefarious way.

Only how in the world do I explain why I lied to him in the first place? I could say I was having a shit day. I could say I know I shouldn't have ever sent him Katie's photo—or let him think I was going to NYU. But how?

My tiny little lies have caught up to me in a way I couldn't possibly have imagined. They've grown much, much bigger—overnight.

"Come on, you guys," Bryson calls from the other side of the bridge, the whole group having crossed while I stood here trying to figure out what the hell to say to Jake.

"Guess we should get over there," Jake says.

"Yeah we probably should," I say.

He steps a little closer and smiles. "I know, I know. It's the horror movies, right? Most people think if you're into horror you have to be some kind of death-obsessed loser. Hopefully you won't judge me too hard on that, since we only just met."

*I don't think that. I would never think that.*

"Let me guess, horror isn't your thing?" Jake says. "It's cool. Promise. A lot of people aren't into it."

My breath catches in my throat. I want to tell him, to tell him everything.

But I feel so high from jumping off that zip line, from something finally working out, I don't want this good feeling to come crashing down. I'm scared to reveal even a hint of the truth lest he figures it all out.

I make a snap decision, just like I did jumping off that cliff.

Only this time, I double down.

"Nah." I force it out, my heart already aching at the lie. "Horror's not really my thing."

# The Bad Decision Handbook:

# Part Two

"Looks like you got some sun," my dad says as soon as I get into the car. "We'll have to load up on SPF fifty for the rest of the summer."

My mom, meanwhile, is just staring at me—no bullshit, as usual. "How was it?"

*Well, Mom, I've begun living a double life. See, the boy I've been secretly messaging and chatting with for months, but haven't told you about because it was too embarrassing, is inexplicably working here, too. So now I have to pretend I'm someone I'm not so he doesn't realize I felt too crappy about myself to send him a photo. I'm officially a catfisher now. Yay! I'll be featured on a Netflix documentary any day now . . .*

"Olivia?" she asks. "It wasn't that bad, was it? I know the heights thing, but—"

"No, Mom," I say, forcing a laugh. "It was great, actually. Everyone was super nice. And I did the zip line and didn't even freak out. Well, I only freaked out a little bit, at least, at the beginning. I actually really liked it."

The smiles on the both of them, like they won the lottery or something.

I smile, too, because what I said is true. It *was* awesome, surprisingly so. Steinway is cooler than I could have imagined, everyone was chill, and I did it. I stepped off that ledge. For once, I stopped being scared, stopped letting that damn *Dracula* audition define me. For once, I felt like me again.

The whole double-life thing is just a blip on the radar. It was still a good day.

"Er, thanks for hooking me up."

My mom laughs. "Anytime!"

As we pull out of the parking lot, I check my phone for the first time. It's a Reddit message from Elm, sent around 2 p.m., just as my shift was starting.

*ElmStreetNightmare84: Hey, Carrie, what's up?*

I stare at it, briefly. At first it's strange, reconciling the witty guy who's been in my inbox for months with the semi-awkward dude making dad jokes on the zip-line course. And then, all at once, it's not. *Queen of the Quizzically Terrifying, Justice of Jump Scares*—all that. He's the same guy, cheesy humor and all, only his humor plays better on the internet, just like mine does.

I want to write him back, talk to him like I always do; but instead, I tap out of the message. Even though I'm safely in the car, it feels too risky to respond right here, as if he'll somehow know the geographic location of my response.

So I shove the phone deep into my backpack, into a zippered pocket, as if I can shut it all away.

On the way home, we stop at the German sausage and meat place my parents like to hit up when we grill outside. We take a number, and women in traditional dresses fill paper bags with bratwurst, kielbasa, and smoked pork ribs. Back at our house, Dad lights up the Weber grill we keep in the yard, and for a couple of hours, I put today's parallel-universe weirdness out of my mind.

We sit on the porch and eat our sausages and ribs, scooping potato salad and coleslaw out of plastic containers. Chrissy texts me, asking how it was, I give her the rundown, and we banter for a bit. The air is cool and the sun is setting, casting the sky with pinks and purples, turning the mountains a darker shade of blue, and for a little bit, it's perfect.

As I'm helping my parents finish the dishes, my phone buzzes in my pocket.

I finish up, dry off my hands, and there it is—another message from Elm.

*ElmStreetNightmare84: Hey, stranger, didn't hear from you all day!*

My silence since his earlier message is definitely unusual.

"I'm going to go to my room," I announce to my parents, who are enmeshed in choosing their documentary for the evening.

"Watching a horror movie?" my dad asks. "Make sure to use your headphones. I don't want to hear any zombie screams while we're trying to learn about the historical context of the Voting Rights Act."

"It was one time, Dad. And they weren't zombies. They were vampires. And it was a really pivotal scene."

He laughs, clicking Play on the TV. My parents like to give me hell about how much TV I watch, but I always want to ask them: Where do they think I got it from?

I shut the door behind me. From my window, I can just barely see hints of the last light peeking over the mountains, the moon hanging in the sky like a shadow. Somewhere, not that far away, Elm-Jake is messaging me from beneath the same sky.

I sink into bed and open the Reddit app, Elm's words staring back at me.

What in the world can I possibly say? If I tell him the truth, it will make me, a person he's going to be working with every day now, look nuts. He'll tell Steinway, and my position as the crew weirdo will be instantly cemented.

I jump. There's another message.

*ElmStreetNightmare84: I can see you're on. I'm like the ghost that lives in your screen now . . .*

*ElmStreetNightmare84: Sorry, that was supposed to be funny but now it just sounds creepy*

*ElmStreetNightmare84: Creepy like bad creepy, not good horror-movie creepy*

*ElmStreetNightmare84: I'm digging myself deeper now, aren't I?*

I can't watch him struggle anymore.

*CarriesRevenge01: LOL don't worry you're only ever the good kind of creepy*

*ElmStreetNightmare84: Aww, how sweet. How was your day?*

*CarriesRevenge01: Pretty good, but busy. Learned a lot.*

(Not a lie.)

*CarriesRevenge01: Talked about horror movies.*

(Also not a lie.)

*CarriesRevenge01: Nightmare on Elm Street, actually.*

(Not-a-lie number three; I'm on a roll, here.)

*CarriesRevenge01: How was yours?*

The tiny dots appear, showing that he's typing, but then they stop. After a moment, they start up again, and it hits me. I already liked Elm, everything about him, from our chatty banter to his adorable photo.

But now that I've seen him in real life, now that I've met Jake, awkwardly awesome dad-joke Jake, now that he's held my hand, helped me get through my first zip-line experience, I *really* like him.

I like him a lot.

Another thought strikes me. Is it possible he likes me, too? Was there something there, when he held me by the arm, calming me down, when his hand laced through mine, leading me to the edge of the cliff? Could he grow to like Olivia as much as he likes Carrie?

The dots pick up again, and I want so badly for him to mention me, Olivia, the new girl he met at work, wanting a hint, even so tiny, that he felt some kind of spark, too.

*ElmStreetNightmare84: Day was good, nothing crazy, just the same ole same ole at work. Tell me about your screenplay.*

The words hit me hard. *Same ole, same ole.* You couldn't find a way to make it sound more unremarkable if you tried.

I shake my head. This is silly. Elm is my internet friend, nothing more. I have to act normal, not like a weirdo who doesn't know how to go about living a double life because she never meant to. What would Carrie say, if she hadn't just met Jake in real life?

*CarriesRevenge01: Screenplay is in its nascent stages still . . .*

*ElmStreetNightmare84: Like when the alien from* Alien *is just a pod thing? Before it invades your body and stuff?*

I laugh. The truth is, it's not even a pod, not yet. It's a pre-pod.

*CarriesRevenge01: You could say that, yes*

*ElmStreetNightmare84: Okay, so describe it in pod form then*

*CarriesRevenge01: I don't know*

*ElmStreetNightmare84: Genre of horror, for starters?*

*CarriesRevenge01: The* Halloween *director said horror is a reaction, not a genre*

*ElmStreetNightmare84: And Hitchcock said you can only have suspense if the audience can see the bomb ticking beneath the table. You have to tell me what's going on! I need to know SOMETHING.*

I smile to myself. Hitchcock did say that, in a cool speech about the difference between surprise and suspense. Surprise is when you're watching two characters talking, and a bomb goes off out of nowhere. Suspense is when you see them talking, and you, the audience, know the bomb is right there, because you saw the villain plant it. It's a tough balance. Mysteries only work if you don't know what's going on, but suspense only happens when you do. The best directors play with both.

I pause. Until now, I've never shared the details of my screenplay with anyone, apart from the NYU application board. I was too damn scared.

But the way I felt today, taking a risk, I don't know, it felt good. Besides, meeting Jake in real life, I know it for sure—even if it's a stupid idea, he won't judge me for it. He'll just laugh about it.

*CarriesRevenge01: All right, it's not really a genre, per se. It's kind of a mix of a bunch of them. Like* Cabin in the Woods, *I guess, only not so many references, because* CITW *does it all, right? This is kind of the same idea but with a "less is more" approach.*

*ElmStreetNightmare84: So like playing off clichés?*

*CarriesRevenge01: Yeah it's tentatively called* The Bad Decision Handbook. *It's a play on the bad decisions people make in horror movies, you know, splitting up to look for the killer, going into an abandoned house alone, not calling the cops until it's too late . . . but the twist is, the person who's terrorizing them, he's a horror director himself, and he's using these people trapped in a cabin or whatever to make his movie. Once they figure it out, they have to use their knowledge of movies and stuff to outsmart him, which includes making some intentionally bad decisions to throw him off.*

*CarriesRevenge01: So it's like poking fun at horror movie tropes, only the characters are the ones in charge.*

There's something nice about laying it all out there, seeing how it looks typed out.

*ElmStreetNightmare84: Wow, that's a lot*

I freeze. Maybe I was wrong about him. Maybe, on the other side of the screen, he's looking at my messages like Ms. Sinclair looked when I messed up my audition.

*CarriesRevenge01: I know, it's kind of overcomplicated*

*CarriesRevenge01: There are a lot of kinks to be worked out, of course. It's just an idea. Probably not even a very good one!*

*ElmStreetNightmare84: No no no, I mean that's a lot like, you've got so much to go on already! I guess I thought, I don't know why because you're amazing, but I thought it would be simpler, kind of like a starter movie.*

*CarriesRevenge01: It probably should be simpler lol*

*ElmStreetNightmare84: No it should be exactly how it is*

A prick of excitement in the tips of my fingers.

A feeling of flying again.

*CarriesRevenge01: Thanks for being my sounding board*

*ElmStreetNightmare84: Anytime, it sounds amazing. Send it to me when you're done! I want to be the first to read it!*

*CarriesRevenge01: Oh, if I ever actually finish the damn thing, believe me, I will*

*ElmStreetNightmare84: Promise?*

*CarriesRevenge01: It's a deal!*

*ElmStreetNightmare84: Awesome. I can't wait! I'm a huge fan of horror, obviously, and what's more, I'm a pro at bad decisions ;)*

Instantly, I think of my stupid mistake, my very own bad decision, sending that photo. I could tell him. I could tell him right now.

Only I don't want to lose Elm. Or Jake.

It's only for a summer, I tell myself. Despite the connection I felt today, the likelihood that it will turn into anything is practically nil.

So online, I'll be Carrie. Horror-loving, screenplay-writing Carrie.

And in person, I'll be Olivia.

It's a clunky solution, but it's the only way to move forward without disappointing both Elm *and* Jake.

The words come easily, almost too easily.

*CarriesRevenge01: I'm a pro at bad decisions, too*

# Carrie vs. Olivia

I wake up newly inspired the next morning. It's not even nine, and my shift doesn't start until eleven, so I have at least an hour to write. I may have stayed up a little too late talking to Elm, but it doesn't matter—I'm *inspired.*

Elm-Jake liked the idea of my screenplay. He liked it a lot.

And even more than that, I proved to myself that I didn't have to be scared anymore. I faced a fear, even if it was a relatively small one, and beat it down. Maybe I can do this, too.

My parents are out on their morning walk, and I grab a banana and return to my room, opening my laptop and sitting cross-legged on top of the covers. My desk, the old walnut one we picked up one Saturday at the Brooklyn Flea, lives in Brooklyn, not here. I could sit at the kitchen counter, but I'd rather not have my parents peeking over my shoulder, salivating at my every productive word, as soon as they get back.

My phone buzzes, but this time, it's not from Elm. It's the group text, the one that Fatima started, so the "French Ladies" can keep in touch over the summer. Eloise has just sent a photo of herself doing yoga in front of a sunrise in Vermont.

Katie responds right away with a selfie of her sipping some sort of sugary drink on a cobblestone street—looks like SoHo.

I could add my own, show them how I'm working on the screenplay, only I don't want to jinx it. Instead, I dash off a response—*gorgeous, ladies, keep the snaps coming!*—then put my phone aside.

On my laptop, I find a Stephen King quote that feels particularly apt, then scribble it on a Post-it.

*Amateurs sit and wait for inspiration, the rest of us just get up and go to work.*

I stick it to the top of my laptop, but it flutters off.

I turn around, tacking it to the space above my headboard instead.

Only problem is, I can't see it now; it's behind me. I scrunch up my lips.

My eyes flit to my laptop, the cursor blinking at me impatiently.

Quickly, I head to my dad's office, where he works remotely when we're here. I grab a few sheets of computer paper and one of the Sharpies that poke out from a WORLD'S BEST DAD cup I made him at one of those pottery studios when I was a kid.

I head back to my room and write the quote out in my best handwriting. It takes a couple of tries before I get the spacing right. If I paste it to the wall next to my window, I'll be able to see it perfectly from my bed—and lord knows, these are words I need to see.

Except, I don't have tape. I head to the kitchen just as my parents are coming back in.

"Morning," my mom says. "If we'd known you were up, we would have asked you to join us on our walk."

"No worries," I say, pulling open the drawer in the kitchen island.

"Did you get breakfast?" my dad asks.

"A banana."

"Want me to make you something?" The man is a scrambled-eggs guru. "I'm back to work this week, but my first conference call isn't until ten."

"I'm okay, Dad," I say, digging through the drawer. "I'll have some cereal before my shift."

"Are you going to pack a sandwich or something? Since it's longer today?" he asks.

It's the Iowa in him, this anxiety over when we're going to eat next. My grandmother feeds us these huge meals three times a day. Mornings begin with some sort of meat sizzling against cast iron.

"What are you looking for?" my mom asks.

"Tape."

"For what?"

I shrug. "To hang something on my wall."

She leans over me, shuffling through the drawer herself, and pulls out these 3M hanging tabs.

"No, it's just a small thing. Like a sheet of paper."

"Oh?"

"A quote," I say casually. "That I find inspiring."

She smiles, and I know she wants to ask me more, but she doesn't. "I think it's in Dad's office."

Tape procured, I head back to my room. It's already nine fifteen. I've lost time for writing, time I should have taken advantage of, if I'd been following the very quote that sits, waiting to be tacked up, on my bed, but it's all good.

Quickly, I tape the quote to my wall, then head back to my bed and open my laptop. I still have forty-five minutes before I have to start getting ready and pack my lunch.

I stare at the blank page, but the words won't come. The cursor blinks at me, my very own demon. I grab my phone and tap out of the text chain and into Reddit. I start a new chat to Elm.

*CarriesRevenge01: Real talk. I think I'm going to write a*

*screenplay about a writer who can't write to save her life . . .*
*LITERALLY*

I wait, staring at the phone, as nine thirty approaches. He writes back almost right away.

*ElmStreetNightmare84: I'm pretty sure that's already been done by Stephen King*

*ElmStreetNightmare84: Like multiple times over ;)*

*CarriesRevenge01: Great, even my jokes are unoriginal!*

*ElmStreetNightmare84: Aww, don't worry. I've never written anything like that in my life! My two-page creative writing essay was teeth-pulling all the way. A screenplay is no joke. But hey, that's what the program's for, right? To help you do it?*

That ache in my gut again, present as a ghost lurking in the shadows, messing with doorknobs. I hate that I've lied to him—not once but twice—but if I fess up and tell him I'm not at the program, he'll want to know what I am doing. Obviously, I can't tell him that—I'll have to make up another excuse—because if he knows I'm in his proximity, he might want to meet; no, he'll definitely want to meet, and then he'll know that Carrie is Olivia.

I'm split in two, like the villain in *Split*, that M. Night Shyamalan movie I actually liked—only that guy was split in twenty-four. Instead, I'm Carrie, a girl who hasn't been honest about where she is and what she's doing. And Olivia, a girl who told Jake that she doesn't even like horror movies. But that's what I've decided. Because the other alternative—disappointing Jake—I don't like at all. I stare at the screen. I need to say *something*.

He types first.

*ElmStreetNightmare84: I know it's scary, but I know you can do this.*

I feel it, like I did yesterday, the warmth of his encouragement, deep in my gut.

*CarriesRevenge01: Thanks, ok signing off to get back to it!*

I return to my Google Doc.

I know I can do this, so long as I stop getting in my own way.

After all, yesterday, I jumped headfirst into the great unknown, just like that.

I pause, because I kind of like that line. I'm not sure where it goes, how it fits in, but I know I like it.

I hit the return key a few times, making space on the page.

And for the first time in ages, I write.

# Close Encounters of the

# Carrie-Olivia Kind

I don't get that far, but I write until I run out of time, getting in a good, solid page. Then I get ready, pack myself a turkey sandwich, and leave Carrie behind.

I'm Olivia now, Olivia, who is decidedly not at an NYU program. Olivia, who doesn't even like horror movies, those lowbrow gory flicks!

The check-in office is empty when I arrive, so I clock in at the computer station, like Steinway showed me yesterday, and kneel down, tucking my things in the bottom shelf of the cabinet behind the front desk and shoving my lunch into the tiny bit of space available in the communal fridge.

"Are you Olivia?" I hear behind me. When I turn, there's a woman, one about my mother's age.

I stand, tugging at the hem of my shirt, which already looks wrinkled—I shouldn't have tossed it so haphazardly on the floor when I got home yesterday. "Yes."

She smiles wide, showing perfectly white teeth. "I'm Marianne," she says, reaching out her hand to shake mine. Her nails are painted shiny red, her hair cut into a neat bob, and she's wearing a seamless black dress, not the Zipline Experience T-shirt I have on. She's nothing like I'd expect the owner of a zip-line company to look like, nothing at all. "Your mom and I were camp counselors together when we were in high school, if you can believe it. Ages ago."

"Thanks so much for"—*Hiring me? Taking pity on me?*—"giving me this opportunity," I say. "Especially so last-minute."

She leans against the counter. "Your mom told me what happened with NYU. You know, I wanted to go there back in the day, didn't even get in. I totally feel for you."

I freeze. As she says it, Jake walks through the front door, smiling at both Marianne and me.

*Don't say anything more. Not another word, Impossibly Chic Marianne! Not another word!*

"That school has gotten so competitive these days. And for a high school summer program. I mean, really? Shouldn't they be *happy* so many people want to go into the arts? Perhaps they should widen the program if there's so much interest."

My mouth fixes into an awfully forced smile—I'm petrified, about to be mortified—as Jake comes around the counter, checking in, tossing his stuff into a cabinet, and grabbing a walkie.

Marianne stares at me, waiting for an answer.

I never even considered my mom would have told Marianne the truth. Steinway said everyone loves her. Marianne will probably bring it up again. Maybe she'll even start some zip-line employee email thread this afternoon, introducing me along with my NYU-failed-application backstory.

*Stop it, Olivia. Be cool. Be cool!*

"I'm just happy to be here," I say finally.

Marianne's smile grows wider. "That's the spirit. Don't know what they're missing, I'm sure!"

Jake stands up then, turning to us, interest piqued. "Who doesn't know what he's missing?"

Time stands still, like it's a sports game—even though I never really watch sports, except for the Super Bowl—when everything is all slo-mo. Marianne is the offense and I'm the defense. And Jake is the ball (or something). Point is, I see her mouth open, to explain that he heard her wrong, that *NYU* doesn't know what *they're* missing. I can't let her say what she's about to say next.

"It doesn't matter!" I exclaim, too quickly, too loudly. Jake and Marianne both turn to me, staring, and I try not to come off as a complete weirdo on day one of meeting my new manager, who (a) seems cool, and (b) is my mom's friend. Eesh.

I tug at my collar. "I just mean, onward and upward! I don't like to dwell on the past."

Jake narrows his eyes but then immediately turns away. Marianne, on the other hand, nods her head appreciatively. "You have your mother's spirit, that's for sure. Now, I heard you did the course to get the hang of it." I steal a grateful look at Jake, but he's no longer looking our way. "Did Steinway give you the rundown on the check-in process?"

I nod. "She showed me everything yesterday."

"Great," Marianne says. "Tennyson will be at the office with you for the first couple of hours, so if you have any questions, you can ask him."

Almost on cue, Tennyson walks in, ducking his head to get through the door without messing up his bandana, which is now tied around his head like he's about to do some sort of hippie exercise class.

"Newbie Olivia," he says, giving me a mock salute.

Marianne clasps her hands together. "All right, team. The nine o'clock tour will be finishing up soon, and the noon tour will be kicking off. Jake, you've got what you need? Bryson and Steinway are finishing the tour now." He nods.

"Tennyson, you'll be here with Olivia for the first part of the shift and running the lift when Cora leaves. All good?"

"All good," Tennyson says.

Marianne digs into a cabinet and comes out with a walkie. She hands it to me. "Just push this button to talk, this one to listen. It's easy. And if you get tripped up, Tennyson can help you. I'll be in my office if anyone needs anything." She disappears into the back.

Jake, still avoiding my eyes, asks Tennyson to help him untangle a huge knot of carabiners and ropes, and I mentally run through all Steinway told me yesterday about checking people in.

When they finish up, Jake smiles wide and gives Tennyson a comically dramatic high five. *He really is a nerd*, I think. *Just like Elm.*

Tennyson starts messing around on his phone, and Jake makes his way around the counter and toward the door. "By the way," I say before Jake goes. "Thanks for helping me on the zip line yesterday."

"No worries," Jake says. He smiles, but it seems, for some reason, forced. Not like the smile he just gave Tennyson, or the smile he gave Marianne as she was explaining our roles. Or the one in the photo he sent me. It's like the mood has changed with him, like happy helpful Jake has turned nervous, awkward.

He pauses a second, shifting his weight from foot to foot, like he wants to say something else, and I look at him, confused, wondering if he's somehow figured it all out—my whole charade—but then he turns on his heel, heading out the door.

My first full shift goes as smoothly as could be desired.

I learn from Tennyson that there are two shifts, early morning, eight to three, and late morning, eleven to six. Steinway works both because she's training to be Marianne's assistant manager—not of her life, of course, like Katie is to me—just of the zip-line company.

As groups file in, I hand them waivers, hook them up with the basic gear, and ring up any T-shirts they want to purchase, while checking their names against our online reservation system.

The computer's a dinosaur, so it's a little slow going, but no one, least of all Tennyson, seems to be in any sort of a rush. Instead, the pace is easy. When we get through one group, we move on to another, and when there are lapses, Tennyson pulls out his phone, and I do, too.

Part of me knows I shouldn't—it feels too risky—but I can't help it. This is the new me, after all. The one who throws caution to the wind. The one who threw my body into the wind, even if it was connected to a zip line.

**CarriesRevenge01: How's your day going?**

I tuck my phone into my pocket, half afraid of what I've done, that some sort of alert will tell Jake I'm messaging him from halfway down the mountain. Instead, I focus on the sunshine filtering in, the cool mountain air breezing through the window, too afraid to do anything else.

At one thirty, Tennyson tells me to take my lunch.

I grab my sandwich and my water bottle and head through the hallway and outside. I wave to Steinway as I make my way past Ropeland, packed with rowdy kids in helmets and gear, to a few bales of hay on the edges of the clearing, near the second lift, the one that doesn't run in the summer.

It's quiet and peaceful, the mountains strong and blue, like giants standing guard, the lift floating upward toward the summit, a flock of birds V-ing across the sky . . .

And Jake, Jake walking toward me.

He takes a seat at the adjacent bale of hay. "I see you found our designated lunch spot," he says.

"Oh?"

"Everyone comes out here. It's the best place to get away from the people but still be outside." He pulls out a bottle of Gatorade and two cold slices of pizza, and I stare down at my turkey sandwich, my fingers leaving indentations in the whole wheat bread, desperate for something to say.

There are so many things I could tell him. Ask him when he's going to watch *Nosferatu*, which I wholeheartedly recommended last night. Tell him how I conquered my writer's block, at least a little bit, this morning. Get details about the film collective—where he interns, when he interns, how it's going, what his aunt is working on now. Only, these are things Carrie knows, not Olivia.

I feel that tug, the one I felt last night, to hear about my other half, to get a glimpse of myself through his eyes. It's strange, but I swear I'm almost *jealous* of Carrie in this moment. "Are you tired?" I ask, remembering how late we stayed up talking, but as soon as the words are out, I know they're all wrong.

"Huh?"

"I mean, did you get much sleep last night?" An awful pause. "Given that you're afraid of the dark and all."

"Oh," Jake says, forcing a laugh that's not remotely convincing. He shifts nervously, tugging at the hem of his shorts. "Not a ton, honestly." He doesn't say a word about my other half. Instead, he turns back to his stale pizza.

I glance over surreptitiously as he makes his way through the last of the slice and the hard cardboard crust. His eyes catch mine briefly. "So, uhh, what did Marianne mean this morning?"

"Huh?" I ask.

"When she said someone's missing out."

My heart thumps in my chest. *Shit, shit, shit.* What can I even say? "I thought maybe you got in a fight with your boyfriend or some-thing," Jake says, his eyes returning immediately to his pizza. "Or your girlfriend. Or whatever."

"Oh," I say, "No, I mean. I don't have a boyfriend," I say, my words hanging in the air. A tickle of excitement, of surprise, sparks in my belly. He wouldn't be asking if I had a boyfriend if he didn't actually want to know.

And he wouldn't want to know unless . . .

"Sorry," Jake says. "Everyone's up in everyone's business at this place. I didn't mean to pry."

"You weren't prying."

He stands up quickly. "I better get back to it." Then he downs the rest of his Gatorade in one gulp.

"Enjoy the rest of your shift!" I say, but it sounds all wrong, too forced, too not-me.

"You too," Jake says. He walks off, sunlight catching the waves of his hair, breeze making the grasses fan back and forth.

As I watch him go, I feel myself smile. Even if what just passed was decidedly awkward, he wanted to know whether I had a boyfriend. That has to mean *something*.

But not five minutes after he walks away, I get a message on my phone.

*ElmStreetNightmare84: Not much, you? P.S. I started* Nosferatu *last night! Got 20 mins in before I fell asleep. Will catch up on it after my work shift is over. How are you? Did you make any progress writing?*

The excitement I normally feel from getting a message from Elm is clouded. Just minutes ago, he seemed super keyed in to whether Olivia had a boyfriend, but now, it's like all he wants to know about is Carrie's progress.

I shake my head. It's too damn complicated, and I'm already in so deep.

All that's left now is to roll with it, keep on throwing caution to the wind and hope the proverbial zip line doesn't snap.

# Carrie vs. Olivia: Part Two

My new way of life is strangely . . . kind of wonderful.

In the mornings, I stumble out of my room, dazed from lack of sleep, grab a bowl of cereal, while my mom peruses the local art pages and my dad pores over the daily crossword, asking us to help him with everything from a six-letter synonym for VIP (bigwig) to a nine-letter birdman (Hitchcock, duh).

And then back in my room, munching my cereal, I write. It's not like I'm Stephen King or anything, words pouring out of me, but guess what? I'm doing it. Turns out that thinking about writing and agonizing over it are actually more difficult than just doing the damn thing.

There's my main character, Onyx, a badass feminist woman, the first one to realize something's wrong. Then there's her woodsy friend, who, the deeper I get, acts more and more like Steinway—minus the red braids, which would be way too obvious. And the male lead, a Jake type—I call him Jimmy now—who's handy and good with an axe, who knows how to give Onyx the encouragement she needs to do what she has to do. There's the stoner kid, tall and lanky like Tennyson, playing the role of the clown in Shakespeare, acting like an idiot the whole time but then saying, at the end of the first act, exactly what needs to be said.

It's not like I don't get stuck. Only when I do, I think about having to step off that cliff, how scary it was to me, but how wonderful it was once I was flying. And I remind myself that putting a few words on a page is far less scary than catapulting through the air. I've already had two *Death Becomes Her* moments now, and this is my *Bridges of Madison County*.

Not to mention, I have plenty of fodder. At eleven every weekday, I leave Carrie and the screenplay behind to work at Hunter Mountain, where I am Olivia, simple, easygoing Olivia, and no one even knows I'm trying to write a screenplay. Most of my shifts are easy, spent checking people in. I haven't had to help out at Ropeland, either—the most I've had to do there is blow a whistle and tell the next group of kids to wait their turn.

At one thirty each day, I take my lunch, and more often than not, Jake takes his at the same spot, something I try not to read too hard into, given that I'm living a double life and I can't very well strike up a real relationship with him.

Sometimes others join us, Steinway sitting on a bale of hay, chewing on beef jerky and nutty trail mix while redoing her French braids, fingers working deftly, only pausing to yell at Tennyson for saying something problematic. But sometimes, it's just us—Jake and me.

Careful not to say anything to give myself away, I tell him about Brooklyn, about the crowded streets and the flourishing beauty of Prospect Park, the way the subway trudges along slowly, full of the sweat of humans packed together, the nervous energy of people about to be late.

He tells me about North Carolina, about the swampy humidity and the suburban sprawl, shopping center after shopping center speckled along highways. He tells me that, after his aunt hooked him up with the internship, he applied here because he worked at a zip-line place back in North Carolina, and he thought he'd be a shoo-in, which he was. He explains that his internship is only two days a week, and I can't help but laugh to myself, because as Elm, he made it sound like that was all he was doing. It makes me feel a little bit better, like we all fudge the truth a teensy bit.

That's not to say there haven't been hiccups. Last week, Jake walked in to the check-in office to get new batteries for his walkie, and after shuffling through the drawer, he began typing into his phone. The notification popped up on my phone instantly, the device thrumming against the counter. Jake spotted it, and, hardly able to think straight, I pretended to stumble, crashing into the counter and sweeping my phone to the ground. It landed with a thud, my extra-tough case preventing it from cracking. I was safe, but I vowed to be more careful, to never leave my phone out like that again.

A few days later, on a day when Jake was working at the film collective, Marianne started asking me how I got into screenwriting. Steinway was right there, and, much as I've come to adore the girl, she's a talker. I knew if she heard too much, it would eventually get back to Jake. When Steinway asked me about it afterward, I claimed that Marianne must have been confused, thanking my lucky stars when Steinway's only response was to laugh.

But for the most part, even I have to admit the Catskills have been good. When I finish my shifts, my parents pick me up, and we have dinner together, sometimes hitting up an art event in Woodstock or just going on a walk around the neighborhood. I text Chrissy funny stories from my "fancy outdoorsy job," as she has taken to calling it, and she responds with stories of her own. I keep up with the French Ladies text chain, seeing Katie's photos from the city, Tessa's from Paris, Eloise's very rare updates from sleepaway camp (she is supposed to be meditating, after all), and Fatima's even rarer updates from Africa. I even send a few Hunter Mountain pics of my own, my earlier anxiety about having sub-par summer plans having largely faded away.

When all that's done, when I'm back in my room and on my own, I fully morph back into Carrie. I talk to Elm often into the wee hours—about movies, about my screenplay, about silly memes and the way Stephen King seems way too focused on female characters' boobs in his books. It's different from the way Jake and I talk at lunch—it's freer, it's funnier, and there aren't any nerves involved. We trade movie recs, like we always do. We make jokes, exchanging barbs and banter.

And the best part is, no matter how long we talk, no matter how late we stay up, we never, ever run out of things to say.


On Thursday afternoon, just over two weeks into my new job and my new life, Jake finds me at lunch again.

"Seat taken?" he asks as he motions to an empty bale of hay.

"Pretty sure it's got your name on it," I say.

He smiles. "Glad to hear."

We go through that same dialogue, or a version thereof, every day it's just us, and it's cheesy, movie-cheesy, but with him I don't even care.

Taking a seat, he pulls out a sandwich and sets his phone on his knee. I can't help it: I think about the messages from Carrie, locked away in there. It gives me a tiny thrill, that I'm part of his life in so many ways, one that immediately makes me feel guilty.

He nods down to his phone. "I usually try not to be glued to the thing but my little sister wants to FaceTime me. She won this art contest at her day camp, and apparently it's a *really* big deal."

I realize, for the first time, that he's never mentioned siblings before. It strikes me then, as much as I think I know him, on Reddit and here at work, there is still so much to learn about him. The thought makes me happy. Knowing more, knowing everything there is to know about Jake. "How old is she?" I ask.

"Eight," he says. "With the opinions of a twelve-year-old, I'd say."

"Into movies?"

"YouTube channels, actually. She's got a whole list of her favorites. She'll watch a food blogger and then whip up this crazy flourless cake thing. She's not even ten, and she's already quite the Renaissance— er—girl, I guess. And here I am, seventeen, afraid of the dark and resigned to making dad jokes all the time."

I laugh. "She sounds cool. Is it just you two?"

Jake shakes his head. "There are four of us kids, actually."

"Damn. It's just me and my parents."

He laughs. "Yeah, it's a lot, and I'm the oldest. My younger brothers are fifteen and twelve. I think that's part of why my aunt went out of her way to get me the film thing. She knew it would be good for my college applications next year and all that, but I think she felt for me, living in all the craziness day in and day out. I also have the pleasure of having my own room for the first time in my life. Where, yes, I some-times keep the lights on when I sleep."

"Hey, no judgment here," I say, biting into my sandwich and swal-lowing quick. "Anyway, that sounds pretty intense. I've had my own room my entire life. Only-child benefits, I guess. Although people say only children are weird. Socially inept or something."

"Well, I think that's quite obviously untrue. I mean, look at you. You're *amazing*."

His cheeks turn bright red, and he looks down.

I feel my cheeks burn as well. He probably didn't even mean to say it. He clearly tripped over the words. And yet, he *did* say it, and went instantly red, as if he'd thought it before—maybe more than once.

I think the same thing about him.

His phone beeps then, and a photo of a little girl pops onto his screen.

"I gotta take this," he says to me.

I nod. "Of course."

He grabs the remnants of his lunch and walks off, and I can hear him, the uptick in his voice as he talks to his sister, the way he obviously cares about her—that makes me happy, too.

I stare down at my sandwich, replaying every minute of our inter-action, delighting in it.

I know I'm playing with fire. I know that this is unsustainable, that it can't go on this way. Only it's so lovely, it's so wonderful, seeing every side of him like I do. How his awkwardness, his nerdiness, his cheesy humor play out in different sides of his life.

The truth is, I liked Elm first, but now I like Jake, too.

And when push comes to shove, I don't want to lose either of them.

# The Haunting of Sophia Blaine

That night, Katie and I finally get a chance to FaceTime. I'm sitting in the living room, tucked up on the couch. My parents are out at a documentary screening, getting dinner after, so for once, I have the house to myself.

"Hey, girlie!" Katie says, flipping the camera around so I can see her dorm—linoleum tiles, cinder-block walls, a poster tacked up of Meryl Streep in *The Deer Hunter*. Across the room, a girl waves to me.

"That's Hallie," Katie says, turning the phone back so she can see me and sliding her earbuds in. "She's a fellow Meryl fan, too. It's her poster—can you believe that?"

I can, given that Meryl Streep is only the most popular actress in the United States, but I don't dare say that to Katie. "That's amazing."

"So let me get this straight," she says, jumping right in. "You're actually into the whole camp counselor thing, per your pic the other day? I *told you* it wouldn't be so bad."

"Zip line," I remind her. "Not camp."

Katie smiles. "Yes, yes, I know." Her hair shines, catching the evening light, and in the background, I can hear the honk of a horn, followed by the wail-shriek of a siren. She's practically radiating the energy of the city. "Let's just pretend it's camp, though, because I think it's great fodder for your screenplay. Isn't horror always about people dying at summer camp?"

I laugh. "That's one franchise. *Friday the 13th*. There are plenty of movies that have been inspired by it, but that's not everything."

"Yes, yes," Katie says, tilting her head to the side. "Horror is nuanced and feminist and cutting-edge and all that. It's not just a bunch of blood and gore."

*"Ding, ding!"*

"So give me the deets—you tie up kids and send them flying into the air?"

"It's actually mostly adults," I say. "And I'm not an instructor, so I don't have to tie up anyone. I usually just hang out in the office and check people in, that kind of thing."

She smirks. "Any hot guys?"

I feel myself blush.

"Oh my goodness, I-told-you-so number two."

I shake my head. "I don't want to talk about it."

Katie shrugs. "Some best friend you are." She scratches at the corner of her mouth; she's sporting a new color of coral lip gloss. I imagine her heading to the flagship Sephora on Thirty-Fourth Street, playing with pots and pots of colors, getting one of the employees to do a demonstration on her. I hear another honk, picture a yellow cab chugging by, just below her window.

"He's really sweet," I say finally. "But it probably won't work out."

"Why so negative?" She pouts.

A million reasons, ones I'm not ready to share with her. "I'm working on my screenplay," I say, changing the subject.

Her smile is genuine this time. "That's awesome. How far are you?"

"A hell of a lot further than before."

"So the mountain setting has been good for you!"

I nod. "Indeed it has."

"Perhaps romance has inspired you as well."

My blush deepens. "Enough about me," I say. "Tell me about your program."

And she does. About the rigorous classes, the Method style of acting, how she had to eat twenty-five blueberries because her character was supposed to be really into them. She tells me they're putting on a play at the end of the summer and auditions were last week—she'll soon find out what part she got, and she's hoping for the lead or the second lead. She details summer evenings, wandering through Washington Square Park, ordering extra-large slices of pizza on Bleecker Street, hitting up the smarmy dive bar that doesn't ask for ID if you go before five.

Her eyes light up as she paints a picture for me, one that could have, in part, been mine. I could have been connecting with would-be writers just like me. I could have been wandering around the city, too.

We get off the phone, promising to talk again soon, and I can't help it, I feel a teensy bit . . . deflated. I know I shouldn't. I've been making really good progress on my screenplay, and I've been making friends, too. But at the same time—I don't have anything to put on my college applications, for all I know my screenplay could be awful, and I've been lying my ass off to Jake—both in person *and* online.

So I do what I always do when I feel that way, the one thing that usually manages to shake me out of it: I decide to watch a horror movie.

Stephen King said we make up horrors to help us cope with the real ones, and he's right. A good horror movie will make me scream at a jump scare and laugh at ridiculous dialogue and spurting blood. The shadows, the spine tingles, the sheer intensity make me feel something outside of me. Not by tugging on heartstrings, like drama, or plying me with one-liners, like comedy. Instead, horror plays on something I know well: fear.

My life is not full of horrors; I know that. It's good, really. But there's a kind of horror in the everyday. Horror in having to acknowledge to your family and friends that you let them down, that you didn't push yourself to the limit—in my case, didn't even give it a real shot. In lying to someone you've grown to care about. In talking to your best friend and feeling jealousy when you *know* you should be happy for her.

Sometimes just being a teenager, trying to cross that invisible bridge between childhood and adulthood, plagued with acne, with new curves that don't feel right, and *not* fall face-flat on the ground, is a horror of its own.

I head to the kitchen, grab the cash my parents left out on the table, order a pizza, and turn on the TV in the living room, perusing my options—I've never watched a horror movie on the screen in here; it's too close to their bedroom. Usually, I'm holed up in my room, laptop close to my face in a desperate attempt to make the screen feel bigger.

I feel a prickle of excitement at what's to come—greasy pizza and a scary movie on a real screen, lights off and everything, no worries about the screams or the score being too loud. A combination that promises to set all my feelings about Katie adrift.

The pizza arrives in thirty minutes, and by then, I've made my selection, a movie Elm recommended a couple of weeks ago, that cost too much to rent then but is free now on Netflix—a ghost story, but maybe it isn't a ghost story—one where the main character is constantly questioning her reality. I grab two slices, turn off all the lights, and sit on the couch.

I message Elm:

*CarriesRevenge01: Finally starting* The Haunting of Sophia Blaine. *Will keep you posted!*

He responds almost right away, a fact that brings my blush right back, gets my heart pumping fast again.

*ElmStreetNightmare84: I hope you like it. No pressure!*

*ElmStreetNightmare84: Well, a little pressure.*

*ElmStreetNightmare84: TBH I'll be heartbroken if you hate it, I loved it so much. Sophia's story is SO INTERESTING. I'll probably re-watch it soon. Shit, I'm overhyping it, aren't I?*

*CarriesRevenge01: A little!*

*ElmStreetNightmare84: Okay, I'll stop, but I demand a full postmortem once you're done. Deal?*

*CarriesRevenge01: Postmortem, good one ;)*

*CarriesRevenge01: And you're on*

*CarriesRevenge01: On like* King Kong

He sends me a silly emoji face, I send one back. Then, face still hot, pulse still thumping, I set my phone on the arm of the sofa, just in case he says anything else, and press Play. I have a feeling this is going to be good . . .

It is good. Too good, in fact. Or maybe it's my setting. Pizza eaten, there's nothing to occupy me but the movie. It's eerily quiet up here, not a single background noise, like I would have in Brooklyn, and I can hear the house settling, almost like a ghost is walking back and forth in the attic upstairs—or that awful husband from the movie *Gaslight*.

In the film's quieter parts, I can't help but hear it—the crack of a twig outside, probably from a deer, or the whir of a solitary car cruising down the rarely trafficked road, its lights casting an unsettling glow through the whole room.

By the time the credits roll, I'm good and scared.

I like to talk a big game about how horror movies never scare me. Most true fans will say the same. We're always chasing that rush, trying to get that thrill, and it almost never works. Only now, it has. Now, I kind of wish my parents would get home sooner rather than later.

I grab my phone, message Elm.

*CarriesRevenge01: I finished!*

He writes back immediately.

*ElmStreetNightmare84: Nice! How was it?*

My fingers shake as I type.

*CarriesRevenge01: I gotta say it's a lot creepier watching horror in the woods*

The phone drops from my hand, clattering onto the floor, and I realize, instantly, what I've done. It's like I didn't think, like Carrie and Olivia were once again one, and I forgot, for a moment, that Elm is not supposed to know I'm here. I grab my phone from the floor and search for a way to delete the message, but there's nothing I can do; it's been sent.

*ElmStreetNightmare84: Huh? I thought you were at NYU*

*CarriesRevenge01: I am*

*CarriesRevenge01: I mean, we took a weekend trip out to the Poconos*

Shit. It's only Thursday.

*CarriesRevenge01: A long weekend!*

There's a hesitation on his part, and I wonder if, somehow, he's put it all together; then he writes me back.

*ElmStreetNightmare84: Oh*

*ElmStreetNightmare84: Sounds cool!*

We talk about the movie, dissecting its ins and outs like I

promised we would, but I can't help but chastise myself for revealing too much.

I have the sinking feeling I've already gotten in too deep.

Just like Sophia Blaine in the movie—for me, it's probably going to get a whole lot messier before it gets any better.

# The Invitation

The next afternoon, just after returning from a lunch that unfortunately—or maybe fortunately, given my flub last night—didn't align with Jake's, Steinway greets me with a smile: "Tell me you don't have plans tonight."

It's just me in the office, the two-thirty tour crowd's all checked in, Tennyson off to supervise the lift.

"No plans," I say. I don't tell her that I never have plans, apart from hanging out with my parents, shooting the shit with Chrissy, and, of course, chatting with Elm—although, after last night's mishap, I'm kind of a little scared to do that.

"Perfect," Steinway says, tugging at the end of her braid. "A bunch of us are going to Pigeon's Landing tonight. It's a swimming hole nearby. I would have texted you last night, but I don't even have your number. Speaking of, we should correct that." She takes out her phone, and I rattle off my digits. She keys them in with freshly painted blue nails. "It's only a little ways up from here."

"I don't have a swimsuit," I say. "Not on me, at least."

Steinway shrugs. "Don't your parents come to pick you up? Just tell them to bring one."

I hesitate. The idea of putting on a swimsuit and splashing around with my coworkers, including Jake, sounds almost as scary as having to jump off that cliff.

"You don't even have to swim," Steinway adds. "It's really about the camaraderie. And I already told everyone you'd come. They can't wait to get a dose of our dear Olivia off the clock. You know, outside work, when we can just be ourselves."

For a second, I imagine Jake and me, splashing around, him moving closer to me in the water, my insecurities drifting away, summer skin on summer skin . . .

Not to mention, I told myself I'd be less afraid.

"Olivia?"

"Sorry," I say. "Sure, sounds great. I'll come."

"Awesome," Steinway says, then turns on her heel, sauntering off, her braids bouncing against her back as she does.

Almost immediately, my walkie beeps twice: "Jake to Olivia. Come in, Olivia."

"Go ahead, Jake," I say, holding down the button and ignoring the uptick in my pulse. He probably just needs a different-size helmet for one of the people in his group. I release the button, and there's another beep.

"Steinway says you're coming to Pigeon's Landing with us tonight. Over."

Jake never radios just me, and yet here he is, asking me over the walkie so everyone can hear. I feel heat rise in my cheeks.

I hold the button down. "Affirmative, Jake. Over."

A smile breaks across my face as the walkie beeps again. Jake's voice: "Cool."

Then immediately, another beep. "Let's keep the walkie to work business, kids."

I push the radio aside. Why would he go out of his way to make sure I'm going to be there unless . . .

Unless a tiny part of him likes me, just like I like him.

Another thought strikes me: I'm getting in deeper and deeper, and pretty soon, I'm not going to be able to find a way out.

My eyes case the room, but there's no one here. The place is totally dead. I pull out my phone, shoot off a quick text.

*You busy?*

Chrissy replies in less than a minute.

*Only waiting for a model who's ALWAYS LATE to finally show up. I shouldn't even book her anymore but I was desperate. Why, what's up?*

My thumbs hover over my phone, trying to think about the best way to phrase it.

*Have you ever lied to someone you like? Like, like-like?* I type finally.

The little dots. She's thinking.

*Well, I guess if you count the fact that I use a photo of me at thirty-five as my online dating profile, then yeah. Why?*

I feel a rush of relief. Chrissy is forty-three, though you'd never tell by her personality. Even she, who couldn't be cooler, wanted to bend the rules a bit when it came to her photo.

*I like someone, and I did something kind of like that. I was chatting with him online, it's not sketchy, don't worry, he's my age, but anyway, he's up here for the summer and the photo I sent before I met him was kind of a misrepresentation. Do you tell them it's an old photo of you?*

She responds immediately.

*Hell no.*

She keeps typing.

*Look, I stare at fashion photography all day, make even gorgeous models appear more perfect. Everyone lies a little bit about their looks. It sucks but it's kind of our culture right now. Do you know how many guys have said they were six-foot-one on their profile and, I swear to god, they're nothing close? As your aunt, I'm honestly more worried about your safety, chatting to someone you don't know online. Have you met him in person? Was it in a safe public place?*

*Yes, of course,* I assure her. *Totally safe. Totally public.*

*And did he like what he saw ;)*

*I think so,* I write back.

*So whatever filter you used couldn't have been that much of a misrepresentation!*

She doesn't get it. Of course she doesn't get it. But I don't know how to correct her.

Chrissy hesitates a moment, dots blinking in and out.

*Sounds like he adores the wonderful, brilliant, hilarious, and BEAUTIFUL person you are. I wouldn't worry about any stupid photos—he's seen you in real life, so it's a moot point. And in person, you're enough to charm anyone, my dear.*

I smile to myself. Chrissy's always been such a great cheerleader.

Maybe, in a way, she's right, even if I've left her a little shaky on the particulars. Maybe we all lie a little bit. Perhaps I should just be Olivia, and see what happens. At this point, I'm not sure what else to do.

It's a half-mile hike to the falls, my sneakers crunching against rocks and ivy. Steinway and I are in the back; she hasn't stopped talking in about fifteen minutes, detailing everything from her plans to open a store of her own one day to the cute girl she met on a hike just last weekend. "Anyway," she says as the trail turns to the right. "Your mom seems cool."

Steinway couldn't resist coming out with me to the car, shoving her hand through the window and introducing herself to my mom, who was more than happy to deliver a swimsuit and a towel. "I'm so glad you're making friends!" my mom had said out loud, while Steinway was right there within earshot. Oy.

"She's not so bad," I say.

"So she's a total Brooklyn OG, right? Born and raised? You can tell by her accent."

I laugh. It doesn't sound like anything to me, but when we go to Iowa, people always comment on it.

"And she knows Marianne from high school?" Steinway asks.

The trail begins to climb before us, mossy and lush beneath our sneakers, and I nod, my breathing getting ever so slightly heavier, the trees surrounding us like tall monsters.

"What does she do now?" Steinway asks as she scrambles up a path of rocks.

"She's an art history professor," I say, careful to follow the path exactly how Steinway made it, careful not to trip over any of the exposed roots. "At Pratt."

"That's cool," Steinway says, tugging at the ends of one of her braids before steadying herself against an overgrown tree. "Are you artsy, too?"

I shrug. "A little."

"Art? Music? Underwater basket weaving?"

We make our way around another bend, the thick of trees preventing us from seeing any farther than about fifty feet ahead. In the distance, I hear the roar of rushing water and echoes of laughter. The rest of them must have reached Pigeon's Landing already.

"Movies, I guess," I say, feeling protected, if only for a moment. Besides, I promised myself I would, you know, *be myself.* Just because

I tell her I like movies doesn't mean Jake is suddenly going to figure everything out. "I'm pretty into movies."

Steinway laughs. "Like Jake? Get him talking about the film collective where he's interning, and I swear, he won't shut up."

We reach the falls, and I take it in. A small waterfall, can't be more than ten feet, that cascades into a swimming hole, surrounded by granite rocks covered in moss, dense trees, and a pink-blue sky. I swear it looks like a painting.

"It's just a hobby," I say. "I don't talk about it too much."

Steinway barely even registers what I've said. In minutes, her extra clothes are off, and she's climbing over the rocks, jumping in, splashing everyone around her.

I take a seat on a rock on the edge, adjusting myself until it's comfortable, stretching my legs out to catch the last bit of sun, and look out on my coworkers, my new friends. Cora is smiling. Per Steinway, she's dating someone new, which is apparently the best way to get over a breakup. Tennyson is swimming in his Zipline Experience T-shirt and khaki shorts, and he looks like a drowned rat. Bryson's got Ray-Bans on, even though shades aren't necessary, the sun already beginning to set.

It's amazing how different it is here from Brooklyn. There's no competition; instead, everyone seems content to move at their own pace. It's not like they don't have any plans. Steinway is training to be assistant manager so she can open her store. Cora is studying biochem at Bard. Bryson is at Rutgers, not yet sure what he's going to study. Even Tennyson, who operates completely by his own unique Tennyson code, is part of a grassroots organization to help get weed legalized in New York State. They're all doing their thing, but it's like, somehow, the pressure is off.

Jake is hovering on the edge, and his back is to me, but I can see the way his curls are even glossier, how the water runs down his back as he stands up and shakes off. I think of how he used the walkie, just to make sure I was coming. How differently would things have gone these last couple of weeks if I'd never met him online? I'd have told him immediately about my love of horror, we'd have bonded over it, most definitely; we'd have had even more to talk about during our daily lunch chats.

Steinway pops up and turns to me. Her braids are undone now, her curls messy and slick. "Get in here, girl!"

"In a minute," I say, looking down. I changed into my suit in the employee bathroom, and yet the idea of whipping off my T-shirt and shorts in front of everyone scares me. There's nothing wrong with my body; there's nothing wrong with *any* body, I really believe that. But even though I don't think we should be ashamed of how we look, I'm nowhere close to living that truth. Like Chrissy said, we all lie a little bit about our appearance, and all I can think of right now is my gawky elbows, the way my thighs rub together, and that one black hair that grows beneath my belly button.

There's a splash, and I jump. Goose pimples rise on my arm and a few droplets of water speckle across the bottom of my shirt. I look up; Jake is right there.

"Sorry," he says. "Seriously, I didn't mean to get you wet. You're not coming in?"

I shrug. "Eventually."

His hand trails through the water. "Do I need to come up with a cheesy joke to lure you in?" His eyes flit around the area. Then he grabs a small rock. "Come on in. It *rocks!*"

I laugh, just as he drops the stone into the water, causing another small splash, sending fresh water droplets onto his chest.

"That was like a two out of ten," I say.

He stares at me a moment, and I remember, instantly, that I used to rate the nicknames he'd give to me when we were first chatting. Shit.

Luckily, he doesn't seem to put it together. "Seriously, what's stopping you?"

*The same self-defeating bullshit that kept me from sending you my picture and giving my NYU application a real shot.*

"There's nothing in the water," he says. "Promise." Then, lowly, he begins to hum the *Jaws* theme. *"Duh-duh. Duh-duh. Duh-duh-duh-duh . . ."*

I hop up as Jake continues to hum. Before I can doubt myself, I shimmy out of my shorts and take off my T-shirt, quick as I can.

I jump, and it's a jolt to my system, a shockwave of cold. "It's *freezing*," I say, my jaw beginning to shake.

Jake steps forward, arms slightly open, as if he's going to wrap me up, keep me warm. But then, just as quickly, he steps back, runs his fingers through the water again. "It's the waterfall water," he says. "Straight from the top of the mountain."

I nod, then take a step to the right, toward a little patch of sun that still remains, but as soon as I do, my foot slips from beneath me, and I'm falling to the side, crashing straight into Jake.

For a second, his arms hold me, strong and tense, and I can feel his heart beating as fast as mine, and our skin is wet and sticky against each other's, and I never, ever, ever want this moment to end.

But he straightens up, quickly, and I find my balance, stepping back. "Sorry," I say. "The water should really come with a warning sign."

Jake's face is red, but he shakes his arms, recovering. "You okay?"

I nod. "Fine."

*More than fine, Jake. Way more than fine.*

He forces a smile. "I suppose the monster in this water is *Degrees Fahrenheit.*"

I laugh, digging my feet into the mossy mud for balance. "*Celsius* for European distribution."

Jake shakes with laughter, then smiles at me. "Have you seen *Open Water*? It's not nearly as good, but it's this *Jaws*-inspired thing, and it's so much fun."

I hesitate.

"Oh, wait, you don't like horror, right? Sorry."

Steinway's voice rises above the din of laughter. "Is he trying to get you to watch B-list movies from like a hundred years ago again? Apparently it's his thing."

Jake ignores her, turning back to me. "I don't always watch old stuff," he says. "*The Shallows* is a newer one, also about a shark. What can I say? I like shark movies. Shit, do I sound like a five-year-old?"

"Well, you *are* afraid of the dark . . ."

He grins. "Hey, I told you that and no one else. Please don't say that out loud. Remember, I'm a newbie, too."

I laugh. I loved *The Shallows*. And *Open Water*, as well. I love high-seas horror. It's so real, so all-consuming. In fact, I'm the one who told Jake about *The Shallows*, where surfer Blake Lively has to basically battle a shark on her own.

"By the way," I say, reminding myself that I promised to be more truthful. "I wouldn't say I don't like them at *all.*"

"What do you mean?" he asks. "Oh. Horror movies?"

"I'm just not that well-versed, I guess." I can't very well go back and un-say what I said to him that first day, but at least I can aim a little more for the truth, try to bring Olivia and Carrie a teensy bit closer together. "I'd actually like to get more into them."

"Really?" Jake asks, eyes wide, water dripping down his forehead.

I nod.

He smiles briefly, then looks down at the water. "There's one I was planning to watch tonight, actually." His eyes catch mine. "If you weren't doing anything, you know, since us newbies have to stick together, I don't know, would you want to watch it with me?"

I feel a warmth course through my veins, a contrast to the super-cold water. I was going to go home and try to get in another page or so on my screenplay—perhaps add a swimming hole scene—but I don't even care about that right now. My heart thumps fast at the thought of us together. Olivia and Jake or Elm and Carrie—it doesn't even matter—right now, we're just *us*.

"I'd love to," I say.

# Fishnado

It's not that he doesn't ask anyone else; it's more that he doesn't do it all that enthusiastically.

"There's this horror movie," he says as we reach the Hunter Mountain parking lot, empty now, except for the group of us. "Er, do you guys want to come watch it with us?"

Cora goes on about meeting up with a new guy she's dating. Tennyson uses the opportunity to take a bowl out of his pocket and crumble weed into it, explaining that he and Bryson are going to chill for a bit and then play video games. Steinway narrows her eyes. "Horror? No thanks."

"You okay if it's just us?" Jake asks quietly, turning to me.

*Most definitely.*

"Sure," I say. "If you are," I add, wrapping the towel tighter around myself.

"You can change at my aunt's house," he says, looking away briefly, as if to give me privacy. "You know, if you don't want to get your clothes all wet. That's what I'm going to do."

I nod, nervous at the prospect of being in nothing more than my swimsuit for the entire ride but not exactly wanting to watch a whole movie with wet shorts either. I tug at the bottom of the towel so it covers me up a little more. "Sounds good."

Steinway smiles as I get into Jake's navy Honda, her grin lopsided and mischievous. "Have fun, guys," she says with an incredibly indiscreet wink.

The car smells like pine air freshener and mint gum. At my feet, a DVD of a B horror he once recommended to me. In the cup holder, an old Starbucks cup.

I text my mom as he pulls out of the parking lot.

*Going to a movie with friends if that's okay?*

She texts back right away.

*Have fun! Be home by eleven please!*

In town, Jake takes a right, heading toward the road that leads to Woodstock. Both of us stay quiet as he drives just a few miles over the speed limit, winding through thickets of trees, lush and green, skirting rumbling creeks, the mountains always in the distance. It's just after eight, the sun not quite fully set, but the darkness is definitely taking over.

The radio isn't on, and the silence is too much. I have to say *something*.

"Do you want to work in movies or something?" I ask finally. "I mean, since you're doing the internship?"

He signals, getting ready to make a turn, and I wait for his answer, one I pretty much already know. "Maybe," he says, after a pause. "I'm not sure I have the guts to be a real-deal artist, to put myself out there like that. I'm kind of getting more into the business parts of the internship."

"The business of film or business in general?" I ask, more than a little bit surprised.

He taps at the steering wheel. "I know this will probably make me even *more* of a nerd in your eyes, but I guess I kind of love math? I mean, don't get me wrong, I'm super into movies, especially horror, but I'm discovering it might be more of a hobby. It's interesting, being at the collective, seeing how they apply for grants and get funding and all that. That probably sounds lame."

I look down briefly at my hands as we enter the outskirts of Woodstock, not far from my home. I had no idea. There're just so many holes that can't be filled through Reddit chatter or workplace lunches. "No," I say, looking up. "It doesn't sound lame at all. It sounds cool."

"I didn't really have any solid plans, but I knew I needed to get away for the summer—like I told you yesterday, four siblings in one house can be a lot—and my aunt told me about this internship, and it sounded pretty good. The rest, as they say, is history."

I laugh. One of the movies he loves most, about a group of friends trapped in a house, trying to figure out who the killer is, ends with that line: *And the rest, as they say, is history.*

"Er, here we are," he says, and he turns right, pulling into a driveway surrounded by thick, dense trees. Before us is a tiny little house, red siding, a roof with a few missing shingles. Paned windows and a porch only big enough for a single chair. As I get out of the car, I hear the trickle of a stream. It's idyllic, similar to our cottage, but even more tucked away—perfect for a horror director.

The two different sides of me seemingly go to war, despite my attempts to reconcile them. As Olivia, I want to be alone with Jake; I really do. But as Carrie, I can't help but feel a little excitement at the thought of meeting his aunt, the absolute real deal. There's so much I'd love to ask her, so much I'd want to say. *Did you ever doubt yourself so much you couldn't get a single thing done? Were you ever so afraid of failing that you couldn't even try?*

We get out of the car and Jake hovers in front of the doorway. "I hope it's okay, but my aunt is shooting late tonight," Jake says. "Up in Windham."

A heat rises in my cheeks. Forget talking to his aunt about movies. The thought of us alone, together, it's almost too much—in a good way, that is.

"Not that I'm expecting anything, to, I mean . . ." He blushes. "I just mean, she's not here. So don't be surprised."

I grin. "Okay, I won't be."

Jake digs in his pocket for the keys. "So you guys come up just for the summers?" he asks, his hands fumbling for the lock and finding it after a second or two too long.

"Yeah," I say as he opens the door. "My parents only got the place last year. We were here for six weeks after they finalized all the paperwork. This is the first summer that we've come up for the whole time."

Jake flips on the lights, and we walk into a smallish living room, a cushy red sofa facing a fireplace with a TV sitting on the mantel. In a corner, tripods and lights, gear zipped into black canvas bags. "Do you want something to drink?" Jake asks. "I mean, like, iced tea or something. Unless you want me to break into my aunt's whiskey, but I won't be able to join you. That stuff smells so gross."

I laugh, his sheepishness—his nervousness—delighting me. "Tea is great."

He takes out two glasses and points down the hall. "Oh yeah, and the bathroom's the first door on the right if you want to change."

I nod and head there quickly, eager to get back into my real clothes, to not feel so exposed. It's one of the few things I hate about horror movies, how the girl will get stuck in some stupid skimpy outfit during the beginning and will conveniently be in said outfit throughout the movie, pieces of clothing tearing away with each new scene. They never do it with dudes, of course. "The male gaze," as my mom is always going on about.

The bathroom is normal, not that I expected something different from a horror movie director—fake blood on the shower curtain in a nod to *Psycho*? A monster peeking out from under the claw-footed tub?—and I change into my regular clothes, hanging my swimsuit on the hooks, then finger-comb my hair. I steal a glance in the mirror—I don't look perfect. Far from it. But right now, I don't even care.

Back in the kitchen, Jake pushes a glass of iced tea into my hand, our fingers brushing ever so slightly, sending a shock to my nerves. "Let me just change real quick, too."

I lean against the counter, guzzling tea and trying to calm my staccato heart. My eyes land on his aunt's equipment. Lenses and black boxes, all the different mechanisms designed to capture something even half as good as what the eye can see.

Jake returns to the kitchen in fresh clothes, dark-washed jeans and a black T-shirt, plus the glasses I recognize from the photo he sent me.

"Nice glasses," I say.

He nods. "I don't like to wear them zip-lining. Too easy to fall off." He grabs his tea and leans against the counter, wiggles a hand through his hair, messing it around, then shoves it deep in his pocket, as if he doesn't know quite what to do with that part of his body.

"So, Brooklyn . . ." he says, his voice trailing off, and I imagine him filling in the gaps.

*I have a friend who lives in Brooklyn.*

*An online friend, actually.*

*She kind of reminds me of you.*

(Yeah, right.)

"I know you said it was crowded and stuff, but do you ever get to be on your own?" he asks finally. "Or are there always people around?"

I smile. "I like to walk down to Shore Road on the bay. I'm not totally alone there, I guess—you're never really *totally* alone—but it feels different. More open. More like this."

He grins, sipping at his iced tea, a tiny bit dripping down his chin. He wipes it off quickly with the back of his hand. "Do you ever kayak there?"

"No," I say with a laugh. "You saw me that first day on the zip line. I'm not exactly the definition of outdoorsy."

The corner of his mouth turns up, just the slightest. "It's okay. You're good the way you are."

I feel myself go bright red, and I practically drown myself in my tea. "Some people kayak, but even if it were more my style, I'd be afraid to have the water splashing on me. There are literally signs that say pregnant women or anyone of childbearing age shouldn't eat fish caught in the East River, which feeds right into the bay."

He raises an eyebrow. "No shit, really? My aunt says the water is super clean up here."

"Yes, up north, before it gets corrupted by the endless filth of New York City."

Jake laughs. "Wow, no one even of childbearing age, huh?"

I shake my head. "No joke. Although, who wants to eat radioactive fish anyway? Childbearing age or not."

He nods in agreement, his free hand pressing against the counter behind him. "Radioactive fish. It would make a good . . ." His voice trails off, but mentally I finish the words for him. *It would make a good horror movie.* If we were online, I'd agree. We'd half plot it out together, tossing banter back and forth. Elm and Carrie thrive on banter. It's why I don't know half as much about him as you'd think I would. Our conversations live in another world, the one of movies. I never in a million years would have guessed he was the oldest of four kids, or the fact that escapism has led to his love of movies. If we were on Reddit right now, I'd suggest that—to really draw an audience—we should blend the radioactive fish with some sort of natural disaster, in the vein of *Sharknado*. Fishnado, if you will. Only tornadoes have nothing to do with New York City. Fishquake? Fishiccane? Fish Bomb Cyclone? I chuckle to myself.

"What?" he asks.

"Nothing important," I say, because I'm glad we're not on Reddit right now. I'm glad it's just us, face-to-face, and that I'm learning things about him I never would have known before. I'm glad Jake is more than his online persona. For a blissful second, it almost feels as if it can all work out. I glance to the film equipment propped in the corner. "It's so cool your aunt's a horror director," I say.

He freezes. "How did you know she directs horror?"

My heart practically stops, but not from excitement this time, from fear. I scramble at the words. "Oh, sorry, I mean, does she do something else?"

He shakes his head. "No, definitely horror, but I haven't been mentioning it to anyone, because the collective doesn't really take it as seriously, and she only just got in. How did you know?"

*It's me, Elm. Me, Carrie.* That's *how I know.*

I shrug my shoulders and force a smile. "Because you're so into horror movies—and the fact that we're watching one tonight. I guess I made an assumption."

He pauses, his eyebrows knitting up, but then his confusion seems to dissipate; he smiles back. "Oh yeah. Duh." He drains his tea, then puts both hands on the counter, avoiding my eyes for a moment. He looks at me. "Should we start the movie now? Does that sound good to you?"

I nod.

"It's super good, even if you're not a horror fan."

"Sounds perfect," I say, finishing my tea.

He grins. "It's called *The Haunting of Sophia Blaine*."

# The Haunting of Sophia Blaine:
# Part Two

The truth?

I have never sat alone on a couch with a boy before. I have never kissed one, either. Despite many a crush, I've hardly even flirted. Not really. Not successfully, at least, given my dating history.

Maybe that makes me a weirdo, just like having a full-on separate Reddit identity does—but it's the reality of the situation.

It doesn't matter that we're sitting about as far apart from each other as possible, Jake on one end, me on the other—it's still clear to me that there's *something* here, more than I've ever had with a boy before. Something charged about the energy, about our mutual nervousness. Something thrilling and dynamic and just . . . sweet.

I know another thing, too. I have 100 percent seen this movie before—last night. But I can't let him know that.

"Oh my god!" I gasp, my hand grasping the cushion. A jump scare I knew was coming. Shit. Am I laying it on too thick? Did I gasp just a second too soon? Am I totally obvious?

*Okay, Jake,* I imagine the documentary producer saying. *How did you know that your coworker was leading a double life? That the friend you thought you'd made online had played you?*

*Well, producer,* Jake would say. *It was when she jumped half a second too quickly at a movie she swore she hadn't seen. That's when I knew for sure. She is not who she says she is. At least, she is not only who she says she is.*

Jake turns to me, his face only half illuminated from the light coming off the screen. He scoots a little closer, giving himself a few inches of space from the arm of the sofa, then sinks back into the cushions. "Wow, it's really freaking you out, huh?"

All right, I'm definitely laying it on too thick. I don't want to be one of those people who can't stand even the slightest jump scare. That's not me at all. "No, I like it," I say, moving a little closer as well, resting my hand on the cushion between us. "Really."

Even in the dim light, I can see his eyes widen, his body lean toward mine ever so slightly. "It's good, right? I'm glad you like it. I mean, if it can win a non–horror lover over even the tiniest bit, I think it's a good thing."

*That's not me*, I want to say. *I love this stuff.*

The movie continues, and I feign surprise with each new development, my gasps getting less obvious each time, but my hand, my body, creeping a little closer—his, too.

Sophia Blaine is asking her husband how they got into this position when our hands are so close I'm sure they're going to touch. They're like magnets coming together, his rough and cracked from tying ropes all day, mine sunburnt, lightly freckled. His hand inches toward mine, and I can feel heat emanating from his skin, and then—

There's a sudden flash of a ghost on the screen and a crash of the movie soundtrack. Another jump scare, but this one actually *does* catch me off guard. My shoulders hunch up, and almost on instinct, Jake whips his hand away.

I sigh. The nerves of what almost happened are too much.

"Er, do you want some popcorn or something? You must be hungry."

I realize I *am* hungry; I haven't eaten much more than a handful of almonds since lunch, but until now, I hadn't even thought of it. "Sure," I say. "I'd love some."

"Great," Jake says, and leaps off the couch, pausing the movie.

I pick at my nails as I wait, listening to the pop-pop-pop coming from the microwave. My heart beats quickly, too, at the thought of Jake returning to the couch. I *like* him, I realize again. I *really, really* like him. Every side of him. But what would he think of me if I opened up about it all? What would he do if I told him everything as soon as he came back? The lies, the photo, everything?

Would he forgive me, laugh it off, understand that it's easy to get a little self-conscious sometimes, widen his eyes at the ridiculous coincidence that made this whole thing a possibility? Or would he narrow them instead, take two steps back. *Are you kidding me? You've been lying to me this whole time?*

An explosion of pops and then the dinging of the timer. I listen as Jake takes the bag out of the microwave and empties it into a bowl. What would his aunt think of me? And Steinway? And Marianne? And everyone I've grown surprisingly fond of?

Jake returns holding a metal bowl, kernels of corn shimmering with grease. I expect him to sit where he was, but instead, he sits much closer, so we're only inches apart. "You know, so we can share," he says.

I nod. "Totally."

He sets the bowl between us, balancing it on both of our legs, and I have wild fantasies of grabbing it, tossing it aside, creating greasy popcorn snowfall, turning to him and leaning in, never breaking away.

Instead, we eat and we watch, and I savor every brush of our hands as we reach for the bowl at the same time—it's more delicious, even, than the salty, buttery popcorn. My body thrums where it almost touches his, our thighs so close but still so far, and the movie, so recently watched, takes on a new meaning. Sure, I saw it last night, but I've never seen it sitting so close on a couch with a cute boy. I've never seen it wondering if I turned my head just so, if he would . . .

I turn my head just so, catch his profile, illuminated by the lights of the screen. The glare on his glasses, the slope of his nose, a pimple on the bottom of his chin. He's imperfect, too, and yet, looking at him now, all I see is perfection.

He catches my eyes, and I look away, embarrassed.

"What?" he asks.

I turn back, try to still my racing pulse. "Nothing."

He doesn't drop my gaze, and his hand reaches for mine on the edge of the bowl, his fingers resting, not intertwining, just there. It's suddenly scarier than anything in any horror movie in the history of time, because I don't know *what* is going to happen, and I've never felt this way before . . .

A sudden screech; the front door practically crashes open.

Jake jumps and scoots back about three feet on the couch, and a woman walks in, wearing jeans and a faded *Carrie* T-shirt. Jake's aunt. I love her already.

She takes me in but doesn't say a word about us, about my being here, and I wonder—is this something he does all the time, brings girls over to watch a movie?

But then I realize, it can't be. He's only been here a few weeks.

She sets down more equipment, and I catch the tattoos running up and down her left arm—I bet she's just too cool to say anything like that, like Chrissy.

"This is Olivia," Jake says, quickly getting up off the couch and helping his aunt with her things.

I stand up, too, and she gives me a wave. "Mona." Her hair is short, pixie-like, and dyed charcoal black. She looks about my mother's age, only she couldn't be further from my mother in every single way. She isn't wearing any makeup, or maybe it all washed off—her face practically swims in sweat. "I'd shake your hand," she says. "Only I'm sweating out to here. I swear to god we weren't supposed to be shooting until eleven."

*Eleven.*

"Shit," I say. "I mean . . ." I glance to Mona, but she doesn't seem to notice or care. "I was supposed to be home by eleven."

My phone is still in my bag. I dig it out. There are three texts from my mom.

*Where are you?*

*It's 11:15*

*I'm worried*

I shoot a quick text back.

*So sorry lost track of time, coming home now*

"I'll drive you," Jake says, before I even have a chance to ask.

"Come back again when I'm not a sweaty mess," Mona says with a smile.

In minutes, I've retrieved my swimsuit from the bathroom, and we're back in Jake's car. Only it's different this time, it's dark and it's nearly midnight, and we almost kissed back on that couch. Even thinking about it now, the way his eyes held mine, the way our hands came together, I feel myself blush; luckily, it's too dark in the car for him to see it.

It's not just the car; it's everything. The winding roads, illuminated just barely by headlights. A darkness that surrounds you and presses on you, the kind of darkness that opens the door to all kinds of possibilities. It's that time of night, and that time in movies, when the monsters come out.

If we were just Elm and Carrie, it would be easy. I'd be cracking jokes left and right. About how we *really* better watch out for deer, because every movie that wants to up the creep factor always has the driver hitting an animal of some sort—even *Get Out* did it, and *Get Out* wasn't much for clichés. Or, I'd talk about how these winding, unraveling roads remind me of David Lynch movies, of early *Twin Peaks*.

I can't say any of that, so I don't say anything at all.

"I'm sorry I made you miss curfew," he says finally. "I had no idea it had gotten so late. I was distracted, I guess . . . by the movie, I mean."

"No, it's my fault," I say, forcing a laugh. "I should have been checking the time." Then: "You can turn up here. Next right."

He slows down, making the turn carefully, and as he does, the headlights illuminate a deer. He comes to a full stop, and she looks at us, then prances off, back into the woods.

Screw it, I'm saying it. Having a loose knowledge of horror is not going to give me away.

"This is like the perfect complementary setting to the movie," I say.

He grins. "Right? This whole area is."

*Of course the horror movie setting isn't horrible at all*, I think. *It's completely lovely, having him here with me.*

But that, I'm definitely not brave enough to say.

I point ahead. "It's that green house right there."

He pulls into the gravel drive.

"Thanks for driving me." I reach for the handle.

Jake practically spits the words out: "We should do this again sometime."

I turn back, nodding eagerly. "I'd like that."

"Should we trade numbers?"

I have to stop my hands from shaking with excitement, but I pull out my phone and hand it to him. He punches his in. "Just text me, and I'll have yours," he says.

I nod. "I guess I should get inside, then. My parents are probably having a conniption."

He stares at me, and I feel myself blush.

"I mean, they're probably freaking out, you know."

Jake nods, but his gaze doesn't break mine, and I want, so badly, to lean in, to take that step off the cliff, just like I did, with his encouragement, before . . .

Finally, he looks away, breaking the silence: "Er, thanks for watching a movie with me—or part of a movie with me, at least—we can do something not-horror next time, promise. Or we can finish this one. Whatever you want."

I nod. "No problem. Thanks for having me."

He adjusts himself in his seat, then twists his body, leaning forward—

An awful beep. I laugh as he whips back his arm from where his elbow laid on the horn. Some timing the two of us have.

He looks away, embarrassed. "Sorry. I'll see you Monday."

I smile, reaching for the door. "See you."

My mom is reading in the living room when I walk in. She narrows her eyes at me. "Have fun?"

I nod. "I'm sorry."

"Don't do it again," she says, but she smiles, like she knows more than she's letting on. Then she turns back to her book like nothing's even happened. My mom might be completely different from Aunt

Chrissy or Jake's aunt Mona—but times like this, she's pretty cool all the same.

Back in my room, I toss my bag onto the bed and pull out my phone, type out a message.

*Hi, Jake, it's Olivia*

As soon as it's sent, I feel the heat rise to my cheeks, and I sink into the bed, stare at the ceiling, feel my whole body coming alive.

I really thought this was going to be the worst summer ever.

*How incredibly wrong I was.*

# The Bad Decision Handbook:

# Part Three

I wake up feeling high, even though I have no idea what that would feel like, though Chrissy has told me some stories. High on good vibes. High on what happened (or almost happened) with Jake. High on the prospect of a whole Saturday spent writing.

My parents and I go to brunch at our favorite spot, ordering the usual—eggs Benedict for me, pulled pork sandwich for my mom, and the farmer's scramble for my dad. When we're back home, I open up my laptop and *The Bad Decision Handbook*.

Over the last two weeks I've amassed a fairly impressive fifty pages. It's not going to be a long movie, probably only an hour and a half, which means I don't have much more than forty pages left. If I set my mind to it, I might be able to finish at least a shitty first draft this weekend.

Most importantly, I've got the fodder, stories, settings, feelings acquired from being here. I've already decided that my Tennyson-inspired character is going to accidentally say something brilliant that helps kick off the climax. And that my Steinway-style gal will call him an idiot before agreeing it's likely the best idea. As much as I wanted to avoid the romance clichés, I can't help it, I definitely think I'm going to have Onyx and Jimmy kiss at the end of the second act, right before the evil director launches his most vicious and terrifying attack.

I write fairly solidly from one p.m. to four, when my phone buzzes and I get my first message from Elm. I take a break, shocked to realize I've added another eight pages.

*ElmStreetNightmare84: Hey, so I re-watched* Sophia *last night, it was great!*

And only a few minutes after, a text from Jake:

*Last night was fun! Hanging with my aunt at her shoot this weekend, but we should finish the movie at some point, maybe this week?*

Then another, from Elm again.

*ElmStreetNightmare84: Well I partially re-watched it, at least, but still great. How are you?*

I push my laptop aside and shake my head. This already feels so messy.

I answer Jake first.

*For sure. Maybe Monday?*

Then I open the Reddit app and start to message back.

*CarriesRevenge01: I know, isn't it the best? P.S. Working on my screenpl*

I stop myself. It's too disingenuous after last night, pretending to be two different people. Keeping up the Carrie façade—it's got to stop. I know it's time to fade her out. Letter by letter, I delete the message. Then I close the app and go back to my messages. I watch as the dots appear, and Jake texts back.

*It's a plan.*

A smile breaks across my face. I set my phone down and grab my laptop again.

My mom pokes her head in. "Dad's going to grill tonight. Probably eat around seven. You're here, right? No late-night plans with new friends?"

I feel myself go red, but she only smiles. "I'm just teasing, Olivia. You look . . . happy."

"I'll be here," I say quickly, and when I don't add anything else, she turns on her heel, pulling the door shut behind her.

*I* am *happy*, I realize.

I like my job, I like the people I've met up here . . .

I like Jake.

I'm *not* going to mess it up this time. I'm not going to hide behind Carrie, the photo of Katie, and the anonymity of the internet.

I'm going to try my best to be me. That's it.

Briefly, I consider deleting the Reddit app, putting Carrie behind me, ghosting, just like that.

Only, it's cruel. Elm doesn't deserve that.

I go back to Reddit, open his most recent message.

**CarriesRevenge01: I'm good but pretty busy, actually. Might not have quite as much time for all our usual chats this week!**

Before I can second-guess myself, I hit Send.


I write the rest of the night. In fact, I don't go to sleep until long after midnight, when I have a grand total of seventy pages.

On Sunday evening, after a long hike with my parents, I get back to it, working through—only breaking for dinner—and I nod off sometime around two a.m., then wake up again at four.

I have eighty-six pages. I'm so very close. I only have to write the final confrontation, which I've got all planned out in my head anyway.

I'm tempted to stop. But when it gets hard, I remember the way I felt standing at the edge of the cliff, before the first zip line. I remember Jake's hand in mine. That I don't have to be the kind of person who's so afraid to fail they're afraid to try.

It's five thirty in the morning before I finish.

The script is a mess, and it's all over the place, and I know it's not perfect, but it's real.

I stare at it, scrolling through the pages, looking at all I've written.

So many words, so many scenes, so many bits of dialogue, action lines, and description.

All mine.

My heart swells, and I feel, again, like I'm zipping over the trees, flying.

Like my fear, my self-sabotaging bullshit, my old neuroses—well, they can go jump off their own cliff, and not securely hooked up to a zip line, either.

Only there, in the back of my head, a niggling thought.

There's no one I want to tell as much as Elm.

I shake my head. I can't. I have to fade out Carrie. Things are progressing too much in real life. My alter ego—she's got to go.

Only . . .

What if I sent it to him anyway? Just this one last thing. After all, I did promise him I would as soon as I finished. It's almost rude not to, after how much we've talked about it.

Wouldn't it be wrong to break my promise?

Before I can stop myself, I hit Share on my Google Doc, and it gives me a link. I know I shouldn't do this, but I have to tell him.

I open Reddit and start a new message to Elm.

*CarriesRevenge01: Told you I was busy because I was finishing my screenplay! Here it is.*

I paste the link and hit Send.

It's only after it's sent, somewhere out in the ether, that I realize what I've done. In my Google Doc, my name. I'm the author. Not Carrie. Olivia Knight.

Shit. Shit. Shit. Shit.

It's five forty-five a.m. He can't have looked at it already.

I head to my Google account and change my alias, turning my first name from Olivia to Carrie, my last name from Knight to Revenge.

I don't even care if the script is rough—I don't even care if sending it was a stupid mistake—it's out in the world.

With the person who I care about seeing it more than anyone else.

Maybe sending it was a bad decision; but right now, it feels like a damn good one.

# Vertigo: Part Two

I can barely keep my eyes open on Monday.

I'm not saying it was a *bad* decision to go on a writing bender and finish the screenplay. I'm just saying that I can hardly focus enough to check in the two-thirty crew. I'm just saying that, five minutes ago, a guy told me his name was Brad, and I asked him how to spell it.

I haven't yet heard back from Elm regarding the screenplay, but honestly, I'm a bit too tired to really give it much thought.

Just before three, Marianne pops in. "How's it going?" she asks.

"Good," I say. "All accounted for. No hiccups. And we sold like ten T-shirts today."

Marianne smiles. "It's my niece; she did the new design. She'll be thrilled to see it's so popular. Anyway, I'm putting you on Ropeland duty, because I need to send Tennyson up to the zip lines. Steinway's leading the tour, just make sure the kids wait and all that—you know the drill. I'll handle the front in case anyone comes in."

"Sounds good," I say.

When I get to Ropeland, the kids are impatiently standing in line as usual. I look up to see Steinway leading a cluster through the ropes in the middle.

The next hour passes slowly and unceremoniously. Steinway finishes her group and begins another. I pass out gear for the next group of kids.

When it's almost four, I get a text from Jake.

*Still on for tonight? Was going to ask you at lunch but stayed up here because the tour ran long.*

I write back quickly.

*For sure, can't wa*

I delete it and go for something a little more casual.

*Sure*

Too casual. I add a little punctuation.

*Sure!*

Then I hit Send.

It's only ten minutes after that when I see a message on Reddit.

*ElmStreetNightmare84: OMG YOU FINISHED THE SCREENPLAY? This is the best news ever! I CAN'T WAIT to read.*

I scroll above and click the link I sent him to the screenplay, checking once again that the author comes up as "Carrie Revenge" and not "Olivia Knight." All good.

Suddenly, I see Steinway, booking it across the lowest rope bridge, the group of kids behind her. She hops down, helping the kids down with her. "I need a break," she says.

"What?"

She's completely pale. "I'm gonna be sick," she says. "Just cancel the next group. I gotta go."

That's when I hear the crying. I look up. There's a boy, maybe eight or nine, standing at the very top, the highest part of the tower, head thrown back, wailing.

"What about him?" I ask, pointing up.

"Uh-oh," she says. "Sorry. He must have gotten left behind." She points to the harness. "You're gonna have to get him. I can't."

She runs off, like her life depends on it, leaving me on my own. The kids all stare at me. Shit.

My heart beats faster, and I glance around furtively, hoping to wave down Cora or Bryson, anyone. Standing here, it looks so damn high.

I push a button on the walkie. "Olivia here. Anyone able to come to Ropeland? A kid is stuck up top and Steinway got sick and had to leave. Over."

There's a beep.

"Jake to Olivia. Too busy here with the tour. Over."

"Marianne to Olivia. Just got busy in the office. Can you handle it on your own? Over."

My heart continues to race, but I press the button again. "Sure thing. Over."

I hook the walkie onto my belt and clench and unclench my fists. I can do this. I *have* to do this.

Quickly, I shimmy a harness up my legs, hook a carabiner and a few feet of metal rope onto the front, and grab a helmet that miraculously fits right.

Grabbing the first rope, I pull myself up. I'm only a couple of feet off the ground, but already, the ropes are shaky; I hook my carabiner onto the safety cable that stretches above the rope bridge, like I've seen Steinway do plenty of times, but still, my stomach flip-flops. I take another step, and I let myself look up.

The kid is still wailing, holding on to the ropes with both hands.

I take another cautious step. I'm going to have to speed up. At this pace, it will take forever. My walkie beeps again. "Jake to Olivia. You okay?"

With a shaking hand, I grab my walkie. "I'm making my way up . . . slowly." Screw the lingo. I don't have time for that right now.

The walkie beeps again, punctuating the kid's wails. "Okay, on the left side, closest to the lodge, there's a ladder built into the course. It goes straight to the top. It's easier than using the bridges and nets," Jake says.

I look over, and from the ground, a young girl points to exactly what Jake is talking about. I walk quickly, not looking down, ignoring the way the ropes seem to barely hold me up. I tug on the metal line that connects me to the safety cable overhead, reminding myself I'm secure, that eight-year-olds do this all the time.

The walkie beeps again. "Find the ladder?"

"Yeah."

Another beep. "Okay. Grab on to the outside corner—that's the easiest way to climb—then go up as fast as you can. Look up, not down. You'll be fine."

I swallow my nerves, then unhook my carabiner from the safety cable overhead. I place my foot onto one of the rungs of the ladder, pulling myself off of the rope bridge. Thankfully, I'm still only a few feet from the ground, but I'm no longer hooked to my safety line. I don't look down, like Jake said.

The ladder is much more stable than the rest of the course, made of wood instead of rope.

I make my way, one rung after another. Below me, I hear a call. "You can do it!"

The walkie beeps again. "Just keep looking up," Jake says. "Step by step. You'll be fine."

I can't talk back—I need both hands on the ladder—but I nod anyway. I think of those scenes in *Vertigo*, when Jimmy Stewart stares down. I know that if I do, I'll never get the guts to do what I need to. It beeps again. "You got this, Olivia."

The air seems to get cooler, the kid's wailing louder, but when I look up, all I can see is sky. Then, like that, there's no more ladder left. I've done it.

I swing around, back onto the highest bridge, quickly hooking my carabiner onto the safety cable overhead. The boy is there, holding the ropes so tight his hands are shaking. *I feel ya, boy. I feel ya.*

Eyes locked straight ahead, I walk over to him. Kneeling down, I give him a quick hug, his tears dripping onto my T-shirt, then stand up. "Follow me, okay?"

He nods, and together, we walk.

The walkie beeps again. "So you'll obviously have to take the long route down, but just go slowly. You got this."

I lead the way. One rope bridge connects to the next, and at each one, I help the boy unhook his carabiner from one safety cable and on to another. We wind around, going slowly, our hands holding tightly to the ropes on each side, keeping our balance, until suddenly, we're back at the beginning, on solid ground. The girl who pointed out the ladder is cheering; the boy looks as relieved as I do.

Marianne appears then, walking quickly over. "Sorry, I was slammed."

"It's okay," I say.

"You good? Those wobbly ropes can be trickier than the zip line sometimes. It's totally safe and everything, but it gives you that feeling, doesn't it?"

I nod. "Definitely."

Marianne takes the boy's hand. "Come on, let's find your parents." She looks up to me. "I'll send Tennyson back down to handle the next group. Just hang tight a second." She saunters off.

My walkie beeps again. "All good, Olivia?"

I hold down the button, smiling as I hit it. Between facing my fear and him cheering me on, I'm more than good.

"All good, Jake."

# The Shallows

Back at the check-in office, shift wrapped up, I grab my things and Jake does, too. We say our goodbyes to Marianne, then head out of the front doors together.

The air is perfect—not cold but not too hot, either—the sun, nowhere near setting but lower in the sky. I marvel at how beautiful it is here, with the mountains framing our views, seemingly from every side.

Jake leads the way to his car but turns to me before opening the door, hands shoved deep in his pockets. "It's so nice out. I was thinking, before the movie, we could go on a short hike, but only if you're down."

Nothing in the world sounds lovelier than that. "I'm more than down."

"Perfect," he says. "I can drive us up to the trailhead. It's just past the swimming hole we went to on Friday."

I nod, getting into his car and shutting the door behind me.

Jake pulls away, gravel crunching beneath the tires, and heads out of the parking lot, taking a left instead of right. We drive along for a bit, the road smooth, the view clear, until he shifts onto a small, unmarked turn-off, leading us back into the woods, the road changing once again to dirt.

"By the way," I say. "Thanks for your help, you know, on the walkie."

He turns to catch my eyes for a moment before looking back at the road. "I know how hard that must have been for you, but you were awesome," he says. "You did it."

I narrow my eyes. "I hardly think getting up the guts to do something a million kids can do is 'awesome.'"

"Kids are fearless," Jakes says. "We get less fearless each year."

"*You* don't," I say as the car curves around a bend, and another view of the mountains opens up before us. "You're leading people on daily flights through the forest."

We wind back into the woods, and a trailhead marker comes into view.

"That's different," Jake says as he puts the car in park. "I'm not scared of that, but I am scared of other things."

I turn to look at him. "Like what?" I ask.

He catches my gaze, then swallows. "Believe me, I'm scared of plenty."

The hike is only about a mile, or so Jake says, at least, but he's a lot more used to the outdoorsy thing than I am.

"How was your weekend?" he asks as I stumble to keep up, sweating slightly.

I stop walking, an ache, deep and heavy, in my gut. I want to tell him, so badly, that it's me who wrote the screenplay, that I was up all night, not Carrie.

Scratch that—that Carrie is me.

"What is it?" he asks, turning to face me.

I imagine it, pulling him close, whispering in his ear—*I haven't been totally honest with you. Can we find a way to start over, please?*

I shake my head. "I'm just tired. I was up late last night."

*I was up late finishing the screenplay that was sitting in your inbox this morning.*

Jake reaches out his hand, letting it land on my elbow. "You okay to keep going?"

I nod. "Of course."

His hand drops away, leaving fire where he's touched me. Then he smiles. "It's just up ahead."

We do another few turns, back and forth, the ground rising before us and my body getting hotter as we make our way slightly uphill. The woods thicken more than ever, and I spot ivy, granite, and moss-covered stones.

Jake turns to me. "Ready?"

I nod.

He does something crazy: He takes my hand in his and leads me forward. "Close your eyes."

"You're not some horror movie villain?" I ask. "Leading me to impending doom?"

He smirks. "I think you're warming up to horror, you know? I swear I'll make a fan of you yet."

"Maybe," I say.

Jake lets go of my hand, and when the woods part, I see it. A waterfall, about twice as wide and tall as the one from Friday, one that crashes against a shallow natural pool that glistens pink in the dusky light.

A smile stretches across his face. "So this is connected to the swimming hole. It's all part of the same current. Come on," he says.

He walks ahead, following a well-beaten dirt path.

"Wait," I say, and he stops, turning to me. "You're a newbie, too. How in the world do you know about secret waterfall spots? What, do you have some woodsy waterfall radar? Wood-dar?"

His whole body shakes with laughter. "Wow, that's even worse than *my* jokes."

"I know, right? But seriously. How do you fit in here so much better than me?"

His face goes red. "I don't, not really."

"But you—"

He tugs at the bottom of his T-shirt, his fingers worrying at a tiny hole. "This is embarrassing, but I Googled 'secret waterfall spots Hunter Mountain area' this morning, and this one came up. It had a lot of good reviews on Google Maps."

Now it's my turn to laugh.

He grimaces. "That bad, huh?"

I shake my head. "No, it's not bad at all. It's cool. It's great, actually."

His grimace turns to a grin. "Thank goodness," Jake says, and together, we walk closer.

Just behind the falls, there's a tiny little cove, shadowed, blue—a world apart. Jake kicks his shoes off.

"What are you doing?" I ask.

"Getting in."

"But I don't have my swimsuit," I say.

"Me either." For a second, I think he's going to suggest some real horror movie shit, skinny-dipping at a secluded falls, which is 100 percent the surest way to make some errant hiker or sea monster want to orchestrate your demise. "Just my feet," he says.

I watch as he sets his socks on top of his tennis shoes, then tosses his phone and wallet next to them. He steps into the water, his shoulders jolting as he does.

"Cold?" I ask.

He nods. "It's even colder up here, closer to the mountain."

"That's what you said on Friday."

He laughs. "Yeah, well, I guess I should have made it clear that this is even colder than that was."

"Great," I say.

He smiles. "It feels *really* good after a hike. I promise."

It's not so much the appeal of feeling chills rise *literally* up my spine—horror movie or not—it's the thought of being in the water with him, of being connected in a way. I look around. The trees surround us, making this our own little globe. I take off my shoes, too. I step in, and he's right, it's colder than it was on Friday. But I step forward anyway, so I'm only about a foot from Jake. He rubs his hands up and down my arms, and I feel alive all over. "Not *so bad*, right?"

I laugh. "No, it's definitely just as bad as I thought it would be."

He looks at me a moment, his chin turned down just so, and in the pink-y light, his eyes look even bigger, even more beautiful. Again, I imagine telling him the truth.

His arms drop from mine. "What is it?" he asks.

I shake my head. "Nothing."

"It looked like you were suddenly somewhere else," he says.

I kick at a bit of water, splashing it against his shins. "Right here. Promise."

He grins. "Just checking." Then he steps closer to the falls, the water beginning to splash against his shins.

"You're *not* going in that, are you?"

"No, that would be crazy," he says, loud enough to drown out the falls. Then he raises an eyebrow dramatically. "Or should I?"

I should tell him definitely not. That would be ridiculous. But in his eyes, I see that spark, the seeking of a thrill, probably the same thing that first got him interested in horror movies. And part of me wants the thrill. Wants that shock of cold on my body.

I don't say anything, but I step closer, the water splashing my shins now, too. The falls crashing only a couple of feet from us, I turn to him, and talking's almost out of the question now, the water is so loud. The truth is, I want to run through that waterfall with him, I want to see what happens on the other side.

He turns to me and steps just the tiniest bit closer, and I swear to god, he's going to kiss me, right here in the water. I swear it's going to happen, just like it almost happened on Friday. He takes a deep breath, and I notice, for the first time, a smattering of freckles on the tip of his nose. His hair isn't wet, but his forehead glistens with sweat from the hike. Again, I have the urge to run my hands through his curls, pull his face close, feel his lips on mine, run my finger along the scar beneath his eye.

"Well, here I go, then," he says, and then, quick as anything, he turns and jumps forward, crashing through the falls and into the cove on the other side.

I gasp. "You're nuts!" I yell, though I can't even see him, the water a white crashing sheet between us. Then he's there again, the water pounding against his hair, turning his curls straight, slick, and he reaches out his hand for mine.

I brace myself. It will be cold and miserable and way too much, but it will be amazing, too. It will be our own little thrill. I grasp his hand, and he gives me a tug.

The water is all-consuming. It beats against me, on my head, on my shoulders, on the backs of my legs, pounding like a hammer, pounding as quickly as my heart, but as soon as I'm in, I'm free of it—I'm in the cove.

Everything else disappears. Elm and Carrie, the number of pimples on my chin, the way I lied, the fear I felt this afternoon. The zip lines.

NYU. My worry that the screenplay is, without a doubt, the worst thing that's ever been written times a million. Everything is gone, everything but him and me.

"Feels good, doesn't it?" Jake asks, talking loud enough for me to hear. His shirt is wet, hugging his shoulders, and mine is, too. We are soaked, water-beaten, like a movie couple about to kiss in the unwavering rain.

"It does," I say, stepping a tiny bit closer, feeling the draw of his body, like a magnet to mine.

He steps closer, too, looking at me, and I'm sure it's about to happen. I see the parting of his lips, the sucking in of breath.

Then he grins. "So now you know I'm afraid of the dark, I have a penchant for shark movies, and the only way I can remotely appear smooth is by reading reviews on Google Maps. But hey"—his grin grows wider—"at least you know what you're getting into."

My throat tightens, the feeling gone, replaced with a weight in my stomach—with guilt.

So badly, I want to just lean in, push the rest of it out of my head, but I can't, not when he puts it like that.

*At least you know what you're getting into.*

He has *no idea* what he's getting into. Not with me.

I take a step back, hugging my arms to my chest.

"It's a little too cold back here."

Then I dash forward, out of the cove, back into the real world.

A world where Jake still doesn't know the truth about me.

JIMMY
Now that we're out of the woods, literally
speaking, I'm gonna go ahead and throw this
out there: Things have gotten a teensy bit
complicated.

ONYX
No shit, Sherlock.

—*The Bad Decision Handbook* by O. Knight

# Katherine Carrie

"We should probably skip the movie, huh? Now that we're drenched."

I laugh. My shorts and T-shirt are already clinging to my body. Soon, I'm going to start smelling like a wet dog. "It's probably for the best. Rain—er—waterfall check?"

Jake gives me a half smile. "I'm sorry if that was weird," he says. "Jumping in and everything. This is what happens when I try to be spontaneous." He starts the car and begins to pull out of the lot.

"No," I say. "It was a good thing. It was awesome. Like something out of a movie. But not a scary one. A good one."

He nods, turning on the road that leads to Woodstock. "Tunes?" he asks.

"Sure," I say.

He rolls the windows down, the breeze fresh and welcome against my wet skin, and flips to the same station my parents listen to—oldies, classic rock.

The Grateful Dead, or something that sounds a lot like them, booms through the speakers, and for a second, there's no need to fill up the space with words. I rest my arm on the edge of the window, feel the sunlight on it, think of how wonderful it is to be with him. Try not, for a moment at least, to focus on all the ways I've lied to him.

"I'll be at my internship tomorrow," he says as he pulls into my driveway. "So I guess I won't see you until Wednesday."

*I wanted to kiss you, I promise I did. It's not you, Jake, it's me! It's probably one of the rare times in the history of relationships that that excuse has actually been true.*

"Have fun," I say. "At your internship, I mean."

"Have fun at the zip line."

Not sure what else to say, I get out of the car, wave goodbye.

"What in the world happened to you?" my dad asks as I step inside.

My mom looks up from where she's making dinner in the kitchen. "Whoa."

"I'm fine," I say. "Just going to change." Still dripping, I rush into the bathroom, shut the door, and get out of my wet clothes, running the shower hot.

I step in, washing the waterfall water off, knowing I can't wash away my secret. Knowing full well now that there's only one way to make this okay.

Phasing out Carrie simply isn't enough.

I've got to tell him the truth.

Jake's words ring in my head. *At least you know what you're getting into.*

He has to know what he's getting into. I owe him that much, at least.

And once I tell him, all I can do is hope he'll understand. Even if he doesn't, I have to be okay with that, too. He'll know the truth, and that's what matters. I get out of the shower, toweling off. I feel a tad lighter already. Back in my room, in fresh clothes—my bones a tiny bit warmer—I grab my phone and fire off a quick text.

*Today was fun, but remind me never to go with you to Niagara Falls ;) P.S. there's something I want to talk to you about. Hang after work on Weds?*

I can see him typing immediately.

*Everything ok?*

I hope so, Jake. I really do hope so.

*Yes, everything is fine! Wednesday good?*

There's a pause, but then he texts back.

*Sweet. Yeah, Wednesday works. See ya!*

Wednesday takes forever to arrive, like a movie that progresses way too slowly.

I chat with Elm as little as possible, telling him thanks for promising to read but not asking too many follow-up questions. Soon, I tell myself, it won't matter. Whatever happens, at least he'll know. My charade will finally be over.

The first part of my shift drags—I'm the only one in the office and Jake and Bryson have lunch up on the mountain—so I spend most of the time on Instagram and checking our text chain. Just after three, and after spotting a serendipitous post about the importance of honesty, I shoot Chrissy a difficult-but-necessary text:

*By the way, I wasn't totally honest with you when I asked for advice the other day. I didn't just send an edited photo to that guy I told you about. When we were chatting online, I sent him a photo of somebody else. So when I met him in person (he's super coincidentally working at my job up here), he didn't recognize me, even though I recognized him. Basically, now we've hit it off in person, and he doesn't even know that we're also friends online. But it's okay, because I'm going to tell him today. Wish me luck!*

I see the dots that indicate she's typing, and my stomach twists nervously. She'll probably be horrified, absolutely appalled. That her own niece could carry on a double life, hash out a catfishing scheme of such magnitude, even if it was accidental.

Then her message appears:

*Oh my! That makes a lot more sense. I was wondering why you were so worried about a photo if he'd already seen you in person. Yes, that is different! And what a crazy coincidence. Reminds me of this one time, I ran into a guy I'd met in a hostel in Europe at a casino in Atlantic City!*

*Anyway, try not to beat yourself up too much. We all do stupid stuff in the name of romance, trust me! Just be honest and I'll cross my fingers that he understands!*

My smile spreads cheek to cheek. I feel better that someone knows, at least. That she doesn't think I'm the worst person on the face of the earth.

She keeps typing.

*Only, why did you send a fake photo in the first place? You're STUNNING!*

I shake my head as I write back.

*Who knows? Because I'm seventeen and I have pimples lol*

Chrissy sends over a shocked-slash-horrified emoji.

*You're beautiful, and I'm not just saying that because I'm your aunt!*

I smile to myself, putting my phone away.

Maybe it will work out. Maybe it will all be okay.

The door bangs open, and Steinway appears.

"Feeling better?" I ask as she walks behind the counter.

She nods. "I was sick as all get-out, but I'm better now. By the way, I heard you did good with the kid-saving."

I blush. "I did all right, I guess."

She puts a hand on her hip. "Hey, I saw how scared you were that first day. It had to take at least a little gumption."

"Or desperation," I say. "Or fear that you'd puke all over me if I argued. Whichever."

She laughs, but then she looks at me, and stops.

"What?" I ask.

She nods down to my fingers, nails ripped apart. I hadn't even realized I was doing it. "You're nervous," she says. I shove my hands in my pockets, hiding away my nails.

Steinway leans against the counter, tugging at the end of one of her braids. "Nervous about *Jake*?" she asks.

*Yes*, I want to say. *But not in the way you think.*

She crosses her arms. "What? You're not going to give me the lowdown?"

I look away, feeling myself go even redder. "There's no *lowdown*."

"Oh, isn't there?" Steinway prods. "That's not what everyone says."

I laugh. "You haven't even been here."

She smirks. "And yet, the gossip mill carries on. It's more reliable than the ski lift, that's for sure."

I can only laugh.

"All right, don't tell me," she says, throwing up her hands. "I'll get the dirt from someone else."

"Oh, I'm sure you will."

Just before six, Jake walks in to get his things. He smiles, eyes wide and eager. "Ready to go? Want to get dinner or something?"

Behind him, Steinway raises her eyebrows up and down dramatically, mouths, "Get it, girl."

I ignore her, turning to Jake. "Yeah, you eat meat, right? There's a burger place in Woodstock."

Jake smiles. "I do, indeed. And I haven't been there yet, if it's the one I'm thinking of. Always down to try something new."

We head out the front doors together, and he lets his hand drop to the side, stretching out his fingers, almost as if he's going to reach for mine; but quickly, I shove it in my pocket. I want to talk to him, get everything out there before anything else happens between us.

We're almost to Jake's car when I stop short.

To my horror, Jake does, too.

I can hardly believe it, but there she is, standing at the edge of the parking lot, blond hair catching the light.

"Olivia!" She breaks into a smile and runs at me, tackling me with one of her signature hugs—so fierce it almost tips me over.

Katie.

Katie, here.

Katie, upstate.

Katie, in a world she's not supposed to be in at all.

She pulls back, letting me go momentarily.

"What are you *doing* here?" I ask, stumbling over the words.

Jake doesn't wait for an answer—or an intro. *"Carrie?"*

Katie doesn't even look over at Jake. "I came to surprise you." She beams and throws her arms out, wiggling the tips of her fingers. "Surprise!"

"Carrie," Jake says again.

She turns her head, only now acknowledging his presence. "It's *Katie.*"

That doesn't stop him. He takes her in just as I do, her long hair, silky and straight, her cool blue eyes, that infectious smile that shows her front teeth, slightly gapped in a way that only makes her look cool and unique. "No," he says. "I mean, it's me. *Elm.*"

Katie's eyebrows knit together. "What?" she asks him.

I step on her foot, hard as I can.

"Ouch!" she says, turning to me.

I try to use all the Jedi mind tricks I have, but she doesn't comprehend. Meanwhile, Jake's confidence doesn't waver. "ElmStreetNightmare," he says. "Well, ElmStreetNightmareEighty-Four, to be exact. Jake in real life, of course. You're CarriesRevenge!"

Katie looks to me, all, *Who the hell is this guy?*

"You know," he continues. "Queen of the Quizzically Terrifying. Feudal Lord of the Fear-Inducing? Carrie!"

I have no choice: "Your handle on Reddit," I say quickly.

"Huh?"

I widen my eyes at her. "In the horror movie community, *right?*"

Come on, Katie. Come on.

"The one you're always going on about, the one you chat in every day?"

Like that, a spark in her eyes, the same sort I've seen when she watches a great scene with Meryl or makes me practice lines with her for a role, and before me, Katie, my dear, perfect, *wonderful* Katie, becomes the actress she's always been meant to be.

"Oh," she says, turning to Jake and sticking out her hand. *"Of course."*

I step forward. "It must be weird for someone to say your Reddit handle in person like that. I mean, even if you've been online pen pals for months," I say.

Jake's eyes flit from Katie to me, me to Katie.

"And someone you've never met," I add.

It's a major no-no in screenwriting, revealing through dialogue like that, but right now, I have no choice.

Katie smiles. "Yes, of course, you just caught me off guard. It's so good to meet you. I'm not used to people calling me Carrie." She shoots me a glance, all, *I got this, Olivia.* "Carrie's my middle name, so I don't normally answer to it."

Jake's eyes narrow slightly. "Your middle name?"

"Right?" I say loudly. "Isn't it *hilarious* that it's both your middle name *and* your favorite movie?"

A flash of fear in Katie's eyes, but she recovers quickly; just like when she flubbed up her line in the spring production of *Romeo and Juliet*. It was supposed to be "Romeo, Romeo! Wherefore art thou Romeo?" Only she said it way too fast—"Where *fart* thou, Romeo"—and she acted like nothing of the sort would dare come out of Juliet Capulet's mouth, like we were all wrong for thinking it had. That's when I knew she was truly a pro.

"It's funny," Katie goes on. "I watched *Carrie* for the first time because the main character had my middle name. I never expected to become obsessed with it like I have."

"That's amazing," Jake says, rocking back and forth on his heels, pure excitement. "You never told me it's your middle name, too."

Katie winks. "Got to keep some secrets, I suppose. Especially from an internet stranger."

Jake bursts into laughter.

*All right, Katie,* I think. *Dial it down a notch.*

Jake turns to me then, as if only now remembering I'm still here. "So *you're* friends with Carrie? I mean, Katie. Katie Carrie." He glances to Katie. "That's a funny name combination."

She shrugs. "Yep, Katherine Carrie. My parents are nuts."

Jake laughs hysterically again, then glances back to me. "So you guys know each other from Brooklyn?"

I nod. "Known each other for years. What a small world!"

Jake crosses his arms, gaze ping-ponging between us. "I know this sounds weird, but if I saw it in a movie, I wouldn't believe it." His face scrunches up, and he turns back to Katie. "Wait a second, I thought you were at NYU?"

Katie opens her mouth as if to correct him, but I butt in. "Yeah, I thought the *screenwriting program* was supposed to go on longer."

Katie stares at me a minute, all, *What have you done now, Olivia?*, then composes her face. She shrugs. "It was nothing like I expected, honestly. I ended up leaving early. Not a good environment for writing at all."

"But didn't you just finish your screenplay there?" Jake asks.

She freezes, deer in the headlights. Shit.

I clear my throat, and they both turn to me. Katie's eyebrows shoot up. *You finished?!?* her gaze seems to ask.

"Didn't you write the best parts *after* you left the program?" I ask Katie.

She nods slowly. Very, very slowly. "Yeah . . . yeah, I left last week because it was pretty lame, and then I made some major progress on the end."

Jake tilts his head to the side. "Really? But you were so excited."

Katie shrugs him off.

"Whatever works, I guess," Jake says. "I'm glad you're here!"

"Yes, me too!" I say, but it comes out all wrong.

Jake's eyes catch mine. "If you're down, Katie should come to dinner with us."

"Of course," I say, my heart racing. "The three of us together . . . how exciting!"

# The Changeling

"We'll meet you there," I call out to Jake as I follow Katie to my parents' car.

As soon as the doors close, like a director calling action and cueing the next scene:

"What in the hell was *that* about?" Katie asks. "I mean, I love a good challenging role as much as the next girl, but really, Olivia, even a true artist needs some warning."

I shake my head, ignoring her question. "I don't understand. What are you doing here?"

"You invited me," Katie says. "Duh."

"But your program."

She shrugs. "It wasn't a good fit. Totally not on my level."

"But you were so—"

Katie interrupts me, raising a hand in the air. "Forget about the program for a second. I thought this would be a nice surprise since you practically begged me to come save you from your summer. Now can you please tell me what in the world I just witnessed slash participated in?"

I watch as Jake's car pulls out of the lot. "Just drive," I say. "I'll explain."

Katie nods. "I'll drive. You spill."

"Take a right up here," I say, already dreading what I have to tell her. "You'll stay on this road for a few miles."

"Good," she says. "That means we have time for a full rundown of what in god's name just happened."

We pull up to a stoplight, the shops of Hunter's main street on one side, the mountains on the other. I tear at a broken bit of nail.

"I did something bad," I say finally.

Katie taps her fingers on the wheel, and the light turns green. The car jerks ahead. "Like, you buried a body bad? Some girl named Carrie who looks like me and inexplicably spends every day on Reddit? I mean, I know you love Reddit and all, but you have to know that's not me at all."

I clear my throat. "I know that. It's me."

Katie shakes her head. *"Je ne comprends pas."* I don't understand.

"I'm the one who's been spending every day on Reddit for months. *Me.*"

"Duh," she says. "In true nerd fashion. But what does that have to do with my likeness? What is this whole mystery girl thing?"

"No, I mean, Carrie is me. I'm Carrie."

Katie tilts her head to the side, and I go on.

"Back in February, right as I was starting to work on my screenplay, I started messaging in this horror community on there. And then Elm and I started chatting on our own. A lot."

"Elm?" Katie asks.

"Jake," I say. "But that's his handle. Like on the threads, you know."

Katie sighs, as if her brain only has enough space for one nerdy handle at a time, as we follow the road along the edge of a meadow.

"Okay. Great. He's a cutie, and you obviously like him. But what in the world does that have to do with me? What the hell happened back there?"

I sigh. "I do like him. I like him a lot, actually." It feels good to say it out loud, even though it doesn't change what I know must follow. "But the thing is, I never expected to meet him in real life. He was just an online friend. This is crazy, but when I came up to work here, the first day at Hunter Mountain, I saw him. Turn here," I say, pointing to where Jake has just turned.

She does, but her jaw hangs there, agape. "Wait, you didn't know he was going to be here? It wasn't, like, a community for horror nerds that *also* live in the Catskills?"

"No," I say. "That doesn't even make sense."

"Hey," Katie says. "You're the one who's woven this twisted web. I'm only trying to make sense of it. That's nuts, though."

"I know. And it's even more nuts, because he's from North Carolina. He only came up here because he's staying with his aunt for the summer."

The road curves into downtown Woodstock. Hippie shops. Organic eateries. Bluestone sidewalks. "You can park in the lot right here," I say.

Katie turns in and finds a spot. She puts the car in park. "So he's here. So that's crazy. Fine. Why didn't you just tell him it was you he was chatting to? How did you even—"

"I recognized him from his picture. He'd sent it to me before."

Katie's face scrunches up. "I still don't get it." Then her eyes widen. "Oh," she says. "You told him you were at the NYU program that you didn't get into. You let him believe that little lie because there was no harm in it, right? You were never going to meet him. But then you did."

I look down at my hands. She's got half of it right, but it's so much worse than that.

"Wait," Katie says. "But then why did he think *I* was you?"

I fiddle with the ends of my hair. "It's embarrassing."

"Just spit it out, Olivia."

"Because of the photo," I say.

"Huh?"

I sigh. "When Jake asked me for a photo, I sent him one of you."

"Of me?" Katie asks. "But why in the world—"

Jake appears then, seemingly out of nowhere, knocking on the window. (A total horror movie cliché.)

Katie's lips are formed into a thin line, but quickly, she turns away, opening the door. "Easy there, slugger. We were having a girl chat."

Jake takes a quick step back and shuffles his feet. "Oh," he says. "I didn't mean to interrupt."

Katie laughs, then shoots me a confused look before turning back to him and plastering on a smile. "Don't worry. We'll make an exception for you, I suppose."

I get out of the car, and the three of us walk through the public parking lot, down to the center of town, where Mill Hill Road meets Tinker Street. Jake walks by my side, hands shoved into his pockets as if he doesn't know what to do with them with Katie right here beside us.

Part of me wants to reach out, take his hand in mine, get us back to where I thought we were not that long ago. But with her here, a physical embodiment of my lie, I don't have the guts.

Besides, what if he likes Carrie, or who he thinks of as Carrie, as much as he likes me?

What if he likes her even more?

The burger restaurant is tiny. A little postage stamp of a place with wood-plank walls, reclaimed lighting, and a bar that stretches across most of the room.

"Three?" the girl asks. I nod, and she leads us to the back corner. I get in first, and Katie takes a seat on the other side.

Jake hovers, eyes flitting briefly from me to her and back again, as if he's making a decision.

Both girls. One on each side. He's going to choose Katie. I just know he's going to choose Katie.

A server scoots by, forcing his hand, and he sits down next to me, but as soon as he's in the booth, his eyes lock on her, on Katie, or Carrie—on the girl he thought he was chatting to all this time. God, this has gotten messy.

We rattle off our orders quickly. Burgers all around. A basket of sweet potato fries to share, sriracha aioli on the side. Menus get taken back, and Katie announces she has to go to the bathroom; she stands up quickly, leaving us alone.

He turns to me as soon as she's gone, his hands on the table in front of him, not even close to touching mine. "I hope it's okay I invited her. I know you said you wanted to talk, I just—it was such a crazy coincidence seeing her like that." He pauses, as if debating saying something else. "I don't know, she and I have been friends for months . . . I guess it just kind of popped out of my mouth."

"It's fine," I say. "I mean, I was surprised, too, but of course I wanted her to come." My smile feels weak and unconvincing, even as I deliver it. "She's my best friend."

Jake nods. "I still just can't *believe* that your best friend is the girl I've been talking to all this time. It's like, what are the odds?"

*Better than you know*, I want to say. *But what are the odds that she'd ditch her dream program to come up here as a surprise? That's another story. What are the odds that you, the guy from North Carolina, would be spending a summer in the Catskills, working at my very same job? That's another story altogether.*

Jake adjusts himself against the hard wooden booth and takes a sip of water. "What did you want to talk about anyway?"

I look down at my hands, nails ripped raw. There's no way in hell I can tell him now, not like this, not with Katie set to return any moment. In minutes, my lies have gotten so much deeper. The girl in the bathroom isn't Carrie. The screenplay I sent is mine, not hers. I was foolish to think I could just ask him out to burgers and tell him the truth while we dipped fried sweet potatoes in freaking sriracha aioli.

"Nothing huge, I'll tell you later," I say; and as I do, Katie comes back out, and our next act begins.

As we wait for the burgers to arrive, it's his eyes I notice. His questions are run-of-the-mill—how long have you been friends, how did you meet, that kind of thing—but his eyes give me pause. They're locked on Katie, wide and eager, taking her in as she details the meet-cute that has come to define our friendship: how she tripped, spilling her LaCroix all over me our first day of freshman year. She tells the story in grand detail, hands flitting about in her Katie way, and I swear his gaze never breaks from her once.

Meanwhile, tucked in the booth, I feel smaller, more invisible than ever, like everything from the last few weeks—trying the zip line, writing my screenplay—never happened. Next to Katie, they seem suddenly like tiny, insignificant accomplishments, nothing compared to her.

When she's done—folding her hands, all, *And that's that*—Jake finally turns to me. "You've been friends since then, and Carrie, I mean, Katie's, er, horror obsession never rubbed off on you at all?"

"I guess not," I say, his eyes already returning to hers.

Katie leans in, conspiratorially. "Olivia likes to think she's above *genre* films like that. She's more of a Meryl Streep person." She winks not so discreetly at me. Luckily, Jake doesn't seem to notice. Or maybe not so luckily, because his eyes are still on her.

"You know what's funny," Jake says, "is Meryl Streep was in two campy comedy-horror movies back to back in the eighties and nineties . . ."

"*She-Devil* and *Death Becomes Her*," they say together.

Yes, friends, they *actually* say it together.

Katie tosses her head back in laughter. She's good, I have to hand it to her, a veritable shapeshifter like the ghost in *The Changeling*, this old eighties movie I recommended to Jake. One he now thinks *she* recommended to him.

As she laughs, I realize something horrible.

I liked Elm from the moment I saw his photo. Scratch that, long before that. I loved our banter, and when I saw his picture, it was like confirmation of all I already felt.

If Jake felt the same way—and part of me knows he did—then it's not just that he likes her, it's more than that . . .

She's his dream girl.

Come to life in the most serendipitous way.

I'm just the girl he met at work, the girl there to accompany him on a hike or to sit next to him on a bale of hay for lunch. *She's* the interesting one, the writer, the horror lover, the *Queen of the Quizzically Terrifying*. I'm just Olivia.

As if confirming my fears, Jake breaks into a smile. "Oh, and by the way," he says. "I still haven't read the screenplay, but I can't wait. I've just been . . ."

*Turn to me, look at me, say you've been too preoccupied with* me.

"Just been busy, I guess," Jake says.

Katie tilts her head to the side and shoots me a quick *I want all the deets* look before resuming her role. "Too busy to read my pièce de résistance? You better get on that."

Jake's eyes finally catch mine, and he must see the look of horror written all over my face. "What is it?" he asks. "Are you okay?"

*What is it?* Only that she's doing it all wrong, turning Carrie into someone she's not at all. Carrie would *never* tease him so casually about not having read the screenplay, would never refer to *The Bad Decision Handbook* as some sort of "pièce de résistance." It's a shitty first draft, at best. I'm thankful he even wants to read it.

More than that, it's that he's sure to be so enchanted by her—all the nerdy-cool elements of Carrie wrapped up in a drop-dead gorgeous, enigmatic Katie package—he's going to forget about Olivia altogether.

"It's nothing," I say. "Just hungry, I guess."

The edges of his fingers, pressed against the booth, find mine for a second. "I'm sure the food will be out soon," he says. Then, just as quickly, he whips his hand away, as if he shouldn't do that sort of thing anymore—not now, not when his Internet Dream Girl is sitting there across the table. As if he's rethinking everything he thought about me.

The burgers come out then, and Katie and Jake dig in, but the mise-en-scène before me makes my gut ache. Katie, as usual, takes the spotlight, going on about how she has to arrange her burger just so to ensure that each bite is the perfect mix of lettuce, tomato, cheese, and meat; talking about how sriracha is the most overrated hot sauce, even though she knows I love it; detailing her entire bus ride up here, every single leaf, tree, and creek, Jake nodding along the entire time, as if he's happy for someone to take charge.

It's hard to blame him; I usually feel that way, too. Hell, I usually like her stealing the show. She's the loud one, the natural star. When we're together, there's no pressure on me to fill the space with words.

When she's in the spotlight, it means it doesn't shine on me, on my imperfect skin, or my moments of awkwardness, on the fact that I feel far more comfortable in an online community like Reddit than I ever did up on a stage.

But it's different now, because she's pretending to be Carrie—and not only is she getting it wrong, Jake doesn't seem to mind at all. He seems to love it.

It's different because for the last few weeks, I've let myself take the spotlight, just a little bit. And I'm not sure if I want to go back to the way it was before.

Jake sets his burger down and looks at me. "What's wrong? I thought you were hungry."

I take another bite of a fry. "I am," I say quietly. "Just going slow."

He nods. "You know what's really crazy is, *The Haunting of Sophia Blaine*—that movie we got halfway through the other night—I originally recommended it to Carrie. I mean Katie."

"No . . . really?" I ask, dipping another fry into the sauce but not quite bringing it up to my mouth.

Katie smiles. "Oh, you know I love a good ghost story."

My pulse quickens, this time not from jealousy, but from fear that it's all about to come crashing down.

Jake's eyebrows knit up. "But it doesn't turn out to be a ghost story."

*This is it*, I think. This is where he figures it all out. It doesn't matter if he likes her or he likes me. He won't want anything to do with either of us once he knows the full truth. Part of me is almost relieved. No more charades. No more lies. He'll never forgive me, but at least he'll know. At least it will be over.

"Remember, it's all in Sophia's head, because of her past trauma,"

Jake says. He turns to me, his face falling to a frown. "Shit, I'm sorry. Spoiler alert. Ugh."

Katie doesn't miss a beat. "I know, I know," she says. "But it's a *metaphorical* ghost story. She's haunted by her past, right?"

Jake's eyes take me in, like he can sense it in me, that something is off.

I look away, picking at a bit of yet unravaged nail.

He clears his throat. "Yeah, I know, but still, I'm not sure I'd really call it a ghost—"

"I mean," Katie goes on, "is there any need for ghost stories anymore, anyway? Isn't it much more interesting to explore the ghost we all carry within us? In our modern world, haven't we moved beyond things that just go *boo*?"

I look up to see her popping another fry into her mouth. The Great Katie Carrie has spoken.

She's wrong, totally wrong, and I wait for Jake to say it, to school her. Ghost stories are a central tenet of horror, have been forever, and while some movies play on the tropes without having actual ghosts, the more traditional ones are not going to take the route of their star specters and disappear. These sorts of films are not ever going to go away.

I glance at Jake, at his face, unreadable, and it feels, suddenly, like it all rides on his reaction. Whether he finds Fake Carrie enchanting or disenchanting.

He breaks into a grin. "You know, that's a good point," he says, eating up her words faster than he scarfed his burger. "I'd honestly never thought about it like that."

I can't help it, I push my plate forward. I can't sit here and watch this anymore.

"Sorry, but I'm not feeling great," I say, eyeing the exit.

Jake stands up to let me pass, and before they can stop me, I squeeze out of the booth, out of the restaurant, and into the fresh air.

Out of my own horror movie. The one I can only blame myself for creating.

# Bridges of Madison County

Katie finds me on Mill Hill Road, a few shops down from the burger place. "What are you doing?" she asks, hand on her hip like she's my mom.

"I'm sorry," I say, shaking my head. "I just can't go back in there. It's all too much."

Katie sighs loudly, then grabs me by the elbow and nods to the crosswalk.

"You're lucky," she says as we make our way across the street and up the stone sidewalk. "I told Jake that you have a food intolerance that sometimes hits out of the blue, and you were sorry for leaving so abruptly."

"Great," I say, nausea coating my stomach, and not from any purported food intolerance, either. "All I need is another lie."

Katie stops just short of the car. "I also told him that you'd Venmo him the money for our portion, so as not to seem *rude*."

"Okay," I say. "I get it."

I shuffle toward the car, and Katie gets in the driver's seat. "My house is just down the road. A left at the corner." She nods, but I can tell she's fuming. "So are you going to tell me why you stormed out like that? I honestly thought it was all going off pretty well."

"Of course you did," I say as she makes the turn.

"What's that supposed to mean?" Katie asks.

"I mean, you didn't have to play it up so much, did you?" I tug at the edge of another nail.

"Are you seriously mad at me for doing too good of a job?" Katie asks. "He totally bought it; all of it."

"Exactly," I say. "I never asked for an Oscar-worthy performance. Turn left."

Katie huffs, but she dutifully makes the turn. "Sorry, Olivia, next time I impersonate someone without any warning, I'll make sure to be a bit more robotic."

My house comes into view, and she pulls into my drive, winding toward the cottage. It's still just barely light, but the sky is purple-blue now, the sun almost set. "I don't mean robotic," I say as she puts the car into park. "I just mean less *dramatic*. Less . . . enchanting."

"Dramatic?" she asks, focusing only on the former accusation. "Seriously?"

I look away so she can't catch my eyes. "It was like The Katie Show in there. I know guys eat that sort of thing up, but I don't even act like that. It's not me."

"I thought the whole point was for him *not* to know it was you?"

I turn back to look at her. "Yeah, but you don't have to make me this completely different person," I say. "Ghost stories will always be important to horror. I would *never* say that."

Katie laughs, tossing her head back. "So you want me to be kind of like you, but not too much, and also not too enchanting. And to do a good job, but not *too* good of a job. *Girl.* You should hear yourself."

I feel my eyes begin to well, and Katie puts a hand on my shoulder. "Olivia, it's okay. There's nothing to cry about. I'll tone it down, okay? Believe me, it's obviously you he's into. You're the one who sent all those messages to him. The only reason he was even talking to me was because he was excited to finally meet *you*."

I brush the moisture from my eyes with the back of my hand.

"I know you think I'm dramatic, but you're the one who's storming out of restaurants, mind you," Katie says.

"I know," I say, feeling suddenly foolish. "I'm being a total drama queen, and I don't want to be."

Katie holds up a hand. "First off, the one true Drama Queen will always be Meryl, so don't you worry your pretty little head about stealing her title. Second, I've known you a while now. I'm used to your antics. This is a bit more involved than most situations we've been in together, but we'll get through it. We always do."

"Thanks," I say, pushing away the sting of jealousy as I realize, once again, that Katie really is the *best* best friend ever. "I'm sorry for dragging you into this."

"Can we go inside now?" Katie asks. "I need some chips or something since I had to leave with a quarter of my burger still sitting on my plate."

We spend the night watching a movie with my parents, their taste aligning with Katie's better than it ever has with mine, passing around a bag of the white cheddar popcorn my dad's been addicted to for years, and sitting stock-still at the sex scene that makes us all feel uncomfortable, no matter how cool my parents try to be about it.

As the movie plays out, I try to focus on the good things: that my best friend, whom I love—who always knows how to make me happy—is with me, saving me from the summer I thought would be mind-numbing. That my world of lies hasn't come crumbling around me just yet. Only problem is, as she munches at the popcorn, digging her fingers down to the saltiest crumbs like she always does, I can't help but feel *off*. Things were going so well before she arrived. I was going to tell him the truth today. Now, with Katie here, that feels impossible. The lies go too deep.

More than that, it's clear to me after tonight that there's a reason she's the star and I'm not. Seeing her at the restaurant—cracking jokes, detailing her bus ride, making up theories about movies she hasn't even seen—it's easy to see what makes her so lovable. It's hard to feel anything but dull by comparison, no matter what's happened over the last few weeks.

When the movie's finished, my mom stands up, flipping off the TV and turning to me. "I forgot to ask," she says. "Were you surprised? Katie's been planning for a few days, and I hope I didn't give it away!"

"Believe me," I say. "I was definitely surprised."

My dad gets up, too. "You know you're welcome to stay as long as you want, Katie."

"Thanks, Mr. Knight," she says politely.

He crumples up the bag of popcorn and takes it to the kitchen, and my parents begin their evening shuffle. Water, vitamins, turning off the lights.

Back in my room, after changing out of our regular clothes and into PJs, Katie turns to me. "Are you feeling any better?"

I shrug. "I guess."

She sits on my bed, and I plop next to her. A smile twists at the corners of her mouth. "Never in a million years did I anticipate my most challenging acting role would be in real life."

"That's what happens when you surprise people," I say.

"Correction, my friend. That's what happens when you surprise people who've concocted elaborate online identities featuring your very own photo." She pauses. "Are you going to tell me *why* you used my photo, anyway?"

I sigh. "Because I looked awful that day, okay? And I just thought, I don't know . . . It was stupid. It was a snap decision."

Katie shakes her head. "Come on, Olivia. How many times do I have to tell you you're—"

"I don't want to talk about it."

She sighs. "Well, which one did you use, anyway?"

I shrug, figuring she might as well know. I grab my phone, load up Reddit, scroll through the hundreds of messages between Elm and me until I find it. I hold it out in front of her.

"That?" she asks. "All this for *that*? It's not even a good photo!"

I whip the phone away, toss it onto my nightstand. "Yes it is. Every one of your photos is a good photo."

"What can I say?" She rests her head on her hands and bats her lashes. "I'm always ready for my close-up."

I don't laugh.

"Oh, come on," Katie says. "I'm telling you, you're just as photogenic as I am."

That, on the other hand, does get a laugh out of me.

"You are!"

"Can we not go down this road, okay?" ·

"The *Olivia Is Beautiful but Doesn't Know It Road*? Right next to *It's Time to Love Yourself Already Street*? Across the corner from *Things Will Work Out If You Only Stay Positive Way*?"

I can't help but laugh. Then my phone buzzes, and I forget all her affirmations: a message on Reddit.

*ElmStreetNightmare84: So great meeting you, even if it got cut a little short! Still can't believe this crazy coincidence. It's amazing!*

My stomach sinks. He's going to choose her. I just know it.

"What is it?" Katie asks.

"Nothing," I say, setting the phone facedown on my dresser.

Katie leans against my headboard. "Anyway, you should have

warned me if my presence would set off some sort of chain reaction. You were the one who *begged* me to come up and save you from your exile in the Catskills. Remember?"

Of course I remember, but it feels so long ago now. I thought that this summer would be hell, but it's been kind of wonderful, truthfully. And now it's all messed up. Broken beyond repair.

I glance over to Katie. "I still don't get it," I say.

"What?" she asks.

"Why aren't you in your program?"

"I told you," she says. "It was beneath me."

My eyes narrow. I'd been hearing about the program for ages, and I can't imagine she'd change her mind about it, just like that. "Really?"

"Yeah," Katie says, eyes suddenly on her hands. I want to ask more, but I know what it's like to not want to talk about things that make you upset.

"Let's just go to sleep," I say instead. "I'm exhausted from all the drama."

She whips her head up, narrowing her eyes at me. "Hey, you're not the one who spent the whole evening acting."

I manage a smirk. "No. I was only director, writer, and muse all in one."

"Just don't get too used to it," she says. "I like to retain some creative control."

I laugh.

"By the way," she says. "What's this about the screenplay? You *finished*?"

"It's just ninety pages," I say. "They're not even very good."

Katie shakes her head in disbelief. "Ninety pages is *insane*, Olivia. I seriously can't even comprehend it."

"Don't act so shocked." I lean back, sinking deeper into the pillows.

"Girl, it's not about me believing in you or not. There are people at the New School, like, studying writing and all that, paying shitloads of money to be there, who have accomplished less, I guarantee you. This is amazing. I'm so freaking proud of you, you don't even know."

"Well, it's just another thing that's messed up now," I say, crossing my arms. "Because Jake thinks *you* wrote it."

Katie sits up straighter, grabbing me by the shoulders. "Olivia, forget about Jake for a minute. Or his nerdy handle, all that. You were afraid you could never do this, and you did. Whatever else happens, that's huge."

"But—"

"No buts," she snaps. "You're a rock star. Own it, for once, okay? Girl, this is your *Bridges of Madison County*."

# The Dexter Incident

I try to own it, like Katie said, but it's not that easy.

I texted Jake this morning—*Sorry for leaving like that. Let me know how much we owe you!*—and I still haven't heard back. Since he's at his internship, I won't be seeing him around the office. Part of me thinks he's pissed. Another fears he's wildly in love with Katie. And a tiny, tiny part hopes that somehow Katie is right, that if I can stop being such a drama queen, this will somehow magically all work out.

When it comes time for lunch, it's too nasty to sit outside, so I find a quiet table in the corner of the lodge and take out my turkey sandwich, the bread's edges stale. Even with all the windows, it's fairly dark in here, the sky so foggy you can't even see the mountains.

"Hey, stranger."

I look up, and to my shock, it's Jake, his face stretched into a grin.

"What are you doing here?" I ask. Between him and Katie, the two are full of surprises, practically walking jump scares.

He takes a step or two back. "Sorry, just thought I'd say hi. I'm on my lunch break at my internship and . . ."

The words spill out of my mouth before I can stop them. "What, did you come just to see me?" It's the kind of thing Katie would say. Bold and unapologetic.

Jake looks taken aback. "No," he says. "I mean, I just, I left something at the check-in office yesterday. Marianne told me you'd be out here . . ."

"It was just a joke," I say, though I guess I thought that maybe, just maybe, he might have. Serves me right for trying to act like Katie would.

The corner of his mouth tilts up. "I thought bad jokes were *my* purview."

I laugh, but it comes out weak. It's like, since Katie arrived, we can't quite get back to us. Even more, I can't quite get back to me.

"Anyway," he says, taking a deep breath, as if he senses the awkwardness, too. "You okay?" he asks. "I mean, after last night . . ."

*No*, I want to say. *No, I'm not. And it's no one's fault but mine. I was scared, I didn't believe in myself, and now I'm in too deep. Now it's all screwed up.*

Most of all, I want to tell him, *I misled you, and I feel sick about it.*

"Yeah," I lie. "I'm sorry about peacing out without saying good-bye."

"Hey," he says. "I get it. When stomach issues strike, right?" His face instantly turns red. "Sorry," he says. "I'm sure you don't want to talk about it. Not that I want to talk about it or anything, believe me. I mean, not that I'm one of those weirdos who likes to pretend girls *don't* have stomach issues. Shit, I'm making this worse, aren't I?"

I laugh. "No," I say. "It's not that. Honestly, it wasn't my stomach, I just wasn't feeling that great."

"Oh," Jake says, eyes turning down at the corners. "Any reason?"

I look down at my sandwich, then back up again. Not lying is one thing, telling the full truth another. "Not really," I say. "Anyway, did you get to finish your burger, at least?"

Jake smiles. "Well, I wasn't going to tell you; but since you asked, I finished mine, polished off the sweet potato fries, and I may have had a little bit of yours and Katie's, too."

My eyebrows shoot up playfully. "You *monster.*"

His eyes widen. "I know, I know. You should have seen the way the waitress looked at me. Went from being the uber-cool guy at a table with two girls to the sad loner eating off of other people's plates."

I laugh. "That's quite the fall from grace."

He pauses, his feet shuffling back and forth, and I know I should say something.

*Let me make it up to you for storming out. Let's hang out again, without Katie this time. Let's get back to exactly where we were before my best friend dropped the bomb that is her dazzling, confusing presence. Let me tell you the truth.*

"Er, how's Katie, by the way?" Jake asks.

"Oh," I say, immediately losing my nerve. Maybe that hike up to the waterfall was nothing, and he routinely jumps in bodies of water fully clothed. Maybe every hand-graze, every stolen look, was imagined. Maybe it all meant nothing.

Only it wasn't, I know that.

Maybe it's just that, now that she's here in front of him, he likes her more than me, simple as that. "She's fine."

Jake nods. "Well, I'm glad you're good." He stands there, hovering, as if he wants to say something else. "I should get going, though."

"Sure, see you tomorrow," I say.

He smiles. "See you tomorrow."

As he walks away, I know in my heart that something has changed. I want to rewind, start everything over, but like the *Dracula* audition and my failed NYU application—like a lot of things—in real life you don't get to do that.

Rewinding is only for movies, after all.

Katie picks me up that evening. As we make the drive back to my house, she details me on her day. She went on a long walk around my neighborhood and even discovered a nearby swimming hole, and spent the afternoon getting some sun. That's Katie for you. Always finding a way to fit right in no matter where she is.

Back at my house, we situate ourselves on the back porch with iced teas while my mom cooks in the kitchen and my dad finishes a conference call.

"So did you see him today?" Katie asks. "Jakey-Poo?"

"Can we just say no to the baby names, please?" It's a favorite habit of Katie's, anytime I get a crush. And it never works the other way around, because Katie, dedicated, passionate Katie, hasn't gotten a crush since her ex, Dexter. It's almost like crushes are beneath her. Along with the New School's acting program and who knows what else.

"Fine." She shakes her tea, ice clinking like it's some sort of timer. "So? Did you?"

"Yes," I say.

"And?"

"At first I thought it was a good sign, because he wasn't even supposed to be at work today. He's at his internship."

"You mean he came all the way just to see if little stomach-issues Olivia was okay?"

"He said he left something there and was on lunch, but . . ." I shrug. "It was nice, I guess. At first."

"So what happened?" She tips back her tea and stretches out her legs. Damn, she really did get sun today. I curse myself for never having discovered said swimming spot on my own.

"I don't know. It just felt friendly. He asked me how I was, said he'd see me tomorrow, that kind of thing. Then he asked about you."

Katie sits up straighter, crossing her legs and turning to me. There's that gleam in her eye again. "So you didn't ask him on a proper date or anything?"

I shake my head. "Something about the whole thing was just . . . off. Plus, I didn't have the guts."

Katie nods, as if taking the situation in. "All good. In fact, this fits right in with the plan I've been formulating all day. I mean, a girl has a lot of time to think when she's alone at a swimming hole."

"Oh, god."

Katie raises a hand, preemptively halting any and all objections. "Hear me out. It's good for me, it's good for you, it's even good for Jakey-Poo."

"You said you'd stop with that."

She nods. "Okay, that was my last one. Only because it rhymed—totally worth it. I will abstain from here on out."

The water trickles down the small stream on the edge of our property—it sounds like softly ringing bells—and it's so nice that for a second, I can pretend that none of this is happening, that all of it is okay. "All right, all right, what is it?"

"I'm Jake's friend, right?"

I scoff. "No, actually you don't know him from Adam."

Katie laughs and runs her finger along the edge of the glass. Around me, the sky seems to darken as the sun sets further, as if someone is up in the sky, messing with a dimmer. The crickets are beginning their chorus, and it feels suddenly like the witching hour, the point in the movie when the people come up with their plan. I make a mental note to make sure at least one of the scenes in *The Bad Decision Handbook* takes place at dusk.

"Look," she says. "I know I don't know him, beyond our thrilling twenty minutes of conversation at the burger place. But what I mean is, my character, Carrie, she knows him, right?"

"Of course."

"She's his friend?"

I pause, trying to parse out exactly what Elm and I were to each other when it was only online. I know there was always something more. The excitement I felt at getting each new message, the way I'd half plan my entire schedule around it. The first time I saw his photo, how cute, how adorable, he was. I'm sure of it now. I wouldn't have freaked out and dashed off that photo of Katie, getting myself into this mess in the first place, if I didn't feel something romantic for him, even then.

Maybe he did, too. I'm pretty sure he did.

But that's the problem—it's like one big sick joke. Even if Elm really did like me, it wasn't long before I sent him that photo of her, which was exactly when our chatting went full on. For all I know, half of why he's been so interested in talking is *because of* her photo. Now that she's here, in the flesh, how can I even compete?

"Olivia?" Katie asks.

"Yes, sorry. She's his friend. I'm his friend, I mean."

"Right? So he trusts her."

The words cut me like a knife. He shouldn't trust Carrie, shouldn't trust her at all.

"Olivia, focus."

I nod. "Okay, sorry. Yeah, he trusts Carrie."

Katie clasps her hands together. "Great. So basically, I'll present myself as the world's most abhorrent version of a woman so you shine by comparison."

"What?" I ask.

Katie laughs quickly. "Sorry, it was a joke. That's the gross, sexist version, the plague of rom-coms and the like. What I'll *actually* do is use my position as his friend to act as, drumroll please . . ."

Katie beats a fake drum roll on her thighs.

"Out with it," I say.

She beams. "The ultimate wingwoman!"

I shake my head. "What are you talking about?"

"He likes you, even if you can't see it. Even if he's maybe a little off the mark about his online pen pal's real identity. So I'll use that power to steer him in your direction."

I sigh. "Isn't that just *more* deception?"

Katie shakes her head vehemently. "Not at all. He likes the nerdy-film-buff you, and he likes the in-person, trying-desperately-to-be-outdoorsy you. It's not our fault that he doesn't realize they're the same exact person." She pauses. "Actually it is our fault; well, *your* fault. But we can't help that now, can we?"

I sip the last of my tea. "Maybe I should, I don't know, just tell him."

Katie's eyebrows shoot up. "Really?"

"Why not?"

"Must I remind you of the Dexter Incident?"

Dexter, Katie's aforementioned ex: a sweet, nerdy guy we used to see hanging out in the library during lunch, when we were all working on a history project. Only Dexter wasn't working on any project. He *liked* spending his lunches in the library.

After a week of observing dear Dexter, Tessa dared Katie to ask him out, for a laugh. It wasn't particularly kind, and Fatima and Eloise gave us hell about it, but we were fourteen. We were freshmen—and idiots. Katie did, and he said yes, and to our surprise, she actually went forward with the date. And then another. And another.

Katie liked Dexter, the guy who'd been so far from our estimation of who someone like Katie would be with that the whole thing had been a joke. A few weeks into officially dating, Katie had made the mistake, in a moment of rare vulnerability, of telling him the truth about how things had started, and it hadn't gone at all like she'd anticipated.

He'd been (rightly) horrified that he'd been the butt of our joke and had broken up with her on the spot. They're still friends; she still spends lunches in the library sometimes; but nothing has happened between them again. It's half of why I think Katie doesn't ever get crushes. She's never gotten over Dexter.

I shake my head. "This is nothing like that."

"Isn't it?" Katie asks.

"We were playing a joke on Dexter," I say. "It was wrong."

"And Jake won't think you were doing the same?"

"I don't know," I say, picking again at a jagged nail. "I hope not."

"He won't think we were laughing behind his back as you fed me hints about what to say about horror movies, a genre in which I have absolutely no interest?"

"It wasn't like that, though."

"Look, you aren't going to marry the guy, right?" Katie asks. "I mean, ninety-nine percent of high school relationships are just trial runs, you know?"

I pause. A tiny part of me wants to be all *never say never* about it. Because as much as it's a bit of a stretch to think about meeting *the one* at seventeen, I've never felt like this about anyone. I've never been around someone who knows and enjoys all the parts of me like this, even if he doesn't yet know that these parts belong to one person, not two.

But that's silly. And even if it were fun to entertain, long-term things don't start out with lies. It's like Rule No. 1 of The Healthy Relationship Handbook.

"Of course not," I say. "I'm seventeen."

"Exactly," Katie says matter-of-factly. "You're seventeen, and he lives in North Carolina. So have your summer romance. Enjoy his company; you obviously adore him. Don't go telling him things that are only going to hurt him. If I could do it again, I would never have told Dexter what I told him."

"It's not *right*, though," I say.

Katie tilts her head to the side. "When it comes to romance, sometimes right and wrong isn't always so black and white."

# I Scream

And so the plan goes forward. Another act begins.

As Carrie, I send a message to Elm:

*CarriesRevenge01: Olivia and I are thinking about getting ice cream after work tomorrow. Want to join?*

He says yes immediately. It's on.

After dinner, Katie and I spend the rest of the night preparing for her second appearance as Carrie. She demands I inform her of all the ins and outs of horror, even though I'm not quite sure it's necessary; but I don't object. I love talking about the stuff, and it's rare that she wants to hear it.

I walk her through the various genres and subgenres, from killer (slasher, home invasion, etc.) to psychological (paranoia and phobias) to monster (zombie, creature feature, and so on) and paranormal (witches, ghosts, haunted houses, and the like).

I explain that many techniques can cross genres, like found footage, which manifests as a ghost story in *The Blair Witch Project* and a killer story in movies like *Creep* and *Creep 2*.

Then I go through a few key directors, making sure to point out that there aren't nearly enough women and that needs to change. And I brush her up on some of the movies Elm and I have specifically discussed.

Finally, I give her a quick rundown of my screenplay, explaining that it plays on a lot of different genres.

A dutiful pupil and dedicated actress, the girl even makes flash cards, insisting I quiz her; that is, when she's not looking up YouTube clips to make sense of my references.

We stay up too late, quizzing and laughing and eventually watching *Carrie*, which Katie has never seen. All in all, it's kind of fun, and I can't help but love her even more—only a true best friend would go to such lengths.

A part of me knows I'm only stepping further into some seriously gray territory, and that part is like the viewer in just about every horror film:

*Turn back. Don't go into the shadows! For god's sake, don't split up! And whatever you do, don't open that door!*

I can't help but shake the feeling, the same I have when I watch any of those movies, that this is not going to end well, as much as Katie swears it will.

Work is busy yet uneventful the next day. It's so hot out, I take lunch in the lodge again, though I don't see much of Jake, and apart from a few words exchanged via walkie, we don't talk much, either.

Still, I know what's waiting. The ice cream date where Katie will fully embrace her role as the perfect wingwoman. Our second chance—one I won't storm out on this time.

Katie's ready and waiting in the parking lot when Jake and I walk out together. "Ice cream time?" she asks, running up and high-fiving us both.

"I scream for ice cream," Jake says. "And horror, of course."

Katie forces a laugh—the only bit of bad acting I've ever seen from her—and I suggest the roadside place, my favorite, near North-South

Lake. Jake offers to drive the three of us since it's not too far from Hunter Mountain.

We pile into the car, me in the front, Katie in the back, and with the classic-rock station as our soundtrack, Jake and I chat about work, how Steinway's feeling better and back to her usual self, the runaway success of Marianne's niece's T-shirt design, and the annoying dad who keeps dropping his kid at Ropeland so he can get drunk in the lodge.

By the time we reach the general store—a side-of-the-road spot that my parents and I discovered after a long hike around Kaaterskill Falls—horror hasn't been brought up even once, a tentative win.

"Oh my god, this place looks amazing," Katie says as she dashes out of the car and up to the front. She turns back to me. "Girl, it's like something out of a movie. So quaint."

Something out of a horror movie, even.

It's like the girl reads my damn mind. "It would be fun to set a *slasher* movie here," Katie says.

"For sure," Jake says, sidling up in line next to her.

"I'll have a cone," Katie says. A girl about our age in a hot-pink T-shirt jots it on a note pad. "Single or double?"

Katie turns back to us. "Do I dare?"

Jake raises an eyebrow. "You should dare," he says.

Again, I feel like Katie's running the show.

"Double," she says to the girl.

"What flavor?"

"Rocky road," Katie says.

"Crazy, that's my favorite, too," Jake says immediately.

Katie laughs. "Coincidence!"

*It's everybody's favorite, you guys.*

They both order, and I step up. "I'll have a double cone, too. Strawberry." The girl writes the order down, and I hand her a few crumpled bills.

"Strawberry," Katie says. "Such a waste."

The strawberry vs. chocolate debate has been a long-standing one in our friendship—I love me some chocolate; just not in ice cream, for some reason—but now it only annoys me. "Rocky road is just too much. Sorry."

Jake shrugs. "Hey, whatever works." He nudges me with his elbow, his skin lingering on mine for just a second; and I think, just maybe, that we're edging back to what we had.

But just as soon, his arm drops back to his side. He looks at Katie and offers a weak smile. "I'm with Katie on this one, though. Rocky road is fairly unparalleled."

My heart sinks once again. He's with her. Shock of all shocks. Why did I think someone as scene-stealing as Katie could *ever* be a wingwoman?

The girl behind the counter returns, holding out the pair of rocky road cones. Katie takes them both, hand-delivering one to Jake. Mine comes out separate and I accept it eagerly, glad to have something to do with my hands.

We walk over to a pair of benches, where Katie stretches herself out on one, taking up the entire thing. *All right*, I think. *She's trying to do her part, at least.* It's not her fault she's so charming that something as small as ordering an ice cream can come off as delightful.

I sit down on the other bench, Jake only a couple of inches away, and we dig in.

He's halfway through his first scoop when he pauses, looking up at Katie. "So I have something to tell you," he says, and I swear my heart stops. I have the sudden, irrational thought that he's going to say that he likes her, right here in front of me, my ice cream melting in the heat but my heart frozen solid.

He takes a deep breath. "This is bad, but I *still* haven't read your screenplay. I'm going to, though. I promise."

"Cool," Katie says, licking her cone with gusto.

"I mean, you want me to, don't you?"

Katie shrugs. "Sure."

Jake's face falls. "I just thought it was important to you—"

She interrupts him. "'Course. You'll see when you read it, but I've just been so inspired by the different genres of horror."

I nod along. She's getting this much right, at least.

But then she goes on. "You know, from your classic killer-slasher sort of thing to your, I don't know, *creature feature*. I just really want to push myself, to explore."

Jake's eyes narrow. "I didn't know it played on creature features. What creatures?"

I catch Katie's eyes, shake my head as discreetly as I can. Katie smiles. "Well, it does in that there's a monster in all of us," she says. "Isn't that what horror is always exploring?"

I could do without any more of her philosophical pronouncements about a genre that until yesterday she knew almost nothing about, but maybe that's just me.

"I *guess*," Jake says, a little less convinced than when she went off on her tangent about ghost stories. "But I don't know, really," he continues. "I think most creature features are pretty cut-and-dried. They don't have to be deep. That's kind of what's refreshing about them. Some are even stupid. Like my bad jokes," he adds, shooting me a smile before fixing his gaze back on her.

"But are they cut-and-dried?" Katie asks. "Really?"

Jake laughs. "Well, yeah, I mean, sometimes a monster is just a monster."

Katie licks at her cone. "That's why I prefer the psychological variety, you know, like Hitchcock's *Psycho*."

I half want to smash my forehead into my ice cream cone. *Hitchcock's Psycho?* Is this a conversation or an essay for her New School program?

Jake laughs her off. "You *know* my feelings on *Psycho*."

I do, of course, but Katie doesn't. He thinks it's horribly overrated. It's one of the very few points on which he and I disagree.

"I mean, doesn't *everyone* love *Psycho*? It's obviously the preeminent film in the psychological horror genre."

Oh, god. I shouldn't have trained her so well. Hell, I shouldn't have trained her at all.

Jake bristles. "It's not, though. Honestly, it's just Hitchcock getting all these accolades because he dared to kill off the lady who we're led to think is his main character in the beginning of the movie. Remember? We talked about this. Like, for an hour."

In his voice, I hear a flash of hurt, and I want to turn to him, tell him I don't forget things like that. I listen to him, even when I disagree. I care about his opinions, even if sometimes I think they're silly.

Katie's eyes flick to me, all, *Help*.

I clear my throat. "I'm kind of a Hitchcock fan, but I wouldn't normally even call his movies horror. I mean, they're not, right?"

Jake turns to me then, and in his eyes is the kind of relief you get from being understood, the kind I almost always feel when I'm near him. "Yes, *exactly*. They have crime and suspense and all those elements, but they're missing the fundamental part. Take the shower scene out of *Psycho*, and it's not horror at all. You said that, actually," he says, turning to Katie. "When we talked about it."

Katie licks a bit of melted ice cream off her finger. "I say a lot of things," she says, voice flat. "You shouldn't take them all so seriously."

Jake looks taken aback, but I'm not so surprised. The thing about Katie is . . . she doesn't take feedback all that well. When Ms. Sinclair, her drama teacher, told her that she had a tendency to overact during more upbeat scenes, it took her a full week of moping before she could even *consider* the teacher's words.

I glance at Katie again, and for once, her eyes catch mine—she knows she's taking this too far. Wowing Jake with her movie knowledge was never the plan: playing wingwoman was. And making him feel like he doesn't matter—that wasn't the plan at all.

Like a good bestie, Katie stands. "I'm going to walk up that way and take some photos."

"Sure," Jake says.

"Have fun," I add.

Katie heads off, cone in hand. I know what she's about to do. She'll chastise herself on not getting the role just right, but I can't focus too much on that now. Jake is beside me, after all. What's more, if I'm not wrong, his feelings are hurt.

"Sorry," Jake says, turning to me. "I guess movie debates can get a little heated."

"It's not just that," I say. "I know you've talked to Katie a lot online, but in person, she can be a little . . . brusque, sometimes."

Jake shakes his head. "It's okay, and I didn't mean to dominate the conversation. It's just . . ."

"What?" I ask.

*It's just that I'm in love with Katie/Carrie, and I thought you should know sooner rather than later.*

*I liked you, kind of, but that was before my dream pen pal entered the picture.*

*Should I go check on her? Do you think she's mad?*

Jake's face tenses up. "It's just funny. I thought, when I found out Carrie was actually here . . . I don't know, I thought it would be different."

"What do you mean?" I know I shouldn't push, but I can't help myself.

"She's so easy to talk to online. We used to chat for hours, but in person, it's different. It's almost like she's got a whole other personality. I'm sorry—I know she's your good friend."

"My best friend," I correct. "But I guess you don't get the full picture online, do you?"

Jake gazes at me, like he's thinking hard on something, and half of me wants him to figure it all out, but I remember what Katie said about Dexter, and she's right. He'd be horrified. This all would be over, and I can't bear the thought of that—not when it feels like this is only our beginning.

"I guess," Jake says, glancing to where Katie walked off, perhaps a little wistfully.

He bites into the top of his cone, then turns back to me. "Anyway, enough about that. Should I entertain you with some bad jokes or something?"

I laugh. "What are you, a factory?"

He chomps at the bottom of the cone, then sucks the rest of the ice cream out. "Maybe. Though I don't have any good ones off the top of my head, to be honest. Mood has to strike me just right."

"I'm sure you can dig up a bad one, though."

He raises an eyebrow. "Hey, even those take work."

It's quiet for a moment, and I feel that thrum again, of our bodies close. I lick at a bit of ice cream dripping down the side of my cone.

"You know what's funny," Jake says.

"What?"

"It's just that we spend so much time working together, you and me, and we don't even know that much about each other."

I feel a blush start to creep to my cheeks and I dig deeper into my cone. "So, what do you want to know?"

Jake smashes the remains of his cone and bites into it like a sandwich. "Well I didn't know you had a best friend named Katie, for one. And I know you're from Brooklyn—and that you're an only child—but I don't know anything about your family. Like, what they do and all that. I assume people have really cool jobs in Brooklyn. My parents are high school history teachers, which is decidedly not exciting."

"Well, Katie is my best friend, that's true. My parents are fairly boring parent types, too; my mom is an art professor, and my dad works in marketing, and my aunt is pretty cool. She's a creative director."

"Wait, like Katie's?" he asks.

"Huh?"

"Katie's aunt, the one who lives nearby, she's a creative director, too." He laughs. "Damn, is that the only job in New York?"

I swallow, my throat thick. Shit.

Quickly, I force a laugh. "Seems like it sometimes!" I'd completely forgotten I'd told Elm that ages ago, when he was going on about his aunt Mona, when we were in the thick of initial conversation, trading cool-aunt stories. Oy.

Jake smiles. "You know, I don't even know your favorite movie."

"*Carr—*"

I manage to stop myself, halfway through.

"Ing," I finish. "*Caring.*"

"*Caring?*" Jake tilts his head to the side.

My heart races. "*Caring for You.* It's with Meryl Streep. She made it right before *The Deer Hunter.*"

"Really? My mom is obsessed with her and I've never even heard of it."

I smile weakly, pushing the lie, the totally made-up film even further. "It's pretty low-key. Kind of like the original indie movie, you know."

I want to smack myself across the head, it sounds so stupid.

Jake smiles, finishing the rest of the cone and licking his fingers. "I never knew you were into indie film. That's how I got into horror in the first place. I was really into low-budget, nontraditional distribution kind of stuff. Just tired of all the superhero movies and all that."

"Right," I say. "Exactly."

His hand drops to the side, and if I dropped mine, too, maybe ours would touch.

In the distance, I spot Katie walking back toward us, and I can't do it. It all feels too shaky, too precarious, like I'm on some kind of tightrope—one wrong step, one more cool-aunt mention or *Caring for You* (oy) slipup, and I'll crash to the ground.

This will all be over before it's even begun—and no amount of hand-grazing, accidental or otherwise, will change that.

# The Invitation: Part Two

"I'm sorry for my behavior," Katie says as soon as we're back in my parents'
Subaru, driving home.

"Geez, you don't have to apologize," I say with a laugh. "It's okay."

Katie shakes her head. "It's not, though. I got too into the role, and
I . . ." She gulps as she turns into my driveway. "I *overacted.*"

She says it so dramatically, as if it's more horrible than anything in
any horror movie, hands down. I suppose, to her, it is.

"Are you okay?" I ask as she puts the car into park.

Katie's eyes are wide, almost glossy.

"What is it?"

She only shrugs. "Let's go inside."

We do, and my parents greet us, asking if we want them to heat up
any food from dinner. We're both so full from our double cones that we
go straight to my room, promising to get real food later.

Katie tosses herself onto my bed.

"Too much ice cream?" I ask as I set my things down and turn
around, quickly changing out of my zip-line T-shirt and into a tank.

"Ugh," Katie says. I can't tell if she's talking about ice cream or her
"role" or something else altogether.

My phone flashes, buzzing to life. I pick it up. It's from Jake.

*Had fun tonight! Going to a party tomorrow up in Cairo, at one
of Bryson's friend's. You guys should come!*

I break into a smile, then flip the phone around. "Don't be so quick to hate on your performance, lady."

Katie grabs the phone from me and gives it a read. For the first time all night, her smile is back. "Oh, girl," she says, beaming. "We're doing this."

"A party?" my mom says incredulously at breakfast the next morning, Katie and I digging into my dad's famous scrambled eggs and turkey bacon. "Will there be alcohol there?"

Katie takes a sip of coffee—she drinks it black, more for the quirk of it than because she likes it that way, I swear. "If there is, we won't touch it, don't worry. I'm driving, and I do not mess around with my shiny new license."

"License!" my dad says, looking up from his iPad. "Seven-letter word for 'Permit, as a government office.'"

"Charlie, we're trying to decide if the girls can go to a party tonight."

"Oh," he says, putting his iPad down. "Sorry. Will there be alcohol there?"

My mom shoots us a conspiratorial look, nodding to Katie to deliver her line again.

"If there is," Katie says dutifully, "we won't be partaking."

My dad looks from my mom back to us. "It's okay with me if it's okay with you."

My mom nods. "As long as you're back by eleven and don't come home smelling like a distillery. And if we text you, you text right back."

"Deal," I say.

"Deal," Katie says.

My mom takes another sip of her coffee. "We're just glad you guys are choosing to be honest with us instead of making up some sort of story. But I suppose that's just the kind of girls you both are. Oh, and Olivia—"

"Yeah?"

"Aunt Chrissy got a few days off her current project and is coming up on Tuesday. So no impromptu parties and hangouts next week, okay?"

I hesitate. I love Chrissy, and I welcome any chance to spend time with her, but I can't help but think of our last text exchange. She thinks I told Jake the truth. I promised her I would.

I promised myself I would, too.

"What is it?" Katie asks quietly, but I only shake my head.

"That sounds great, Mom. Can't wait to see her."

We spend the day at the swimming hole, before having dinner with my parents. I ask Katie again whether I should just tell Jake the truth, but she reminds me of the Dexter Incident, promises it will all be fine if I just trust her to do her wingwoman job.

Chrissy texts me after dinner, while Katie and I are in my room, getting ready for the party, trying on sundresses and asking each other's opinions, as we always do.

*Did you hear my change in plans? I'm coming to see you, my dear sweet niece!*

I pull one of my favorite dresses of Katie's over my head, then text her back.

*Mom told me this morning, can't wait!*

She sends me a smiling emoji, then:

*P.S. Did you tell the boy? How did it go?*

I hesitate, then type quickly.

*No, actually I didn't. Not yet, at least.*

*Okay, good luck. Truthfully, I don't blame you for putting it off. It sounds difficult and complicated, but I know you can do it! We can dish all about it when I'm up, but go easy on yourself, Olivia. None of us are perfect, you know.*

I smile. Chrissy always makes me feel better.

"Texting your boo?" Katie asks as she tugs at the bottom of her dress.

"No." I laugh. "Chrissy."

Katie approaches the mirror, then begins to draw on her winged eyeliner, her official going-out look. "Do you think we need to brush up on any more horror movies?" she asks.

"No," I shake my head vehemently. "I think you're good."

Katie smiles, blinking a few times as she finishes up. "I won't overdo it this time—promise."

It takes us thirty-five minutes to get to Cairo, and we wind down country roads until we reach the address that Jake gave us this afternoon. Cars line both sides of the road, a few pickups speckled among them.

"So many cars," Katie says as she puts the Subaru into park. "I have a feeling we're not in Kansas anymore, Toto."

I laugh. "I think you might be right."

Together, we amble up the gravel road. There's a meadow on one side, but the house in question is nestled in the woods.

"This has got to be the way, right?" Katie asks as we follow two guys up a winding drive.

I nod. "Either that or we're going to meet some kind of awful death, *Deliverance*-style."

Katie laughs. "Hey, no horror jokes for you tonight. That's *my* expertise now."

"You promised you wouldn't overdo it," I say. "Don't forget that."

Katie smiles. "I won't."

We follow the guys around the house and through the woods, to a clearing in the backyard. In the middle, there's a fire pit crackling and blazing. Around it, twenty or so people spread out on camping chairs and coolers. On the edge, near the deck, a couple of guys are hovering over a grill.

Katie points toward the fire to where a guy is standing, separate from any group. "Look. There's Jake." She steps confidently toward the crowd of people, not missing a beat. "Jake!" she calls, and as he turns, a smile breaks across his face. He runs up to us, and he looks like he's going to hug Katie, but in true wingwoman form, she sticks out her hand. It's a little awkward, greeting a friend with a handshake, and by the time they're done, all I can manage is a wave. Oy.

"Do you guys want a drink or food or something?" Jake asks.

"Water for me," Katie says.

"Me too," I say in solidarity.

Jake dashes off to a cooler and returns promptly with three waters. "This way," he says, leading us toward the grill. "This you have to try."

At the grill, I spot Bryson, who gives me a requisite nod. I don't think he and I have exchanged more than two words since I started work. Jake sidles up to him. "Can I get some of that grilled pineapple? Three."

Bryson puts the trio on a plate, and Jake nods to us. "Come on. There's an awesome spot to sit back there."

He leads us back, deeper into the woods, to a log turned on its side, and takes a seat. I hesitate at first, but wingwoman Katie gives me a nudge, and I take the spot right next to Jake. Katie sits next to me.

"Dig in!" Jake says a little too enthusiastically, grabbing a piece and passing the plate to me. "I already had three."

"Not stopping you from taking another, though," I say.

"Hey," Jake says. "Only a *monster* passes up grilled pineapple."

I grab a slice and pass the plate to Katie. It's sweet and charred, like sugar and smoke mixed together. Juice drips sticky down my chin, and I wipe it away with the back of my hand.

"Damn, this is good," Katie says as she devours some, too.

We talk about work—I ask if Steinway or Tennyson or Cora are coming, and Jake says no, and we discuss how Bryson's robotic demeanor doesn't change too much off the clock—and we talk about how nice it is to be in the mountains, away from the muggy heat of North Carolina and Brooklyn. Jake even tells us about his little sister, Emma, how she FaceTimed him today just because she missed him, and to tell him she learned a new song in day camp, which she sang in full—all four verses.

For a little bit, I let myself imagine that this is just regular life, that no lies have been exchanged, that Brooklyn is far away, and Katie and I are the sort of girls who regularly go to parties in the woods. Jake is no more than the guy I met at my summer job, talking about his cute little sister, and everything will unfold like normal, like it does in books or movies. And for a moment, as the sweetness tickles my tongue, and Jake's warm summer skin is so close we're *almost* touching, it's just lovely. My crush and my best friend and me, sharing a log in the woods, eating grilled pineapple.

But then Jake changes up the game, taking the conversation in a new direction. "I was thinking about what you said," he says, leaning forward so he can see Katie. "About creature features. Maybe you're right, you know. Maybe they really are always about the monsters inside us, and that's what horror is all about."

"Nah, I was just bullshitting," Katie says. "Sometimes, I take this stuff too seriously."

"Don't we all. Except Olivia." He elbows me playfully, his arm warm against mine. "She knows better than to obsess about the ins and outs of creature features."

I have a feeling I should say something. Agree or disagree. Do anything but shove pineapple into my mouth. But I don't know *what* to say.

I don't know how to be myself when I'm pretending to be somebody else—and when somebody else is pretending to be me.

"By the way, I was meaning to ask," Jake says to Katie. "Did something happen to make you leave your program?"

"Huh?" she asks, her body tightening.

"Your screenwriting program?" I give her a quick nudge.

She doesn't look at Jake. Instead she stares at me, her eyes going suddenly cold.

"Only because you were *so* excited about it," Jake says. "When we talked before."

Katie's steely gaze disappears. Now she looks almost . . . crestfallen. For a second, I'm not sure what she's going to say, but she looks away. "Like I said, it wasn't the right environment." She stands. "I'm going to go, uh, get some more water." She walks off without another word.

Jake frowns. "You think she's okay? I didn't mean to upset her."

"She's just sensitive," I say. "About the things she cares about. Let me go make sure, though."

He nods. "I'll be right here."

I find her back near the deck, staring intently at her phone.

"Hey," I say. "Are you okay?"

Katie looks up, and for a second, her eyes are glossy. I could swear she's about to cry.

"What's wrong?" I ask.

"Nothing! This is all just a part of the plan. I was trying to give you guys some time together. I didn't want it to turn into yet another movie discussion."

"What is it?" I ask. "Just tell me."

"Just go back to your little log of love, okay?" she says. "I'm good. Doing my part and all that. Embracing the only role I've got right now."

Before I can say anything more, she smiles, and I can't tell if she's acting or not—which is, I suppose, the mark of a good actor. I turn around just as Jake approaches.

"Are you guys okay?" he asks.

Katie's smile grows wider. "Of course! It's just these damn mosquitoes."

"Mosquitoes?" he asks.

"Yeah," Katie says, scratching the back of her neck, though I haven't felt a single bite. "Talk about a creature feature!"

Jake laughs, but Katie keeps scratching. "You know, they're really getting to me," she says. "Would you mind terribly if I bounced? Jake can drive you home," she says. "Right, Jake?"

"Oh," he says, and I can't tell if it's an *oh* of surprise or excitement or disappointment. "Oh yeah, of course."

"Great," Katie says, before turning on her heel and sauntering away.

Jake watches her go, then turns to me, shoving his hands deep in his pockets. "I'm sorry she left, but at least we won't hassle you with horror trivia anymore."

"Thank god."

He grins. "Would you judge me if I got one more pineapple slice?"

I shake my head. "Never."

We top off on pineapple, and then, without either of us saying a word, we head back to our log and sit down, separate from everybody else. The air is warm but the breeze is cool, and the crackling of the fire in the distance makes a perfect soundtrack.

When Jake finishes his slice, he sets his hands on his knees. "I don't want you to think I can only talk about movies," he says.

"It's okay," I say. "I don't."

He sighs, tugging at the frayed ends of his shorts. "It's just that, when I'm nervous, sometimes it's my default."

My heart catches in my throat. "Nervous?" I swallow thickly, then force myself to speak. "How can you be nervous?" I half laugh. "You've been up in the Catskills only a tiny bit longer than me and here you are, getting invites to cool parties with grilled pineapple."

He laughs, but then, abruptly, he stops.

"I have a confession to make," he says.

*I have so many confessions to make, Jake.*

He doesn't wait for my response. "I don't even like parties. For someone who lives in a house full of people, I never know what to do in big groups."

"What are you talking about? You're great with the zip-line groups," I argue.

"That's different," he says. "I stick to the script there. Places like this"—his eyes flit around—"I don't know what to do with myself. Why do you think I've been bingeing on pineapple?"

I laugh, but I understand. It's how I've felt so many times. It's why Katie's presence always calms me, because she does the work for me in these types of situations.

And yet, a part of me doesn't want to be like that anymore. I came up here; I started a new job, even if my mom got it for me; I got to know people. I met Jake. I'm never going to be Katie, with her natural ease and charm—just like Jake will probably never feel perfectly comfortable at a party where he doesn't know many people—but it's okay. I can still be me.

I don't have to hold back so much, just because my best friend doesn't hold back at all.

I don't have to be an observer in my own damn life.

"The truth is," Jake continues, "I don't even think Bryson really wanted any work people to come—that's why Steinway and Co. aren't here—but I kind of begged him for a hint of plans this weekend, you know, so we would have something to do." He clears his throat. "So I would have something to do with you."

Back near the house, I can hear that someone has put on music. A bass beat thumps toward us, echoing the drumming of my heart.

"I mean, we already did burgers and ice cream, and I was running out of food groups, after all."

I laugh again. And then, I feel his hand, warm and rough against mine. I'm scared, just like I was the first and only time I did the zip line, and I want to pull away, only I *don't* want to pull away even more.

"Truth is, you make me even more nervous than this party does," he says.

"I do?" I close my eyes, breathe in and out, and open them again. I'd thought he liked Katie, was wowed by her beauty and charm, but I can feel it now, in my pumping blood, the connection that he and I have—just Jake and Olivia, just the two of us in person, in the flesh. It's more than banter and movies and even screenplay discussions. It's learning about his family, about social anxiety, about real things.

I've spent too much time—way too much time—being scared. I turn to look at him, and he's looking at me.

I remember what he said when he helped me rescue that kid at Ropeland.

*Don't look down, only up.*

And I do.

His lips press against mine, and his arms wrap me tight, and it's warm, our bodies together, warmer and sweeter, even, than charred pineapple in a Catskills summer.

I kiss him back, and I feel a thrill, so blood-pumping, so intense.

It's better than the thrill of any horror movie, that's for damn sure.

# What Would Meryl Do:
# Part Three

Jake pulls up to my house at 10:58 exactly.

"I had a lot of fun tonight," he says, and he leans in, pecking me on the lips, as if this is something normal now, something we just do.

"Me too," I say, feeling my pulse quicken.

"Don't tell Katie how glad I am that the evil mosquitoes attacked her."

"I won't," I say, trying to hold back a blush.

Before either of us can say anything else, I open the car door and bound off to my house.

My mom is smiling, sitting in the living room and watching some kind of documentary, when I walk in. She hits Pause. "Just in time. Have fun?"

I nod. "Thanks for being cool about it."

She grins, sinking deeper into the couch. "Oh, you know, that's me. Cool Mom, always."

I can't help it; I laugh.

"Is Katie okay? She said she got attacked by mosquitoes?"

"Yeah, they were pretty bad," I lie. It seems easier than explaining that the ultimate wingwoman had to fake a mosquito invasion to fulfill her role. "I'm gonna go check on her." I walk toward the hallway that leads to my room. "Good night, Mom."

She presses Play on her documentary. "Good night."

Once I'm out of sight, I rush to the door, ready to tell Katie everything. She was a success, a huge one. This whole plan of hers actually, miraculously . . . *worked.*

But as I approach the door, I see from the crack just above the floor that the light is off. I open it slowly. Katie is in bed, turned on her side.

"Katie," I whisper. I don't think the girl's gone to bed before eleven in her entire life. Maybe she really didn't feel well. "Katie?"

No answer. It will have to wait until morning.

I grab my phone and text Jake instead.

*Thanks for the ride*

He texts back right away.

*You're welcome*

*Good night, Olivia*

*Sweet dreams*


"Feeling better?" I ask Katie when she wakes up the next morning, just after ten.

I barely slept at all; my head was too full of thoughts of Jake, of our kiss.

Of my first kiss, which was better than I could possibly have ever imagined. Despite my lack of sleep, I feel more alive, more energized, than I have in such a long time.

Katie stretches and sits up in bed. "Fine," she says.

"You must have slept a long time," I say.

She rubs at her eyes. "Yeah, so?"

"You're sure you're okay?"

Katie doesn't say anything more.

"Guess what?" I ask, sitting on the bed next to her.

She looks at me apprehensively. "What?"

I hold back a smile, hardly able to contain my excitement. "Jake kissed me last night . . . twice."

Katie smiles—she does give me that—but still, something about it is off.

"What's going on with you?" I ask.

"Nothing," she insists, looking down at her hands.

Before I can stop myself, my mind starts to turn. What if? No, it can't be. I rack my brain. She said he was cute that first day she met him, and she's been so eager to impress him, going off script to make her pronouncements about horror movies. She practically stormed off at ice cream, and last night, though the plan had always been for her to go home a little early, I didn't expect her to leave as soon as she did.

Is it possible? It can't be. It's Katie. She doesn't even *get* crushes. Is it possible she's actually jealous?

Before I can ask her anything else, my phone buzzes, the notification from Reddit flashing at me.

*ElmStreetNightmare84: I have something to confess . . .*

I drop the phone on the bed.

"What is it?" Katie asks.

"Look at that," I say, pointing to the phone, a blight on everything that transpired last night.

Katie picks it up, then drops it again. "So?"

I shake my head. "Why would he text you that?"

My mind rushes, filling in his words.

*Even though I kissed your friend, I knew as soon as I did that I'm really crazy about you.*

*I had to tell you before I got in any deeper.*

*I had to be honest.*

Katie rolls her eyes. "First off, he's texting *you* that, not me."

"No, he's not," I say. "He thinks it's you now."

Katie laughs bitterly. "Oh yeah? And whose fault is that? Besides, didn't you *just* tell me that you guys kissed last night? Isn't it time for you to stop projecting your low self-esteem on me for absolutely no reason? Jealousy isn't a good look, Olivia."

"I'm not jealous." I practically spit the words out.

Of all the things I've said this summer, that's maybe the biggest lie of all, and Katie knows it. She scoots out of bed, standing up. "Whatever," she says as she changes out of her PJs and into shorts and a tank. "I think I'm going to leave today anyway."

"Really?" I ask. "But you just got here."

Katie sighs, crossing her arms in front of her. "Actually, I've been here almost a week. Entertaining myself while you worked all day."

"Hey," I say, trying to lighten the mood. "At least you got a good tan."

Katie ignores me, tossing her clothes into her bag. She's serious.

"Come on," I say. "What's wrong?"

My phone buzzes again.

ElmStreetNightmare84: *Okay, so here's my confession. I know you said it wasn't a big deal if I read it or not, but I stayed up super late last night reading your screenplay, and then this morning, I took the liberty of telling my aunt all about it. She thinks it's an awesome idea and would love to meet you. She's actually shooting tomorrow in Woodstock. I was hoping that we could go by, catch a little of the shoot, and go to dinner with her? I told her Olivia would come, too—if you guys want to.*

ElmStreetNightmare84: *Hopefully you're not mad. It was just so good I had to tell her about it!*

My pulse quickens, but it's not because of Jake or Elm this time. My screenplay. The one that he, my favorite fellow horror snob, actually liked. That his aunt, an actual horror moviemaker, seemed to like, too.

"Oh my god," I say.

"What now?" Katie asks.

I look up at her, the smile already breaking across my face. "He read the screenplay. And he liked it."

"Okay. Great," Katie says. "I told you it was a big accomplishment, didn't I?"

I shake my head. "No, you don't get it. He told his aunt about it. She's a real-deal indie horror director. She wants to meet me. Well, meet you."

I look at Katie's bag, half exploding with clothes. "So?"

*So?* Katie doesn't get it. She's an actress. She has loads of opportunities to share what she loves with others, to perform, to get recognition. Writing a screenplay, it's just me and my Google Doc. Maybe it would have been different if I had a whole group of peers from the NYU program, but I don't. I want to hear what Jake's aunt has to say. I want to feel that delight of being understood, appreciated, just a little bit—even if I have to pretend that Katie wrote it the whole time.

I know it's probably risky, I know I probably shouldn't, but I don't care—it's something. After this, Katie can go back to Brooklyn like she obviously wants to, and I can go on pretending to Jake that I've never so much as written a single line of dialogue. But I want this, badly. I don't want to pass it up.

"She wants to meet you tomorrow."

Katie crosses her arms, staring at me.

I sigh. "I'm sorry for being a jealous asshole, okay? I'm sorry for pushing my issues on you. But I need you. This is my chance to talk to a real-life horror director about my screenplay. It's a chance to hear feedback, since I never did a program or anything. I don't want to miss it."

Katie narrows her eyes at me. "Really?"

I look down briefly, then back up at her. "One last performance. I know you've got it in you."

She humphs.

"Come on," I say. "What Would Meryl Do?"

For the first time all morning, my best friend smiles, just a little bit.

All talk of leaving off the books, we spend the afternoon preparing. Katie is back to classic Katie, ready to do anything for a role. We take our flash cards back down to the swimming hole.

"All right," Katie says as we unfold our beach chairs and slather on sunscreen, reaching our toes into the water. "Tell me everything I could possibly need to know about this screenplay of yours. I know it's about a lot of genres mixed together, but I need more. Every character. Every plot point. All the twists and turns."

She pulls her oversized sunglasses down just the tiniest bit so she can really look me in the eye. "And I'm serious. All your inspirations. All the directors and movies that have acted as your muses. It's not just Jakey-Poo anymore. This woman is really going to know what she's talking about. This is the Method Acting challenge I've always dreamed of."

I cock my head to the side. "If it were Method Acting, wouldn't *you* have to write a screenplay?"

Katie laughs. "I think embodying a character your best friend has created through online conversations for months and doing my best with limited training time is Method enough, okay? Plus, you leave the acting definitions to me. I'll leave the gory suspenseful horror shit to you. 'Kay?"

I laugh. "'Kay. Where should we start?" I ask.

Katie jumps up. "With this." She runs into the creek, wading until she's fully submerged. She pops up screaming at the cold, but it doesn't stop her. "Get in here!" she calls.

And I love her. I really, really do.

We splash around, soaking up the sun and pruning our fingers; but we do our homework, too. First I start with the plot of *The Bad Decision Handbook*, including all its twists, turns, and complications.

"So you're saying the bad guy in the movie is actually a director?" Katie asks, rippling her fingers through the water. "And he's using this little episode of terror *as* his movie?"

"Exactly," I say.

"How meta," Katie says.

"Right, so the main characters, Onyx and Jimmy—"

"Nice name choices." Katie smirks.

"Shut up," I say. "Anyway, they have to anticipate what would come next in the movie, like who he's going to go after, in order to defeat him. They have to get into the director's head."

"And that's where the bad decisions come into play?"

"Yeah, they make it sound like they're splitting up, that kind of thing, but really, they're always one step ahead of him. The idea is, what if you actually found yourself *in* a horror movie? Not in one of the situations depicted in a horror movie, but in a horror movie itself." I shrug. "I know, it's complicated."

Katie laughs. "Oh, it very much is."

"It's what I wanted to write, though."

"Truly Olivia, and I don't throw this around lightly, it sounds *amazing*. NYU or no NYU, you did this. You made it happen." Katie splashes me.

I splash her back, a smile on my face now, too.

I did make it happen. I really did.

# Day of the Dead

A real-life horror shoot and a real-life horror director. I can hardly stomach the thrill of it all.

Not to mention all that's going on with Jake. Completely electric, but completely natural, too. Even though the energy feels charged between us, it feels like it was supposed to be that way all along.

He asks Marianne if we can leave work early, just this once, and we pick up Katie and are at the shoot location just outside of Woodstock by four fifteen.

"You excited?" Jake asks as he pulls the car into a gravel lot where about five other cars and a van are parked. I know he means Katie, and I don't say anything, but still, I can feel the tingling in the tips of my fingers. This is really happening.

"I couldn't be more thrilled," Katie says convincingly. In a way, she's not even lying. This is the pinnacle of the role she's been playing all week. Her swan song, if you will.

As soon as I'm out of the car, I hear it: a piercing, chill-your-bones sort of scream. My eyes widen in appreciation of the cool factor, if nothing else, but Jake, mistaking my expression for fear, tosses his arm around me and pulls me closer to him. "You going to be able to handle all the gore?"

*Oh boy*, I want to say. *You don't know the half of what I can handle.* But it feels so good, his skin on mine, that I don't disabuse him of that notion. Instead, I force a laugh. "I guess we'll see, won't we!"

There's a marked trail, and we walk down it, Jake's arm falling away from me as we make our way deeper into the woods. It's a beautiful day, the sun far from setting, the air warm, the leaves fat and green. It doesn't seem at all like a day for shooting something awful, and yet, as we get closer, another scream pierces the air.

We follow the curve of the path, and then suddenly, as if we only happened upon it in the woods, the trees open up, and we're at the edge of the clearing. There are two people who must be actors in the middle, a man lying among the dirt and leaves, a woman standing above. They're both covered in what looks like blood, surrounded by three different crew members. Jake's aunt stands to the side, not in a director's chair or anything—just standing. A guy on the edge yells, "Quiet on set."

We freeze, not wanting to cause so much as another leaf rustle.

"Rolling," another person yells.

"Action!" Jake's aunt Mona says.

And then, it happens. The actress drops to her knees, so quickly you'd think she should be wearing kneepads, and maybe—beneath the skinny jeans that are speckled with fake blood—she is. "No," she says, lifting the man's head almost frantically. "No, no, no." She lets him go, his head dropping to the ground, and jumps up. "Help!" she screams, and I know the cries I heard earlier were definitely hers. "Help!"

She sinks again to the ground and rips open the man's shirt, and I can't see exactly what's there, because the camera is closing in, but it must be some sort of fake wound, and she presses her hands to his chest, and as her head drops, she says, more quietly, but still loud enough for me to hear: "I'll kill the psycho who did this to you."

"Cut!"

Immediately, the mood changes. The woman, who was pretty convincingly distraught just a second ago, smiles. "How was that?"

"Better," Jake's aunt says. "But I still think you can push it a little more."

The man props himself up and starts re-snapping his shirt.

"Come on," Jake says. "I think we can get a better view from over here."

He leads us around the edge to a smattering of wooden boxes tucked among the trees. He grabs one, and Katie and I follow suit, me next to him, her next to me.

Across the clearing, his aunt smiles, giving us a wave. Jake waves back. "You're sure it's okay that we sit here?" I ask, leaning closer to him.

He nods. "This is out of the line of sight of the camera. Don't worry. If we were in view, I definitely would have doused you with some fake blood first."

I laugh, then turn to Katie. To my surprise, she's captivated; and for once, I don't think it's a part of her act. "The acting's not so bad, huh?" I say under my breath, nodding toward the set.

She turns. "I'm more interested in the horror elements," she says, eyes practically twinkling. Girl's not one to break her role. "But the actors are pretty good, I have to say."

I knew it.

"Quiet on set!" the guy yells again.

And then, "Action!"

They go through the scene five more times, to different effect with each take. Sometimes the woman is more desperate than angry; other times, she's seething, the rage completely taking her over. I wonder how she doesn't get hoarse from so much screaming, but she delivers her cries convincingly each and every time.

When they're not rolling, the grim veil comes off completely. The actress becomes a regular person, despite her cries of terror only moments earlier; the guy on the ground re-snaps his shirt; and the makeup artist adds a bit more fake blood. It's so relaxed, so chill; people working, messing around on their phones to pass the time, only springing to action when they have something to do. It's not so different from the way Tennyson and I hang around the check-in office, waiting for the next group of zip-liners to arrive. After all, they're just doing their jobs.

But as soon as Mona calls, "Action," the mood changes. The blood feels suddenly real as the actress delivers her lines. The pain, anger, and fear are almost palpable in the air. Katie wasn't wrong. I, as Carrie, have always been more interested in the horror elements than the acting—post–*Dracula* auditions, at least. Maybe I always was, even if I didn't realize it back then. The jump scares and quick cuts, the sense of foreboding and the twists and turns of every story, even the campy scenes and occasionally comically bad lines. Acting always seemed secondary, but seeing it now, like this, I get why it's so important, why someone like Meryl Streep is Katie's everything. Because when you get right down to it, all the fake blood is nothing without someone to convince you it's real.

There's something else, too, something I know surer than I ever have before:

I want this, I really do. I have to stop being so scared of failing that I don't even try. I have to go for it. Look at all you can have when you do.

"What do you think?" Jake asks, and I know he's talking to Katie, but for once, that doesn't stop me from answering.

"I think this is the coolest thing I've ever seen."

# Carrie vs. Olivia: Part Three

They wrap at sunset, having successfully completed two more scenes.

As the crew packs up equipment, and the actors use baby wipes to clear away the fake blood, Mona comes over.

"Hi, Olivia," she says, wrapping me in a quick hug before turning to Katie. "And you must be the famed auteur of *The Bad Decision Handbook*."

"In the flesh," Katie says, sticking out her hand. "I'm Katie."

"Mona." She pulls Katie into a hug, my heart beating fast with jealousy. When Mona pulls back, she clasps her hands together. "You guys have fun? You sure picked the day for it. You definitely got to see some of the more exciting scenes."

"We loved it," Jake says, briefly glancing to me. "We all did."

"Great," Mona says. "Let me just clean up, and then we'll all go to dinner. I hope you're hungry, because shooting all day makes me starving."

Mona agrees to meet us at the restaurant, and the three of us drive to the Italian place off the highway that is a favorite of hers, as well as my parents'.

They seat us at a table in the corner, and we wait for her—Katie to my right, Jake to my left. Beneath the table, his feet reach slowly, cautiously toward mine, eventually resting against them, and again I feel a thrill, an awe, that this is normal now.

And then the Carrie part of me feels that other thrill—that I'm about to speak to a real horror director about my screenplay.

I grab a piece of bread from the basket in the middle, and pick at it with lightly shaking hands.

"You okay?" Jake asks, squeezing the top of my knee.

I nod, dropping the uneaten bread onto my plate and finding his hand under the table. "Just excited for Katie," I say.

But as Jake's hand squeezes mine, my mind can't help but spin. What if Mona says she hates it and wants to tell me everything that's wrong with it before I even think of showing it to anyone else? What if Katie flubs up everything, and we both embarrass ourselves in grand fashion?

I look to my right, but Katie is dunking her bread in olive oil, apparently not nervous at all.

That's when Mona walks in. She looks so normal in her black jeans and T-shirt, you'd never know she was a director at all.

Jake moves to get up, but she brushes him off. "Please, sit, sit," she says as she grabs a chair and peruses the menu.

"Can I get a glass of pinot noir?" she asks the second the waiter comes over. "Whatever you have that's driest."

She turns to Jake. "So you guys had fun?"

Jake nods, his hand not leaving mine. "Thanks so much for letting us crash the shoot."

Mona smiles. "Anytime. I'm just glad it was when something exciting was happening. I'd have hated for you guys to see the day when the main character is sitting in her office for practically every scene."

Katie clears her throat. "What part of the movie were the scenes we watched from?"

"Actually, fairly near the beginning," Mona says.

"The inciting incident?" Katie asks, making use of one of the terms I used to explain my screenplay yesterday.

"Close," Mona says. "Actually more of the break into act two. But I like the way you're thinking."

The waiter comes back with Mona's wine and details the specials, and for a few minutes, all talk of the shoot wanes as we explore the menu and put in our orders, Mona adding fried calamari for the table.

"So," Mona says, turning to Katie as soon as the menus are cleared. "Jake told me about *The Bad Decision Handbook*, but I'd really love to hear about it straight from the horse's mouth."

*Here we go*, I think. *Time to act your heart out, Katie.*

I steal a look at Jake, and his eyes connect with mine, his mouth stretching into a smile before turning back to his aunt. He's happy, happy to be with me, happy to be helping my friend.

He leans in, voice low. "Mind if I nerd out about horror a bit?"

I laugh. "Of course not."

Katie takes a deep breath and a sip of water. "Well, I got the idea because there are so many bad decisions people make in horror movies, right? As I'm sure someone as seasoned as you knows."

Mona nods. "Oh, believe me, I do. To a certain point, characters need to make some missteps to move the plot along, but some are just ridiculous."

"Exactly," Katie says. "You know, splitting up when it would be much safer to stay together. Leaving your one weapon behind when you go out to face the killer. Purposely entering a bad situation. That kind of thing. But I thought, what if you could really call them out, play off of them, you know?"

"Kind of like *Cabin in the Woods* plays with all the different genres and tropes," Jake says.

Mona nods. "Exactly what I was thinking."

"Right," Katie says. "Only I wanted the characters to be really aware of what was going on. So I thought, if I make it kind of meta, have the bad guy be a director using this whole setup for his next film, it would be a really fun way to explore these tropes. My characters have to use what they know about the director's movies, and horror movies in general, to stay one step ahead. They make some bad decisions, of course, but it's all intentional. Like, what if one day, you actually found yourself *in* a horror movie? Not in one of the settings of a horror movie, but the movie itself? How crazy would that be?"

Jake leans forward. "It's really a brilliant idea, if you ask me. So fresh and original and just, I don't know, cool. That's why I wanted to tell you about it."

Across from me, Mona takes a sip of wine, then sets it down, turning to Katie. "I agree with Jake. I have to say, these are very astute observations for an eighteen-year-old."

Katie smiles. "I'm actually only seventeen."

Mona laughs. "Even more impressive!"

I chug on my water as Jake smiles. "I know, pretty brilliant, right?"

It's all going so well. Katie is pulling it off beautifully. And yet . . .

"I have to admit," Mona says, twisting her wineglass on the table, "after Jake told me about it, I only had the chance to read a couple of scenes, but I can say this: Your ear for dialogue is fantastic, and you've got a great sense of pacing. Of course you have learning to do, as anyone your age would, and as all of us do to a certain degree, but I really just recommend keeping at it. The best way to improve is to keep writing."

"Thank you," Katie says with a smile. "Thanks so much for reading."

Mona demurs. "Oh, of course. Always happy to pay it forward. And I really do think the crux of your idea is special."

"I *told* you," Jake says. "I told you it was a great idea." His hand is still in mine, but he suddenly feels far away. I know he's talking about me—the boy I like likes something I wrote—but it feels . . . it feels again like that damn *Dracula* stage. Like I put in all the work and Katie is killing it while I fade into oblivion . . .

Katie smiles. "I wanted to do something that was a classic killer scenario but had a really strong psychological component as well."

"I mean, don't we all," Mona says. "I feel like you used to get away with just slashers, gore for gore's sake, all that. Now, most horror movies that really take off are very smart and clever. It's a different world. On the plus side, there are more voices than ever, more stories being told by people who have been traditionally left out of the discussion. On the negative side, it can be very hard to get funding for yet another movie about a killer that takes place in the woods." Mona shrugs. "But this is the business we've chosen, I suppose."

Katie beams. *"The Godfather."*

"Yes, dear," Mona says. "I can see you're well-versed in cinema even outside of your genre of choice."

The waiter brings out our food, chicken parm for me, a steaming plate of spaghetti for Jake, steak for Mona, and a chicken Caesar salad for Katie.

Katie digs into her salad. "I mean, that's part of why I wanted to get into horror, you know, because there's so much crap out there, right? So much of the genre is just *dumb.*"

I cringe, shaking my head. *Stop it, Katie. Just stop.*

"I wanted to make smart horror," she goes on. "You know, horror that's just as good as anything that Coppola could make."

Jake lets go of my hand, twisting a bit of pasta on his fork. "I've never heard you be so hard on horror," he says.

"Yeah, me neither," I say, maybe a little bit bitterly. She's getting it all wrong. I love horror because so much out there inspires me, not the other way around.

"I'm just saying," Katie continues. "I want to make the kind of horror that would attract an actor as serious as, say, Meryl Streep."

Mona cuts into her steak, listening, and I hack away at my chicken parm, but I can tell she disagrees. "There is certainly some bad stuff out there," she says finally. "But there's a lot of good stuff, too."

"Tons of good stuff," Jake says, taking a bite of pasta.

"Of course," Katie says, before rattling off a few directors I plied her with yesterday. "But what's interesting is that so much of it is one-note. A creature feature or a ghost story. It's important to add another layer, I think. To not do something that's been done a million times before."

My knife drops to my plate. This is just too much. "Oh, like other genres don't do the same thing a million times over?" I say. All right, to be totally honest, it comes out more as a snap.

"What do you mean?" Katie asks.

I tick off my fingers. "Rom-coms, family dramas, oh my goodness . . . boxing movies. People act like horror is formulaic, but it's really not at all. It's got some of the most inventive work in all of film."

Jake laughs, but it comes out almost nervous. "I told you there was a horror fan in there somewhere," he says, twisting together another bite of pasta. "But I honestly didn't expect you to come around so quickly!"

"I'm sorry," I say, hands dropping to my sides. "It's just that everything she's saying is wrong."

Mona nods. "I have to agree with Olivia a bit. I do think the genre leaves the door open for more experimentation, not less. Traditional cinema has gotten extremely formulaic, especially in recent years. And you didn't even mention superhero movies!"

Jake's eyebrows shoot up. "Don't get me started on superhero movies."

I can't help myself. "That's why I think, with *The Bad Decision Handbook*, it's kind of honoring what's been done in horror, more than making fun of it," I say.

"It *is* making fun of it, though," Katie says firmly. She eyes me, all, *I got this. Just back off.*

For once, I don't care. I can't let her steal the show, not when it comes to this, not when she's so wrong about everything I care about so deeply. "Not like that," I argue, tugging at the bottom of my shirt. "The *intention* was never to hate all over horror and be snobby."

Katie scoffs. "It's *my* screenplay, remember? Perhaps I know the intention a little bit better than you? If you want to write your own, go ahead. But, it's kind of like a photograph, know what I mean? It's a reflection of the person. You can't just take someone else's and then suddenly have an opinion about it."

Jake and Mona exchange a look of confusion. Then Jake sets his fork down and clears his throat. He scoots his chair just a little closer to mine, and under the table, he takes my hand in his, lacing his fingers through mine. "It sounds like two sides of the same coin, if you ask me," he says, quite obviously trying to keep the peace.

"Sometimes the *only* way to elevate a genre is to make fun of it," Katie says, pursing her lips.

"It's not about *elevating* the genre," I say. "Horror doesn't need to be elevated."

"Nothing wrong with adding a little subtext," she snaps back.

I shake my head. "No, sometimes a monster *is* just a monster. Like Jake said."

Jake sits up straighter in his chair and attempts to laugh it off. "Hey, leave me out of this argument. Any more heated, and Mona's steak is going to overcook!"

He turns to me, forcing a smile, but I look away. I don't even have time to focus on his cheesy jokes now.

Katie taps her fork on the plate. "Well, that's not the sort of screenplay *I* intended to write."

I shake my head, my heart thrumming drumbeats and my chest tightening with anger. I can't take it anymore. I can't listen to this. "That's because *you* didn't write it!"

There's silence, heavy as a corpse.

I've given myself up. I've given it all away.

Mona looks from me to Katie, staring, confused.

Katie glares at me, taking in my look of embarrassment, of hurt, of shame. Then, in true *show must go on* fashion, she, at least, attempts to pick up the pieces. "I'm so sorry," she says with a light, bubbly laugh. "Olivia's a great writer as well. She cowrote a few scenes with me. As you can see, we can sometimes get a little combative when discussing our writing process!"

Mona bursts into laughter and motions to the waiter for another glass of wine. "Oh, I've had plenty of similar arguments with fellow creators. All I can say is, it's so energizing to see two young, smart, and passionate horror fans. I can tell you are both going to go very far."

I feel a whoosh of relief, and I look to Katie, thankfulness in my eyes, but then I realize, suddenly, the emptiness in my hand. Jake has unlaced his fingers, let my hand go. He's scooted his chair back, too.

I turn to him, wanting to apologize, to say I'm sorry, to explain, but when I see his face, I know it's too late for that.

He's staring at me, jaw dropped, eyes narrowed, as if he doesn't know me at all.

I know it surer than I've known anything all summer:

He's figured out my secret.

And he hates me for it.

                    ONYX
      What do you want me to say? People make
      mistakes. They take the wrong turn, they
      make stupid decisions, they hurt each
                     other.


                    JIMMY
         Not like this, they don't.

  -*The Bad Decision Handbook* by O. Knight

# A Quiet Place

Jake is silent.

Silent as we finish our meals, which I feel too sick even to touch.

Silent as Mona insists on paying because, as she says, it's rare she gets to treat two budding young horror writers to dinner!

Silent as we say our goodbyes, as Mona promises to look us up next time she's in the city.

Silent as he drives Katie and me back to my house.

"Tell your aunt thanks again," Katie says from the backseat. "And I'll probably be leaving tomorrow, so, uhh, bye. It was nice getting to know you . . . better, at least."

Jake doesn't turn around, only sits stock-still, hands on his knees.

If he were in that movie, the one I actually managed to drag Katie to the theater to see because she's always thought Jim from *The Office* is cute, the one where you have to be super quiet lest the monsters get you, let's just say Jake would be aces.

I listen as the door shuts, watch as Katie heads inside. With the windows rolled up, I can't even hear the crickets outside or the musical trilling of the creek.

"We need to talk," I say, reaching out for Jake's hand, but he flinches, as if I'm the monster now. What can I say? Maybe I am. Maybe Katie was right all along, and it's *all* metaphorical. Perhaps nothing in any horror movie on earth even halfway compares to betraying someone you care about, as I have done to him.

"I don't want to talk to you," he says stonily.

"I know, and I get it. I just want you to know . . ." My voice trails off. "I want you to know that I never meant to—"

Jake interrupts me. "So you're Carrie . . . you've always been Carrie."

I swallow, my chest tight.

"Only Carrie would defend the screenplay like that," he says. "Tell me if it's not true."

I'm the one who's silent now.

"I mean, I should have seen it, right?" Jake says. "Was that the test? To see how long it would take before I figured it out? Were the two of you just laughing at me behind my back?"

I shake my head, and I can feel my eyes glistening. "What do you mean? No."

"The whole time?" he continues. "When Katie showed up, and then when we went to get burgers, and at ice cream, and when I took you to Bryson's party—all that time, it was just a big joke? Better than any of my bad jokes, that's for sure. You really went all out."

"No. It wasn't a joke at all. It wasn't like that."

He grips the wheel so tight, his knuckles go white. "I always knew *something* was off. She didn't sound like Carrie, even when she was going on about movies. She never sounded like . . ." His voice goes quiet. "She never sounded like you."

I tug at the elastic hair tie on my wrist, feeling it snap. As Carrie and Elm, we talked for so many hours, exchanged so many messages. How could I possibly have thought that, with the aid of a few flash cards and YouTube clips, Katie could fool him? She's a good actress—

maybe even she's on her way to becoming a great actress—but no one's *that* good.

This isn't a role, it's real life.

"You know, I thought it was weird—a coincidence, I guess—when the shop in *The Bad Decision Handbook* seemed so similar to our place at Hunter Mountain, but I figured Carrie had just been to summer camp or whatever. I thought it was weird when I plugged *Caring for You* into IMDB and nothing turned up, but I thought I just remembered it wrong. You almost said *Carrie*, didn't you? You slipped."

I nod. "Yes. I slipped, and so I made something up."

Jake sighs. "It all fits together, but why? Why would you do that? Why would you take it *so far*?"

"I didn't *want* to," I say, my voice wavering.

"But you did," Jake says. "If you ever cared about me—even a little bit—why would you try to make me think she was you?"

My throat tightens, because even now, it feels stupid. It's so *embarrassing*.

"I just—"

"You just lied," he says. "Over and over again."

It started out with such a tiny lie, as so many lies do. Like in a movie, where one action, one little decision, leads to everything, threatens to bring the whole house of cards down.

My fingers shake with nerves. "When you asked me to trade pictures, I got scared."

Jake shakes his head. *"Why?"*

I pick at the bit of skin around my nail. "Because we had this great connection, but it was based on the things we said, on movies and horror and just, easy things. I thought if you saw my photo . . ."

"You thought I wouldn't want to talk to you if you weren't, what, blond? What kind of person do you think I am, Olivia?"

"I got nervous, okay? Yours was so . . . nice. You were this horror-loving nerd, and yet you looked like . . ." I glance up at him. "You looked like *you*. Meanwhile, I had this huge zit that day, and I just generally looked a mess, and then Katie sent me this selfie for no reason, like she does, and it looked so perfect, so I sent it to you."

"Just like that," he says.

Maybe he doesn't get it, maybe he's naturally braver or better than I'll ever be, but life is a series of *just like that*s. You do stupid things—or I do, at least. Sending Katie's photo. Not giving NYU a real shot. It's remarkably easy to make the wrong decision, to be a coward.

Maybe that's why I love horror like I do, because it's nice to see people who have no choice but to fight. It's comforting to imagine that, if I were trapped in some sort of house with a ghost, I'd fight, too. But I know now that real life is so much scarier than any shadow monster.

Being close to people, being honest with them, not being afraid to fail—that's the scariest thing of all.

I blink back the moisture in my eyes. "I thought it wouldn't matter, because I thought I'd never meet you. And then I got here, and in this insane coincidence, you were here, and I didn't know what to do."

"You could have told me then," Jake says, shaking his head. "I would have probably laughed about it. It could have been just another joke between us."

"I should have," I say.

He turns to me and for the first time, his eyes catch mine. "Do you know what I would have said?"

I don't drop his gaze. "What?"

He looks down. "I would have told you you're too damn beautiful to be pulling shit like that."

His words strike me, a sudden weight in my stomach. It's crazy, but even after the last few weeks, after the time we spent together, our hike to the waterfall, our kiss at Bryson's party, I still thought that somehow I wasn't quite good enough. I was still finding reasons to be jealous of Katie's picture-perfect looks, still waiting for the other shoe to finally drop.

I know it's stupid to feel this way. I know about the messages that magazines and fashion ads send us and all that. I know people like Chrissy turn photographs into something that isn't real—impossible perfection you should never strive for. I know you have to love yourself before someone else can love you.

But sometimes, when your boobs are growing faster than you expected and your elbows feel all gawky, and your legs are scratchy even though you shaved just the day before, sometimes it's hard to really believe it.

I shake my head. "I'm so sorry."

"We could have spent the last few weeks actually getting closer instead of you playing some stupid game with me for laughs," Jake says, talking more quickly now. "Did you ask Katie to come up so you could play director or something? Really put your skills to the test?"

"No," I say. "I swear, I never even knew she was coming."

"Did you make up the whole thing about NYU just because, I don't know, you're obsessed with lying? You were here with me the whole time, not doing some kind of program."

"You were the only one I was honest with about my writer's block," I say desperately. "You're the only one I even shared the screenplay with. I was as honest with you as I could be. You're the one I trusted."

"That's some way to show it." He practically spits it out.

"Just listen," I say.

Jake shakes his head. "I'm done listening to your lies. Get out of the car."

My eyes well. "Please?"

"No, Olivia. Just leave me alone."

# Drama Queens

"Everything okay?" my mom asks as soon as I'm inside. I can still hear the sound of Jake's car, backing away.

"Fine," I say, hardly looking her way. Instead, I walk down the hall as quickly as I can and slip into my room. The tears spill over then, tears for all that's happened, every lie and betrayal, but also for what Jake said.

*You're too damn beautiful to be pulling shit like that.*

Katie is on my bed, reading a book of monologues. She looks up, but she doesn't say anything, doesn't ask what happened or if I'm okay.

"Jake figured everything out," I say. "He's furious."

Katie goes back to her book. "What did you think was going to happen?"

Her words cut like a knife. "Sorry, I thought you'd care that the guy I really like despises me now."

Katie rolls her eyes. "You're so dramatic."

I shake my head. I can't believe she's acting like this. "Oh, *I'm* dramatic."

Katie tosses the book down. "Yes, actually, you are. Say what you want about actors, but apparently budding screenwriters are an even more difficult bunch."

More tears course down my cheeks, but Katie doesn't stop. "Why did you have to go and start this huge fight with me in front of his aunt? Everything was going fine. They totally believed the whole thing, but you just had to butt in with your opinions. You had to make it impossible for me to do what you asked me to. The fact that that woman doesn't think you're a total nut is only because I swept in with an excuse about us cowriting."

I cross my arms. "Yeah, well maybe I wouldn't have *had* to jump in if you hadn't completely hammed it up. Going on and on with this pseudo-intellectual bullshit about adding layers to the genre or whatever. You always have to overdo it. You always have to take the spotlight, no matter what the occasion."

Katie scoffs. "Oh yeah, I just *love* stealing the spotlight from you. I *wanted* to be forced to assume an alternate identity when I came up to visit my best friend, who, by the way, practically begged me to come and save her from her awful summer."

My hands ball into fists at my sides. "What are you talking about? You loved it. I'm the one who wanted to tell Jake the truth in the first place, and you're the one who started going on about Dexter. You just wanted another role, but you couldn't have played it like a normal person. It had to be The Katie Show. No wonder Ms. Sinclair told you that you overact."

Katie's jaw drops, and as soon as the words are out, I know how cruel and awful they are.

"I'm sorry," I say. "I didn't mean—"

Katie interrupts me. "Go ahead. Criticize my acting, fine. Tell me I'm shit. Everyone else does, anyway. You're not exactly alone. But whatever you think of me, at least I have the guts to try and go after what I want instead of just sitting on the sidelines waiting for stuff to magically happen. At least I'm not *stealing my best friend's photo* for no reason."

"That's not true," I say.

"Yes it is. You totally—"

"No, I mean, it's not true about you. You're a great actress. Everyone knows that. I knew it from the first second of the *Dracula* audition. I was just being an ass. I'm sorry."

"Everyone does *not* know that, Olivia. And if you hadn't been *so* distracted and tied up in your own drama and machinations, maybe you would have thought to ask me why I just up and left my program like I did."

"But I did ask you," I say weakly.

"Barely. Jake seemed more concerned about why I'd left my program, and I don't even know him. He could actually see that I was upset about what had happened there," she says.

"You made it sound like you didn't want to talk about it."

"And when has that ever stopped us from being there for each other before?" Katie snaps. "Couldn't you tell that I was torn up about something? Couldn't you at least *try* to put it together that the last time I spoke to you, I was telling you about the auditions being posted, and then the very next week, I was showing up at your house? Shouldn't that give you a little pause?"

The awful truth is, she's right. Katie and I have *always* been there for each other, caring about and anticipating each other's needs in a way that only best friends can. Like on that last day of school, how I didn't have to tell her how embarrassed I was that everyone else had these amazing summer plans. She just swooped in and saved me herself.

I've been so caught up in my own drama, I haven't even opened my eyes and really looked at my best friend.

"Not to mention," Katie goes on, "in addition to having to save you from this mess you've gotten yourself into, I have to reassure you at every turn while you play this pity card."

"It's easy for you to say. You're . . ."

"I'm what, Olivia? Blond? I have blue eyes? What?"

"You're pretty," I say finally. "Everyone knows that."

"So are you! With your curls and your big doe eyes and your boobs like twice the size of mine. You know that one of Dexter's friends told him I looked too 'basic' after he broke up with me? You think you're the only one who's ever had to deal with self-esteem? We all do. Only the rest of us don't catfish our crushes—we deal with it. You're gorgeous, Olivia. It's not my fault you can't see it."

I shake my head. It can't be that simple. It can't only come down to fear. It *has* to be easier for Katie, if for no other reason than that's the story I've been telling myself for so very long . . .

But what if she's right? What if the biggest difference between her and me is that she's willing to try, to put herself out there, and I'm not?

With the back of my hand, I wipe the tears from beneath my eyes. "What happened?" I ask, my voice soft.

"What happened with what?" Katie snaps.

"With your program."

She laughs bitterly. "They posted the cast list. I was cast as, ready for it? Townsperson Number Three."

Shit.

"I tried to ask the instructor what had gone wrong, but she told me that I should be happy with that part, that lots of people would be thrilled just to be in the program at all. She told me that there's a whole world outside of community theater in Bay Ridge, Brooklyn."

"Ouch," I say.

"Let's just say I didn't exactly handle it well. It seemed easier to leave than to grovel at her feet, making apologies. Plus, I didn't want to be Townsperson Number Three—I don't care what she said about gratefulness. My parents are still freaking out about it, are going to make me earn off the tuition money I wasted. I think the only reason my mom even let me come up here was so she and I would stop fighting."

I sigh. "I'm so sorry."

Katie's face stiffens. "Whatever," she says.

"No, really. I feel awful."

"Don't, Olivia. I don't want your pity."

I stare at her. "I never meant to—"

"Just stop, Olivia. Please. If I never have to hear another one of your excuses, I'll be happy as a clam. Now can you please shut out the lights?" she asks. "I want to go to sleep."

My best friend turns over, away from me, not saying another word.

# Firestarter

There's only one way to describe work the following day: horrible.

The only thing I have to look forward to is Chrissy's visit, and even that feels tainted, because I have to explain to her that I didn't actually fess up to Jake, that instead, it all blew up in my face, in worse fashion than even I imagined.

Jake normally doesn't work on Tuesdays, but because Bryson called in sick, he's rearranged his schedule with the internship. At first I think that might be a good thing, giving us a chance to talk, only when he comes into the check-in office, he goes so out of his way to avoid looking at me, he might as well be the girl in *The Exorcist*, twisting his neck all the way around.

At lunch, I go out to my bale of hay, and though I see Jake walk past, he heads straight to the lodge, avoiding me completely.

In the afternoon when the place is fairly slow, I stare at my phone, trying to think of what I can possibly say to him. There are no texts from him, no messages on Reddit, either. The jig fully up, I don't even know *how* I would go about apologizing—as Olivia, as Carrie, as both?

The walkie dings, and I hear his voice.

"Jake here. Sending a guy down on the lift. He's too scared. Can we give him a partial refund?"

The walkie beeps again. "Marianne here. Approved."

I push the button. "Olivia here. Will do. Over and out."

Not so long ago, Jake had gotten on that walkie and guided me through my first and only battle with Ropeland. He'd asked, in front of everyone, whether I was coming to hang out at the falls after work. How did it all get so messed up, so quickly?

Oh, right. Because of me. My bullshit.

Just after three, Steinway breezes in, puts two elbows on the check-in counter and gives me a look, her braids pinned up around her head like a crown. "Tuesdays, right?"

I offer a weak smile. "Yeah," I say. "Tuesdays."

She stares, not moving from her spot. "What's going on with you?"

My cheeks go red, and once again, I feel like crying.

"Jake's in a horrible mood, too," Steinway adds.

I focus my eyes on my screen, on the reservation list for the day's final group, but Steinway keeps pushing. "Something off between you two? It was all sunshine and rainbows with you guys a few days ago."

"What can I say?" I offer. "Rainbows go hand in hand with rain, right?"

Steinway raises an eyebrow. "Seriously. Are things okay?"

Maybe because she's always been so nice to me, or maybe because now that the secret's out to the person it matters to most, I don't feel like lying or evading anymore, but I tell her the whole story, from the online chats to the way I sent a photo of Katie to the surprise coincidence of discovering Jake was working here, and then the even bigger surprise, that Katie was up here to visit. When I finish, Steinway stares at me, shaken.

"I know," I say. "It's awful."

"Damn, girl," she says. "And I thought *I* was messy with romance. This is like the plot of a romantic comedy or something."

"I wish," I say. "Those always have happy endings."

Steinway laughs. "So he's pretty mad?"

"Wouldn't you be?"

Steinway nods, a little gravely. "I would, indeed. This is a tough one. I mean, it's not cheating or whatever, but—"

"It might as well be," I finish for her. "I know."

She crosses her arms. "Why did you let it go on so long?"

I pick at a piece of the cheap linoleum counter, one that's about to come off. "I don't know, because I liked him? I didn't want him to hate me for lying."

"So you *kept* lying . . ."

"Hey, I never said it was logical. I didn't actually think anything would really happen with us. This is embarrassing, but Jake was my first kiss. I didn't think we'd actually become something real—nothing ever had before."

Steinway taps at her braids. "Look, all I have to say is—and I'm a few years older than you and maybe I have more experience in the romantic department and all—but never, ever, *ever* be afraid of who you are, of what you look like, of *who* you like, okay? Because it *never* ends well, believe me."

To my surprise, Katie picks me up after work that day.

"I didn't think you'd still be here," I say as I climb into the Subaru. "I thought you'd have gotten my mom to take you to the train station, after everything that happened last night."

Katie doesn't look at me, only pulls out of the Hunter Mountain parking lot, turning toward Woodstock. "Don't get any ideas that everything's all good between us, okay? My mom texted me this morning, said that when I get back, we need to have a *long* talk about responsibility and following through on my commitments.

I'm avoiding the reprimands and punishments for at least another day."

I look out the window, watch the mountains roll by. "I really am sorry."

"I don't want to talk about it, Olivia. Chrissy is here now. Let's just pretend everything's okay."

"Come on, Katie," I say. "Talk to me."

She doesn't say another word the rest of the way to my house.

Chrissy knows. That's the sense I get all the way through dinner, which we have on the porch, my dad grilling up burgers, my mom scooping out potato salad she picked up at the farmer's market. As Chrissy sips wine and regales us all with tales of the advertising shoot she wrapped only yesterday, I'm sure of it: Chrissy knows something's off with me. Chrissy knows it all went down horribly. Chrissy can read me like a book.

After dinner, Katie complains of a headache and retreats to my room, and when the dishes are done, Chrissy sidles up. "Want to build a fire outside?"

I nod.

"Cam?" Chrissy asks my mom. "Want to come out to the fire with us? Girls' night?"

My mom shakes her head. "I'm deep into this new art history book and am finishing it tonight if my life depends on it. Did you guys know that Picasso was once considered a suspect in the theft of *The Mona Lisa*?"

"I bet he did take it," Chrissy says. "That guy always seemed messed up. I mean, the blue period. Oy." Chrissy elbows me. "Anyway, her loss. Grab the logs. I'm going to top off my wine."

Outside, the crickets seem to be going double-time, and the stars are bright in the sky. It's a perfect summer night, the sort they make movies about. Chrissy's even here, which makes everything more fun. Only problem is my best friend is sitting in my room right now, furious with me. And the guy I like, he's furious, too.

"All right," Chrissy says, pointing to the fire pit surrounded by stones, the one my dad and I made together when my parents first bought this house. "Lincoln Logs," she says.

"You mean log cabin?" I ask, referring to our fire-building method of choice.

"Exactly," Chrissy says. "Remember, you're the country girl here. Not me."

She sinks into one of the Adirondack chairs that surround the pit and sips her wine. "It sure is lovely out here, though, I have to say. It's good to get out of the city for a bit."

I arrange the logs carefully, adding kindling and the package of fire-starter to the middle. With the extra-long lighter, I get it going. Immediately, it sparks to life, and I sit back, waiting for the kindling to catch.

"You're good at that," Chrissy says.

I laugh. "It's really not that hard."

Chrissy tips back her wine. "Well, I wouldn't know where to start, so I'm going to pretend like it's this really specialized skill."

I sit down in the chair next to hers. The kindling has started lighting now, and I slip my feet out of my sandals, reaching them toward the warmth of the budding flames. "Any celebrities on set?" I ask.

"Oh, you know," she says, running through a list of models and B-list actors and the like. "They're all people, too, when you get down to it. Just doing their jobs. Anyway"—she takes another sip—"how's that *zip-line* company? Learning all sorts of new fancy outdoorsy skills and stuff?"

I lean forward, using an extra-long stick to poke at the fire so it catches even better. "If you count checking in people's reservations and ringing up T-shirts as outdoorsy skills. It hasn't been that bad, though. Much better than I thought it would be."

"Your mother always has something up her sleeve, that's for sure. She's usually right, though." Chrissy narrows her eyes. "Anyway, more importantly, how's that *boy*? What happened with him?"

I remain silent, focus my eyes on the fire.

"Oh, shit," she says.

"It's nothing."

"You told him, and it didn't go well?"

"I actually didn't tell him," I say, shaking my head. "But he found out anyway. 'Didn't go well' is the understatement of the year."

Chrissy sits up straighter in her chair. "I'm sorry, Olivia."

"Well, my summer's been eventful, at least. I'm definitely not *wasting away* anymore," I say quietly.

Chrissy sets her glass of wine down in the cup holder carved into the chair. "Wait, what did you say?"

"Nothing," I say.

"No, really, Olivia. What did you say?"

My eyes tear up. I swallow, holding the emotions back, and look up at the stars instead.

"Did you hear a conversation between me and your mom?" Chrissy asks.

My vision blurs from tears, the stars blending together.

"Oh, Olivia," she says. "I'm so sorry."

I swipe at my tears with the back of my hand. "It's fine. She was right. I *was* wasting away, just like she said. No wonder she's disappointed in me."

"No," Chrissy says. "She's not disappointed in you. That couldn't be further from the truth. She adores you."

"Sometimes I think it would be easier for her if she would just accept I'll never be who she wants me to be. Then it wouldn't be such a drag when I keep disappointing her."

Chrissy reaches out, resting her hand on top of my arm. "Olivia," she says, but I don't look her way.

"Olivia."

I turn finally. "What? I know it's true."

"Olivia, your mom and I have been angry and snippy with each other in some fashion since I was two years old. And in that conversation, which I really wish you hadn't had to hear, your mom was right."

"That I'm wasting away?" I force a laugh. "Thanks."

Chrissy shakes her head again. "No, she was right that, as much as I love you, as much as you are one of the great blessings of my crazy little life, I'm not your mom. She is."

I shrug. "So?"

"So she knows what's best for you in a way that I don't. And I know she didn't word it the best way, because we don't always phrase things well about the people we love and care about, but I do think she was right about getting you that job. I understand now that it wasn't okay for me to question her like I did." Chrissy leans forward, taking my hand in hers. "Olivia, she could not be happier with you. I know she can be particular—even difficult. I know she expects a lot. But you are her dream, you always have been. Believe me on that one. You, all of you—every misstep, every success, every part of you—are exactly what she loves most about her life."

I take a slow, steady breath. "I want to make her proud of me, but sometimes, it seems like she can only be proud of me if I'm perfect. And I get so scared I'm going to fail that I don't even want to try."

Chrissy gives my hand another squeeze. "She's already proud of you, Olivia. She's crazy about you. You've got that one in the bag. Trust me. Whatever is going on in your life, good or bad, you can turn to me, of course, but you can turn to your parents, too. Believe me. They're ready for anything you've got to throw at them."

# The Bad Decision Handbook:
# Part Four

My mom is still sitting stretched out on the sofa in the living room when I walk inside.

"How's the fire?" she asks, looking up.

"Good," I say. "Chrissy's still out there."

She smiles. "I'm glad you guys are getting some time to catch up."

I nod, shifting my weight from foot to foot. "Er, Mom, can we talk?"

Her eyebrows perk up. Immediately, she sets her book down. "Of course." She pulls her legs back, making room on the couch for me.

I sit on the edge.

"Is everything okay?" she asks.

I nod. "Yes." And then: "No. No, it's not." I turn to her, and she's staring, patiently, at me. "I haven't exactly been honest with you."

My mom folds her hands in her lap. Her eyes don't betray even a hint of surprise. She nods, urging me on. "The NYU program . . ." My words hang in the air, but my mom doesn't help me along, only waits. "I told you I didn't get in, and while that's technically true . . ."

My mom blinks a few times and unfolds her hands.

"It's more than that I didn't get in," I go on. "I didn't even really give myself a shot. I waited until the very last minute, so what I did send in was just kind of mumbo jumbo. I basically sabotaged the whole thing."

She stares at me. Then, after what feels like forever but can't be more than a few seconds, she smiles. "I know that, Olivia."

"What?" I ask, shaking my head in disbelief. "How? I told you I was working on it like every day."

"I'm your *mom*," she says. "I'd walk in your room, when you told me you were working on it, and see another horror movie queued up on your screen. I know to a point it was research, but no one needs to do *that much* research."

"But . . . but why didn't you say anything? Why didn't you just call me out on it? My procrastination and all that."

"I didn't want to pressure you. I thought you'd learn a valuable lesson if you didn't get something you really wanted. Maybe even a better lesson than you'd learn in an NYU program."

"Are you mad at me?" I ask.

"Mad?"

"For messing it all up? For not giving myself a chance?"

My mom laughs. "Of course not. The things I put off in my day—the lies I told my mother, you don't even want to know. Much, much worse than saying I was working on an application when I wasn't. I know what it's like to be scared to go after something you want. I hope now you understand that it's always better to give yourself a real shot. When Marianne told me about the job, your dad and I really thought that getting you out of your comfort zone would be good. And we're so proud of you for following through and giving it your all, even if it's not what you wanted."

"Me too," I say, because even with all that's happened, even if Jake will never, ever speak to me again, I'm glad I'm spending the summer doing something I wouldn't have before. I'm glad she pushed me, and I'm glad I took the literal leap off that cliff.

"You don't always have to be so hands-off, you know," I say. "I mean, I know I should get better about being honest with you and telling you things, but I don't care if you ask me what I'm up to every once in a while, or hassle me if you can see I'm messing everything up."

My mom beams. "You know, Olivia, you're right. Maybe I've been so afraid to pressure you that I haven't been as involved as I should. Let's make a pact to both be more open with each other. Deal?"

I nod. "Deal." I hesitate. "In the name of openness . . ."

Her eyes widen.

"I wrote a screenplay, even though I'm not at NYU."

"Really? Like a *whole* screenplay?" She clasps her hands together. "That's, what, like—"

"Ninety pages."

Her eyebrows shoot skyward. "*Ninety pages?* That's amazing, Olivia. That's just, that's crazy. Ninety pages!"

I feel myself blush. "You're not going to like it, though, because it's a horror movie screenplay."

"Olivia," she says, playfully hitting me on the shin. "Your dad and I like anything that you like, okay? We're not *that* old and fuddy-duddy, after all."

I smile. "Really?"

She nods. "Of course."

"Thanks, Mom," I say.

"Anytime. Oh, and Olivia. In the name of more openness on my part, I've noticed that you and Katie—"

"I don't want to talk about it."

"That's fine," she says. "I just wanted you to know that friendships are important. And you have to take care of them, especially the good ones, like everything else."

I stand up. "Thanks, Mom." I give her a hug, and she holds me tight.

"I'm always here for you, okay?"

I nod. "Okay."


Back in my room, the lights are off, but I can hear, by the way she's breathing, that Katie isn't asleep.

"Is your headache any better?" I ask.

Katie scoffs but doesn't turn over. "I don't have a headache. You know that, Olivia."

"Do you want to talk?" I ask, my voice soft.

Katie doesn't say a single word.

"I'm sorry," I say. "I'm sorry for not being a better friend to you."

"I don't want to talk, Olivia," she says, to the wall more than me. "I'm leaving tomorrow. It's fine."

I know it's not, though. I get up from the bed, and leaving the lights off, quiet as I can, I change into PJs, head to the bathroom, brush my teeth and wash my face. My mom is no longer in the living room; my dad isn't in his office. In the kitchen, I grab a glass of water, and through the windows, I see the fire still going. But to my surprise, my mom is walking across the yard, straight toward Chrissy.

In the firelight, I can see Chrissy stand up and then, after a few seconds, they hug. For a long time. Ten seconds, at least. I don't know what my mom said, if she apologized to Chrissy or the other way around, or maybe they both did; but I'm pretty sure my mom took her own advice.

Friendships are important. And Chrissy and my mom have been friends—and sisters—their whole lives.

I return to my room, quietly grabbing my computer, then head into the living room. Then I open Reddit and do what I know I need to do. I start a new message to Elm.

*Figured I'd start my apology here, because I've known you here the longest. Where to begin? I'll start with this. I always loved talking to you. About movies, about your aunt, about what was going on in your day. I know we didn't really exchange a lot of specifics; and I liked that too. It's not because I was trying to be someone else with you, but because I felt like I could really be myself with you. I know that sounds stupid, but it's true. It was always me, then. I was always trying my best to be real.*

*When you asked for that photo, I freaked out. I was worse than any character in any horror movie. It was out of fear, but there's no excusing it; it was a bad decision. And then, when I had already lied, it felt easier to let you think I really was going to the NYU program, one I hardly even had a real shot at because I was so nervous about failing I kept putting it off. That was another very bad decision.*

*But the worst bad decision—again, worse than anything I'd done before—was not telling you this crazy story as soon as I saw you here at Hunter Mountain. It was not trusting you to like me the way I am, even with all my quirks.*

*For that, I'm truly sorry. I've always liked you—when I talked to you online, and when I saw you in person—just the way you are. I should have given you the same chance with me.*

*Anyway, thank you for helping me figure all this out, even if you were an unwitting helper! I will never forget your encouragement, from helping me do that damn zip line to helping me finally write my screenplay.*

*Thanks, and I'm sorry.*

*Carrie/Olivia/The Worst Person Ever*

I read it over three times before I get the guts to hit Send.

Then I close out of Reddit and open up Google. Like my mom said, friendships are important, and I've got some work to do.

# What Would Meryl Do: Part Four

Katie tells us over breakfast that she's taking the ten o'clock train.

"Just as I'm getting here!" Aunt Chrissy says, between bites of her extra-sugary cereal, the one my mom won't let us keep in the house.

Katie smiles her Katie smile. "I think I've imposed enough."

"Never," my dad says. "Plus, between you and Olivia, we have a full range of movie knowledge for the crossword. By the way," he says, looking at me. "What's a twelve-letter word for badass?"

I raise an eyebrow. "I don't know, Dad."

I can feel a joke coming in three, two, one . . .

"Screenwriter!" he says.

I feel myself blush.

"Seriously, Olivia. Mom told me this morning. I'm so beyond proud of you. I mean, completely on your own. It's amazing. You're a rock star."

"Your mom told me, too," Aunt Chrissy says. "And I gotta say, I *told* you you didn't need that bougie-ass school. You're an inspiration all on your own."

"It's not that big of a deal," I say.

Katie takes a sip of orange juice, then adjusts herself in her chair and looks right at me. "It is, though, Olivia. It really is."

The two of us are quiet as Katie loads her bags into the Subaru.

My mom drives, and we get to the station a few minutes early.

"I'll hang out with you on the platform while you wait," I say.

"You don't have to do that," Katie says.

"Hey, it's fine by me!" my mom says. In the rearview mirror, I see her not-so-discreetly wink.

"Thanks again, Mrs. Knight," Katie says.

"Anytime, Katie. Please come up again soon."

I grab Katie's backpack while she takes her suitcase, and we walk, quietly, up the stairs and onto the platform. It's a slow day, and only a couple of other people are waiting for the train.

Katie sits down on a bench and looks at me. "It's okay, Olivia. We don't have to talk about it. I'm just disappointed in myself. I couldn't cut it in the program. I couldn't even play Katie-Carrie without over-acting. It's stupid, but it's cool. I'm not even mad anymore."

I shake my head, reach into my pocket, and pull out my phone.

"Oh my god, did you write some sort of speech? And you think *I'm* the dramatic one? Geez."

I ignore her and clear my throat, reading off the notes I jotted down late last night.

"Scarlett Johansson was overlooked for a role in *Jumanji*. She lost to Kirsten Dunst. Marilyn Monroe was told she should be, no joke, a secretary. Lea Michele was told her nose was too big. Keira Knightley was told she couldn't act." I scroll down on my phone. "Okay, this one's especially bad, but Kerry Washington was fired from two pilots because she didn't seem 'hood' or 'urban' enough. Sally Field was told she wasn't good enough to get into film. And here's maybe the best one, one I'm sure you already know, but Meryl Streep was told that she was 'too ugly' to be in *King Kong*."

I steal a look up, and Katie is staring at me, the corners of her mouth creeping into a smile. "You looked all that up for me?"

I smile right back. "I looked all that up because *everybody* gets rejected, and some stupid casting director at some stupid New School program doesn't know what they're missing. You care about this more than anyone I've ever known, and unlike me, you have *never* been too scared to go after what you want. That's something—not everyone has that drive."

Her smile is wider now, and I catch a sheen of moisture in her eyes.

In the distance, a rushing whooshing sound, the feeling of movement beneath our feet. The train is approaching.

"I love you, Olivia," Katie says, wrapping me in a tight, fierce hug.

"I love you, too."

The train pulls up, and we break apart. "I can't wait until you're back in Brooklyn again. And next time we see each other"—she beams—"I'll even let you pick out the movie."

# Friday the 13th

On Friday at eleven a.m. sharp, I enter the check-in office with a racing pulse.

It's been two days since I sent Jake my apology message, and I haven't heard a word. I haven't seen him either, given that he was at his internship yesterday.

Marianne is in the office, rifling through the cabinets, and Tennyson is at the counter, looking at his phone. I clock in and get onto my computer. The place won't pick up for another half hour, when the noon group needs to check in.

Jake will be arriving at any moment. I know he probably won't so much as look at me, and I don't blame him, but still, I can't help but keep glancing at the door.

"Olivia?" I hear behind me.

I turn. Marianne is staring at me, like she's been waiting for an answer for a few seconds, at least. "Distracted, are we? I know it's Friday . . ." She lets out a laugh. "And Friday the Thirteenth, no less."

"Sorry," I say.

"No worries. I only asked if your walkie needs batteries. I'm putting in an order today."

I click the button, and it beeps to life. "I think I'm good."

I turn back around, and there he is, walking through the door.

Jake's eyes briefly catch mine, but he walks behind the counter as quickly as he can, tossing his things into a cabinet and loading up on carabiners. There is so much I want to say, but I can't. I've already said it, sent it via missive straight to his Reddit inbox. If he doesn't want to hear it, I can't make him. That's his right.

I feel the weight of disappointment wash over me, but there's nothing I can do. I've made my bed—I've dug my grave—it's time to crawl right in. It's Friday the Thirteenth, anyway. Nothing good is supposed to happen today. Sure, there's no Jason, waiting in the woods of Camp Crystal Lake, but I don't need a crazed killer; I've done enough damage for one movie on my own.

I pretend to be engrossed by my computer screen, and only when Jake is no longer there does the full weight of what I've screwed up— what I've lost—hit me.

"Trouble in paradise?" Tennyson asks.

"I don't want to talk about it," I say.

"You know Ten always treats the ladies right," he says.

I roll my eyes, but his voice goes serious. "I'm sorry, whatever happened," Tennyson says. "I can tell you guys really liked each other. I hope you can work it out."

"Me too," I say, even though I know there's no way we can.

Eleven a.m. crawls to five past, then ten. I wipe down the counters, organizing the T-shirts and the other gear we sell in the shop.

Back at the desk, I check the time. Eleven thirty-five.

And then, like magic, like delicious, amazing relief: a message. A reply on Reddit, from ElmStreetNightmare84. With shaking hands, I tap it open.

*The worst part of it all is that you were so afraid of being you, you didn't believe in yourself. And that sucks, because I think you're awesome.*

*P.S. Happy Friday the Thirteenth*

# Friday the 13th: Part Two

My hands shake, hovering over the message.

He's right. I was afraid of being me. I didn't believe in myself. But there's something else there, too: He thinks I'm awesome.

"Can you cover me?" I ask.

"Huh?" Tennyson looks up.

"Just for, like, a couple of minutes."

"*Un*trouble in paradise?" he asks.

"Can you?"

"Anything for love," Tennyson says with a smile.

"Thanks." I rush around the counter, through the hallway, and out the back doors.

It's sunny out, the light temporarily blinding, the air warm and thick. I turn left, running quickly toward the ski lift. I don't have much time. Soon, the first tour group will be here.

Cora is there, reading a book. There are only a few people in line.

"I need to go up," I say.

"Why?"

I shake my head. "I just do."

She shrugs. "Go ahead." Then she blows her whistle. "Hold the line!"

I rush up and wait, heart racing as the seat comes around on its conveyor.

It hits the back of my legs, and I sink against it, the ground leaving my feet and the lift deftly sweeping me up. Fingers tingling, I pull the bar down. It's only the second time I've used the lift.

I chance a look down, and my stomach flip-flops, but I remember what Jake said. "Don't look down, only up."

And that's what I do. As we climb up the mountain, as my feet dangle, I look up at the sky, blue and barely clouded and perfect. I look inward, too, because I'm not going to be afraid to be myself anymore. I'm not going to be scared to take a chance.

Even if it doesn't work out—even if you get cast as Townsperson Number Three (or *Dracula* stagehand)—it's still important to know you tried, to know that you can get right back up and try again.

I reach the top, and I lift up the bar. My feet hit the ground, and I don't hesitate to walk toward the beginning of the zip course.

Steinway sees me first. She's standing with a pile of harnesses and helmets, ready to hook up her next group. "What are you doing here?" she asks. "Is everything okay down at the office?"

I nod. "Where's Jake? I need to talk to him."

She points to the top of the course, about a hundred feet away. "He's about to zip over to the next checkpoint. That's where his part of the tour starts."

"Jake," I call, but he doesn't turn around.

"He's got his earbuds in," she says.

I consider using the walkie, but then everyone will hear. I watch as he reaches up, hooking his carabiner to the zip line.

"Harness me up," I say suddenly.

"What?"

"I need the harness," I say.

"Why?" she says.

"I'll explain later. Please."

"I thought you didn't like heights," Steinway says, but she grabs the harness anyway. "Is this some kind of forced immersion thing?"

I ignore her question, stepping in as quickly as I can and helping her tighten everything up. She tugs on a few pulls. Out of the corner of my eye, I can see Jake still standing there, his clip hooked on.

"Good?" I ask.

Steinway tugs on it a couple more times. "Good," she says, handing me a helmet.

"Thanks," I say, breaking off into a run as I pull the helmet on and clip it tight.

"Wait!" she says, but I'm not stopping now.

I run, half losing my breath, toward Jake. But before I get there, I see him step off the ledge, disappear along the zip line into the woods.

I run faster. In mere moments, I'm at the jump-off point. I don't hesitate. I don't let my fear take over. Most of all, just like he said, I don't look down.

I grab the carabiner and hook it onto the line, tugging on it to be sure it's secure.

Then I take two steps and . . .

I'm flying, rushing through the trees, just like that first day. I look up, see the sky, and it's so beautiful, and I promise myself this: I'm never going to let myself be too scared to take a risk.

I'm flying and rushing, but then—

Suddenly the line is buckling, slowing me down, like the weight of both of us on here at once is too much. I see, up ahead, that Jake is slowing too, moving backward now.

Flying toward me.

# Friday the 13th: Part Three

"What the hell is going on?" Jake calls, twisting his body to look back at me.

"Watch out!"

There's no way to stop what I've put in motion. We crash into each other, his back smashing against me, our bodies ricocheting like two pendulums.

There's a screech of metal as we jolt apart and then come together again, his back against me once more. The weight of both of us buckles the line.

Jake reaches up, grabbing the zip line, using it to twist his body around so he's facing me.

I grab on to his shoulders so he doesn't turn back around.

"Are you hurt?" he asks. "I smacked right into you."

I shake my head, a little shocked. I didn't expect it to go *quite* like this, but still, I'm okay. "I'm not hurt," I say. "Just a little . . . jolted, I guess."

Jake's eyebrows scrunch up. "What were you *thinking*?" he asks.

I interlace my hands behind his back, so he won't flip around. Our bodies hang there together, practically swaying in the breeze. "I wanted to show you I'm not afraid anymore."

His eyes widen. "And *this* is how you do it?"

I grimace. "It was going to work better in my head. I just saw your message, and I thought, I don't know, if we could just talk, I could explain. I'm so sorry for everything. You were right. I didn't believe in myself, but I'm trying to change that. I'm sorry I lied to you, and I'm sorry I wasn't myself from the very beginning."

Jake stares at me a moment, and it's like he's making a decision, but then his arms wrap around my shoulders, and I can't tell if it's because he forgives me, or if there's just nowhere for them to go, the way we're smushed together like this. "I know what you mean," he says finally. "It's easy to want to make yourself look cooler online. The truth is, I took ten photos before getting the one I sent to you."

I shake my head. "No you didn't."

He nods. "I did."

"But you shouldn't have had to do that. You're perfect the way you are."

He smiles. "I could say the same thing about you."

His head tilts toward mine, and I look up at him, and suddenly, his lips are on mine. His kiss is soft, then stronger, and his arms tighten around me as mine clutch tighter to his waist. I kiss him back, because no matter what happens—where the future takes us, whether I'll even get to see him again after this summer, or whether we'll go back to chatting on Reddit like we've done for so long—I know one thing: I'm not afraid anymore.

To be myself. To go for what I want. To fall in love, even if it is messy and scary.

Jake pulls back, and his eyebrows raise. I twist my head around to see Steinway calling to us. "What the *hell* do you think you're doing, Olivia? The tour is supposed to start any minute, and it's going to take forever to get you both down!"

I turn back to Jake. "This was a bad decision, wasn't it?"

He nods. "Worse than any character in any horror movie, that's for sure."

I grin, then kiss him again.

"What can I say?" I pull back. "It is Friday the Thirteenth."

# Acknowledgments

An enormous thanks to the many many people who made this book possible.

First a huge shoutout to Anne Heltzel and the entire team at Amulet Books. Thank you for incredible editorial guidance, patience, and for indulging my horror-loving heart—even when it comes to writing a romance.

And to Hayley Wagriech, Sara Shandler, Josh Bank, and the Alloy family: you are plot and character masters, and this book would not be what it is without your leadership and know-how.

To Danielle Chiotti, Michael Stearns, and all of Upstart Crow, many thanks for years of dedication, advice, and passion.

This book certainly would not have been possible without two things: Reddit and horror movies. Thanks to my husband, Thomas, for introducing me to the world of Reddit, in addition to providing invaluable first-hand knowledge about the inner workings of a film set. And to my horror-movie lovers, I could not have done this without you. Thank you to Julia and Andrea Bartz for creating the Horror Movie Google Doc and getting frustrated when I fail to update it (it's an incredible resource!). Thank you to my sister, Kimberly, for watching all those *Friday the 13th* movies with me in high school. And to my dog, Farley, who snuggled up by my side for many a binge-watch.

To my parents, thanks for always supporting me and encouraging me to do what I love. I owe this to you.

Finally, to *The Shop Around the Corner* and *You've Got Mail*, you gave me so much to riff on. Thank you.